Paradise Interrupted

Tom Levine

Illustrated by K.C. Weller

Defiant Worm Books

Paradise Interrupted © 2007 by Tom Levine

Color Separations by JCS Image Center, 407-856-5758
Orlando Sentinel back cover quote: March 2000

To order, contact Defiant Worm Books
defiantworm@yahoo.com

Paradise Interrupted by Tom Levine
Fiction
ISBN: 0-9729390-1-6

Cover art and illustrations by: K. C. Weller

Invaluable technical support by: Eyal Goldshmid

Typesetting by Atlantis Productions, Edgewater, Florida

*for **Michele***

Also by Tom Levine

BITE ME! Tom Levine's Most Excellent Stories

defiantworm.com

Author's Note

My 11- year old son has requested that I publish this book without a particular cuss word in it. What kind of father would not try to reach such a standard of good taste, when presented it by his child? As a cuss word "#$%!" is overrated and overused anyway and I do not miss it.

There are characters who surely would be speaking that way if they were allowed to, so clues are provided for the reader to plug it in for realism. The dialogue *is* lightly sprinkled with the equally popular and more potent feces and faith based swearing.

Paradise Interrupted

Tom Levine

*O*nce upon the sixties, anonymous buyers quietly assembled parcels of pine flat and cypress hammock. They got them cheap and the sellers felt lucky. When Walt Disney descended and revealed Himself, the former land-owners writhed in remorse while businessmen groveled and scraped and rejoiced that their neglected Eden had been selected for plundering.

Buildings sprouted from crashing treetops as cars multiplied like amoebae, pushing fur-splattered tongues of asphalt through instantly retreating swamps. Flower plants surrendered to power plants, busy replaced the bees, fresh air became an oxymoron and the water was poisoned in the blink of an alligator's eye. Nature was eclipsed so suddenly that it hovered above the pavement in a dream world, maddeningly close as the last vestiges were swept away.

"Time, not fire, roasts a marshmallow," nature's mother reflected. "Disney is a mosquito fart in a gardenia hedge." She waited impatiently to reclaim the heart of her exquisite peninsula. Even in this bleak period emerged signs, however indistinct, of her second coming...

1994

Squirrel-size dolphins roasting marshmallows in the lawn eroded into steaming dog-piles of consciousness as he failed to sink deeper into the Yucatan hammock's snug embrace. Prehensile feet dropped to the peeling orange planks of the front porch. The string bed swung slightly as he stood in boxer shorts, stretched and urinated over the railing.

As Cohen hosed an uninspired oval in the dirt, a puff of delightfully April air rippled his arm hairs. He recognized the perfect mixture of breeze, solar energy, humidity, cosmic rays, oxygen, car exhaust, mosquito farts and factors beyond the pale of knowledge. In his curly, black beard grew a smile like fresh pelican guano spreading over a moonlit piling. It was one of those spring mornings he considered a recurring miracle and every pore, every brain cell, every nose hair in a crescendo of exaltation started shouting, "I FEEL LIKE POPEYE ON SPINACH!"

Mortecai Cohen knew where he belonged on such a day: drying off on a breeze-catching sand bluff over the Econlockhatchee River, his enduring love, most splendid, inviting, irresistible in April. He also knew his van lay dead in the oil- spangled driveway.

Long, sentient toes dodged risen nail heads as he turned with sudden purpose and entered the open door. He squeezed two oranges, made peanut butter and banana toast, and blended breakfast orally. Over the small bathroom sink Cohen combed teeny black balls out of his toothbrush and wished again that the roach toilet might not be his instrument of dental hygiene.

1

In the chronic struggle for leverage in his marriage, Ray Macon stockpiled points when he could, to be applied to future recreational opportunities. Time spent with his family, sacrificed fishing trips and other related suffering boosted his bargaining power while fun eroded it. Like a farmer in his fields, he watched over these points, protecting and cajoling them lovingly toward their harvest of freedom. To trim the cost of weekend escape, he usually arranged for Mortecai Cohen to call him and shoulder the blame. Ray's wife came to believe he would be satisfied to fester away life in his overcrowded house and small dog-doo covered yard were it not for Cohen.

Daisy Macon heard the white dial telephone ring in the kitchen and her sturdy body tensed. From the bedroom she watched Ray bin a pooey nappy in the bathroom, then trudge to his deliverance through baby rattles, Stinker Toys, girls' clothing, Naked Barbie and Ken, a clap-activated puppy and two prepubescent female offspring.

"If that's Mr. Footloose and Fancyfree, you tell him you ain't goin' nowhere today. There's plenty to do around here," Ray's bride screeched over The Power Rangers with a newly diapered baby dangling from her left zeppelin.

A limp, spotted banana peel lay across the receiver. Between bended thumb and index finger, Ray lifted the peel by its little black butt and tossed it onto eleven- year old Andrea's tow-head. Like he hoped it wasn't Mortecai disrupting his home life again, he slowly put phone to ear.

"Hey, let's go," urged a voice from the world of liberty and joy, throwing a temporary lifeline into the Tampon Stockade. "We gotta get out to the Econ. It's one of those days."

"Yeah, I know. But I've got a lot to do around here," Ray said loudly; then softly, "I sure would like to get out somewhere."

Mortecai thought he heard a tomcat getting deep-fried in the middle of its mating yowl. "What do you mean you'd like to get out somewhere?" Daisy had exploded. "Your sorry butt just got here. When's the last time I went anywhere? All you ever do is go fishin'. Fishin', fishin', fishin'!"

"Just come on by," Ray whispered, his motive exposed. "And keep the motor running."

"Ain't got no motor."

"Jesus. You haven't got that thing going yet?"

Dangerously close to the phone, the fried cat apparently was stapled to the floor in Sanford accent.

"Still can't figure out what's wrong with it."

"Alright. Give me fifteen minutes. I can't stay here now."

The line went dead. With Daisy Macon detoured by the now howling baby, Ray made good his escape, on the way out yelling something about having to go to Mort's.

"How'd you get away from Daisy?" Mortecai asked as they sped out of town.

"Promised I'd never try to enjoy myself after today."

Mortecai shook his head solemnly. "That's a rare, understanding woman you're married to. I hope you appreciate it."

With a hand at the top of the steering wheel, it didn't matter. In Ray's mind, his house had just become the victim of an airliner running out of fuel. There was nothing left there for him. "Damn lucky Cohen called me when he did," he thought.

"You know, I wish just once you'd call me in front of Daisy. She's gonna hate my guts."

"Already does."

Mortecai "Whooped" and punched his pal in the arm. "What a day!"

"I need to get gas," Ray hinted.

"Cut it out. You've always got gas."

Sulphuric fumes emanated from the driver's seat. Mortecai's head yelled from outside the car, "Roll your window down, Goddammit."

"For the car," Ray clarified with a grin. "Do you have any money?"

The Honda Civic lunged east from the IDEAL filling station onto Highway 50 in search of adventure and country air, its course plotted to include Cohen's favorite orange grove.

"Isn't this some shit," Ray said, zooming up to a traffic jam.

"Yep. The tourists don't go home anymore," Cohen observed, as if that were Ray's fault.

Suddenly engulfed in a stomach-resonating bass beat, Cohen craned his head around and spied a young skinhead in a brown Toyota. "Is it just me, or is there more stupidity in the world these days?"

Ray pulled onto the right shoulder and sped ahead. "Watch for Arnold," he warned in an historic allusion to Fred Ziffle's pig. "It's not that there is more stupidity. It just has more intrusive ways of presenting itself. It used to be, you could be near an idiot and you wouldn't know it. With today's advances, that's less likely."

"You're saying technology brings out the human potential."

"It empowers the stupid." Ray bounced the car back onto the pavement.

Ten miles east of Ray's house the Civic broke free of traffic like slingshot ammo, leaving suburbia's last outpost diminishing in the rear view mirror. Mortecai became silent and Ray saw him staring in horror at a distant highway overpass.

"It's been awhile since you were out here, hasn't it?" Ray noted, omnisciently twirling his moustache. "That is the new beltway; the latest urban blight spreader; another layer of fat around the heart of Orlando."

"Oh, that's just great." Cohen shot an accusing look at his friend. "Why don't you write a poem about it?"

"You can't stop them. You can only make a statement," Ray said in defense.

"Well, it would've been nice to make a statement. As it is, they didn't hear a peep from us. Probably think we like it." He felt his spirits sink into his feet as they passed under the long, appallingly stalwart pre-stressed concrete statements of things to come.

"You can't understand because you don't have a family."

"I can't streak the mall. I got a family. I can't hop a train. I got a family. I can't go to Borneo....you might as well be dead."

Ray sifted this indictment and found it full of truth. "What are Daisy and the kids suppose to do when I go to jail?"

"Applaud comes to mind."

"Alright," Ray admitted, "you won't relate to this but I couldn't stand the humiliation of getting arrested."

"So you're chickenshit."

"Yeah," Ray resigned, his hand dropping to the bottom of the wheel.

They turned off the four lane Hwy. 50 onto a two lane blacktop.

"Finally! Safe from civilization," Mortecai said and breathed deep. "Those trees should be around this next curve; melt-in-your-mouth mandarins, a skin full of the sweetest juice you ever tasted. There they..."

A surveyor's stake punched through Cohen's light cotton shirt and plunged into his abdomen as he saw his favorite orange grove laying on its side. Its orbs of juicy delight looked brown, shriveled and hard, their promise gone like a field of nubile girls suddenly struck into mummies.

"Goddammit, there oughta be a law against removing fruit bearing trees," he railed as Ray rubbernecked slowly by. "They should be considered a public treasure. Some grove owner wants to sell his land to a developer? Tough shit. Well, Ray, we gonna let this one go in too?"

Cohen quietly mourned the peels not unwrapped, the hopeful seeds not spat to mother earth, nature's own best flavor he never again would know.

Ray just kept driving, envying his friend's faith in his own opinions and his willingness to act regardless of consequences. Ray's thoughts drifted back to when he was four and his farm-bred, stupidly jovial Georgia aunt came swaggering up the walkway. She had arrived to keep him and his two-year old brother alive while their divorced mother vacationed at the Holiday Sanitarium. Aunt Tallulah was too absorbed watching herself take charge of the situation to consider the sensibilities of anyone little. She spied Ray playing with the pet duck he'd raised

from an Easter egg and loved with all his heart. She snatched it up by the neck, swung it over to the kitchen counter and before his bewildered, crying eyes, beheaded it. In retrospect it seemed to be the day his life began. With his best friend on the table as the Thanksgiving turkey, little Ray Macon substituted absurdity for a reality he no longer wished to sponsor. He never really found the track back, though not for want of trying.

Ray was unremarkable of stature; slim, medium height and not particularly muscular. However, where many faces aspire little beyond the proper arrangement of the senses, every feature on his head seemed to have been lovingly molded and painstakingly set in place, as if the job had been overseen by his penis. Macon's Bacchanalian aspect blended the perfect with the primitive, the low forehead under a canopy of wavy brown hair evoking Michaelangelo's Neanderthal David with Kim Bassinger's lips. His narrow, finely crafted nose was mounted prominently between high cheekbones, less an air passage than an accent between eyes that glistened like sunrise on a lime popsicle. The whole presentation was softened by a beauty mark on his lower left cheek.

He was not a heartbreaker in the usual way. Many women had been enchanted by this sweet mask of feminine allure riding its solidly masculine skull and they imagined the lovely children it promised. Some of these were seduced by his grin, a wonderfully guileless expression of heathen delight. When they saw the man behind it scrabbling for a foothold in life like a one-legged crab on a surf-washed rock, they had to let go.

Ray eventually pushed his crippled personality as far as the altar and he spawned a family in the real world. At thirty-five years old he was still trying to reach them there.

"Ray," Mortecai interrupted his musing, "stop trying to fit into society. It's a terrible waste of energy."

"Right," Ray countered. "That's easy for somebody to say who goes around screaming, 'This is me. If you don't like it, there's something wrong with you.'"

"What's not to like?" Cohen asked sincerely.

Mortecai's sense of loss dissolved into raccoon droppings of joy as he neared his beloved Econlockhatchee River like a St. Bernard with its head out the window. The patched and pitted road carried the men to the village of Chuluota, signified by a couple weed infested, boarded up roadside motels, the overgrown nine-hole Chulavista Golf Course and a plywood BUSHOG FOR RENT sign nailed crooked to a pine tree.

Hardy sandspurs pursued solitary lives in the dull, fissured asphalt fronting a Pakistani convenience store, the last gasp of someone's New Urbanism dream. Fortified by a stale banana Moon Pie each, Cohen and Macon cut through a low income 1960's subdivision where a front yard without a boat or a truck on it marked an abandoned house. Then they shot back into the country and rode Snow Hill Road to the concrete bridge. There the sand-banked tributary showed itself briefly to the modern world before diving back into the timeless obscurity of the jungle. They jounced down a washed-out dirt track to the Econlockhatchee's edge. The car doors swung open simultaneously as two friends eagerly stepped out. They gazed with a city-born lust upon this narrow conduit bearing into subtropical forest its gift of prehistoric freedom. Confronted by the usual dilemma of upstream or down, each with its own favorite places, they chose downstream for its unlimited potential. After all, that is where the river was going.

Each man grabbed a light spinning rod out of the trunk.

"You using six?" Ray inquired as he lifted the jack-knife from his tackle box.

"Nah. I'm goin' with eight out here ever since that monster broke me off. You got eight, right?"

"I wouldn't use less, except to make sure I don't catch anything big."

Each carefully chose a pocketful of suitable lures and hooks and Ray pocketed a stringer should they catch a nice bass as dusk led them back. Eager to lose sight of the bridge, they struck off along the beach before ascending into forest.

Though the ride to the river had betrayed its promise, the marvellous air lived up to hers, flailing about them like an ethereal balm. When the sound of passing cars no longer reached them, Mortecai relaxed and said, "Days like this make me think humans might be native to this planet."

After months of dry season the river was low, fifteen to forty feet wide with plenty of exposed bed. Cohen always marvelled that this wild place was so user-friendly with no help from human landscaping. After breaking through the undergrowth and forest barrier at the bridge, they entered a meandering playground of rolling grass hills and sugar-sand beaches. At the inside of each deep bend lay the sugar sand - fluffy white playgrounds perfect for rolling down, hopping across and scrunching into. On the outside of each bend rose eight-foot banks, forested on top. Random live oaks and cypress trees offered dappled shade along the way.

In cut-offs and T-shirts Ray and Mortecai picked their way along animal trails, brushing aside saw palmettos on the high ground without touching the knife edge stems. When they walked among trees, the fishing rods went first to meet webs and avoid terror from the vibrantly colored banana spiders trapezing between stunted sweet gums. At every opportunity they stopped to suck in the outrageously yellow fragrance of the yellow jasmine, its small, potent flowers entwined about spindly elms. Mortecai picked a sweet gum leaf and crushed it between his fingers to carry along, urging Ray to do the same, sniffing it a few times before dropping the remains into the sparse leaf litter. The pleasure of feeling their feet on the earth was worth enduring occasional patches of thorny ground cover, painful but the thorns remained on the plant. When jungle tangles of vines encroached to the edge, the river granted clear passage on the other side and Ray and Mortecai slogged across and kept running. They trotted to the tops of sugar sand hills, then leaped down them. Where the trails dipped low among cypress roots, they guarded their toes against stubbing on the random wooden knees that pushed through the ground like practical jokes. Then the stream flattened out and the contented men sloshed through the middle in shin deep water, feeling mussels in the sand with their toes and scattering occasional schools of mullet that had swum hundreds of miles from the ocean to be there. The farther they went, the more they became a part of the river and the better they felt.

They couldn't resist stopping at the second bend. Ray looked for furrows in the sand near shore, then buried his fingers and pulled out a large, black mussel. The alert shellfish clamped tight so Ray slipped in the point of his knife near the hinge, then slid it along, twisting the blade to pry open the shell against the desperately straining inhabitant. When it was partly spread, he slipped his thumbnails into the space and pitted his muscles against the mussel within, a remarkably even battle given the size differential. As always he prevailed and scooped out the plump loser. Ray threaded its tough foot onto the small hook tied to his line. He added a split-shot sinker for weight, then tossed the juicy morsel into a deep eddy, hoping to start the trip with a catfish. Mortecai did a shallow dive downstream and zoomed along with the current, twisting and turning around logs as he imagined an otter would do. Then he ran out, ran back upstream to the deep bend and jumped in several more times at every possible angle, stood in waist deep Econlockhatchee and splashed and whooped. He smiled at his orange feet.

"Are you finished?" Ray asked. "I don't think there's any more you can do to alert the fish."

"Yeah," Mortecai said and floated back downstream, spouting reddish water out the hole in his head. "Time for phase two." He stepped onto the beach and walked to the top of a high grass-covered bank. There he plopped down cross-legged, drying in the breeze, his taut skin dancing in an ecstasy of refreshment. His brain was thoughtless, simply open and gathering sensations as he gazed downstream. He was dazzled by the red-black water held by sparkling white banks, bright green cypress shoots against the blue sky, the palms high overhead and the amazing light of it all.

"I just love the racket out here on a windy day with the dry palm fronds shakin' all around and the trees rubbin'and squeakin' on each other," Mortecai confided.

"Well, that's alright for a nature lover," Ray said, re-tossing out his mussel. "I'd like to hear the crunch of those trees under a bulldozer. What bugs me is there's no place to get a hamburger out here. We've got to think to the future. How are we going to get tourists to come out here if we don't pave it and put some food concessions along the bank? Think about that."

"I see what you mean," Mortecai conceded, a changed man, "but today I wouldn't add a thing."

A yellow canoe slid silently around the upstream bend and Mortecai recognized Violet Chance guiding it clothed only in a wooden paddle. Her blue shorts and shirt hung from the middle brace. "I might add one thing," he said, thunderstruck by his good fortune.

"What's that?" Ray said, looking up from his line. "Sounds like a chainsaw heading this way."

As Mortecai stood to heighten his vantage point, the source of the noise burst into view. "It's a goddam jet-skier," he yelled, "and another one. What the hell are they doin' out here?"

"About thirty miles an hour and they don't appear to be slowing down."

"They're gonna hit the canoe," Mortecai said, hardly believing this could be in his sanctuary from the industrial age.Previously unaware of the canoe, Ray found it and registered for all time a vision kneeling on the fiberglass bottom and gripping the sides. "No, I think they're just going to spray her."

"Count on jet-skiers not to slow down and view a naked woman," Cohen remarked.

"They can't help it. They don't know what one is," Ray said, blindly setting down his rod on the grass, his gaze riveted by the canoer.

The Sea-Doo brand sit-down jet-skis skated along the far side of Violet's twelve foot craft, eroding the root tangled bank with great tannic waves.

From the edge of the bluff, Mortecai erected a wall of verbal abuse the invaders would have to endure in order to pass, drilled home with an adamant finger.

"Did you see that? They just smiled."

"Well, you did call them carnivorous assholes from Mars," Ray explained, faithfully monitoring the rocking canoe, about to receive backwash off the bank. "Jesus, they swamped her," he yelled with weakly camouflaged delight.

Ray sprinted up the beach. About to dive in, he was tackled hard. "I don't think so," Cohen said, holding him down. "You don't even know her."

"Are you crazy? She could drown out there." Ray tried to struggle to his feet but was returned to the ground by his larger, inspired adversary.

"Thanks. I'm alright now," the men heard.

With an arm around Ray's neck, Cohen looked up at the finest vehicle for goose bumps he'd ever seen, about 5' 6", midnight hair down to her shoulders and the dimple cheeked face and butt of an imp. She was tying up her submerged canoe to a cypress knee five feet away, a little afraid to ask what Cohen and his friend were doing.

"Stay calm," she thought. "Surely they've seen all this before."

Twenty-nine year old Violet Chance had abandoned life in corporate America to be proprietor of Eco-Logic, an Orlando store devoted to converting people to environmentally friendly goods, selling planet-savers ranging from organic produce to pricey natural soap and her recycled flagship item, Eco-Asswipe (made from trees that haven't even been born yet). Competing with Publix, which carried its own line of less sincere feel-good products, it was an uphill battle in the rain with a headache. After a day of trying to start a revolution by example, she liked to drink wine and tell jokes. This was how she met Mortecai at Ann Hinga's Fish House and Tavern. Cohen's apparent cavalier attitude toward a world in peril had poisoned the instant attraction they felt.

Seeing clearly how much was at stake, Mortecai frantically tried to compose something conciliatory to say, that they might start over fresh. "Great breasts," he blurted the thought filling his brain, releasing Ray's head and standing up. "I had no idea."

"Breasts?" Ray gasped under his breath. "Look at her butt!"

"Shut up, Ray," Mortecai whimpered back down. "How about a little respect?"

"I'm sure glad chivalry isn't dead yet," Violet said, wringing out her clothes and trying not to pose for Cohen's friend.

She shook her sparkling head like it was a small dog as the much admired breasts remained preternaturally stationary. Mortecai was insufficiently chivalrous to look entirely away and his brain nearly fused, his entire history topped by this primal revelation of his exact target in life. More of a butt man, Ray was in a similar state of shock over how he had seen that article perform during the head shaking.

"I guess you're Larry and Moe," she continued, stepping into her pants. "Is Curly about to fall out of a tree on me or something?"

As Violet completed her ensemble, Mortecai stepped in front of Ray to get his attention. "We'd like to stay and chat, Violet, but me and my friend have things to do back at the bridge."

"I'm coming, too."

"Alright. We'll take the canoe."

Violet stood on the bank and watched Mortecai bail the canoe with his wide hands while Ray lifted it, finally achieving buoyancy, then tipping it out. With Cohen reclining in the middle and Macon in front to warn of submerged logs, Violet deftly guided her craft around snags and bends back toward the dirt clearing by the bridge.

"Boy, this is the only way to travel," Cohen said with satisfaction, stretching out.

"It's a whole different perspective," added Ray.

"This is amazing," Violet said. "I do appreciate you telling me about it, Mort."

"So you always take your clothes off in a canoe? I never thought it would be this easy to see you naked."

"Being out here just made me feel so free. And I sure didn't think anybody else would be around, let alone jet-skiers. There was just that Honda Civic, and the way it looks, I figured it was abandoned."

"Thanks," Ray said. "They must have put in after you, then. We'll have plenty of time."

"I just have to tell you, Violet," Mortecai said, turning around. "You look damn good. Doesn't she Ray?"

"If optical satisfaction is what you're into. Personally, I'm more interested in a woman's political beliefs."

"Save it for Daisy, Ray."

"So Mortecai," Violet changed the subject, "you use toilet paper, don't you?"

"That's a little personal, but if it's your standard for mating, absolutely. All the time."

"Go left," Ray said.

"Then why haven't I seen you in the store?" Violet asked, ruddering on the right to avoid a submerged cabbage palm.

"Up until today, because it's cheaper everywhere else. But from now on, I'm an Eco-asswipe man."

"But you think recycling is a scam."

"He's been enlightened," Ray clarified.

"Am I onto something here? Do I have to stand in front of the store naked to get people to see the light?"

"Beats the heck out of a wooden Indian."

"Shove it."

"You think everybody's a bad person if they don't shop at your store. We've got the same goal, just different ways of going about it," Mortecai said, wishing they could talk about something else.

"And how are you going about it?" Violet accused. "By driving your gas-guzzling old van to county commission meetings?"

Mortecai felt like a mummy at a pool party. "At least I don't buy new vehicles."

"Great. By all means, stick with 1970 pollution standards."

The concrete bridge loomed into view as they rounded the final turn and Ray was becoming elated. "Quit saving the world, you two. There it is."

Details emerged as they drew nearer. "Boy, they all have the same little shiny plastic-looking imitation pick-up type things," Mortecai noted.

"The whole thing comes as a package," Ray said. "The trailer's actually part of the vehicle." The canoe coasted up to the small gray beach and stopped.

"Do we have anything to let the air out of their tires with?" Violet asked.

Ray pulled out his pocketknife. "This'll probably do it."

"Oh, man. That'll let the air *all* the way out, won't it?" Mortecai said, opposed to tire slashing for the sake of the tires, more beautiful than any he had owned.

" 'Spect so," Ray said, popping out the four inch blade. He turned it slowly until sun flashed off the shiny steel.

"I'm not up for this. Let's just get a stick or something to push in the valves," Violet pleaded.

They sat in the canoe, restrained by a learned barrier to destroying personal property.

Mortecai said, "I just wanted to send 'em a message."

"They'll be able to read this one." Ray stepped out of the canoe and pulled it up on the sand, tipping out Violet and Mortecai. Soon the quietude was broken by a rush of compressed air heading for freedom as they saw the left front of the truck droop.

"As long as we're doing it, I guess we need to do two," Mortecai said.

"On each side?" Ray asked innocently.

"That might be a bit much."

"I agree. We'll leave them one tire. Let them wonder why."

More air rejoined the atmosphere.

Violet was only slightly dismayed by her enjoyment of the retribution. "Hey, I get to have some fun, too," she said, grabbing the knife. "The trailer doesn't match the car now." Squatting by a trailer tire, she jammed the blade in. "Wow! That feels good. Must be that penetration thing you guys like so much. I think I want to do the other one, too."

"My turn," said Mortecai. "We must share the guilt."

Cohen took the knife and walked to the left rear of the truck. There he held the point between raised white letters on the sidewall, unable to slay the innocent child of Vulcan. He glanced up at Ray. "Look at this tread. You've got a jack and a four-way. Why don't we just steal it?"

"Give me the knife," Ray said.

"No, I'll do it."

"Think of it as collateral damage," Ray advised. "It's the owner you're actually hurting."

Mortecai pictured the jet-skiers swamping Violet and plunged the blade.

Violet, Mortecai and Ray stood back, critically assessing their work.

"I don't know. I think the shitbrains will be pretty unhappy when they see this," Ray said approvingly.

"Probably won't be coming here anymore," Mortecai added.

"But I might as well key the thing just to be sure."

Mortecai sighed. "Yeah, might as well. Violet - you wanta t-p 'em, just to ice the cake?"

"Best not to hang around and see the reaction, huh?" Violet judged as Ray doodled on the driver side door.

"Best not. What we've done is probably illegal."

"Look at it as an investment in the future," Ray said, finishing up.

Ray and Mortecai helped Violet reattach the canoe to the roof of her Volvo. Hoisting the back end, Mortecai smiled at the bumper sticker "Earth First - We'll Screw-Up the Other Planets Later." Then they all headed for some exploration around the upstream S.R. 419 bridge, because the beautiful day still was young.

"You know, Ray," Mortecai began, oddly somber as they bounced back up the track to the road, "I used to think this was as beautiful as a place could be. I could just walk around out here all day; but from now on, I'm afraid the Econ is going to be like Eden without Eve."

Ray received this information with genuine surprise. "Maybe you ought to do something about it, then."

As they drove back by the weathered Bush Hog sign, the pine tree released its rusty nail. The plywood slid unnoticed down the bark and lay flat on the needles to create a community of pill bugs and earwigs.

2

V incent Barbarosa sucked seriously on a Camel. "Boy, I love it out here," he gushed with the windows rolled up.

"I thought you hated nature, Mr. Barbarosa," Attorney Tom Blunck released like an audible smoke signal.

"I don't hate nature, Tom, I despise her. There's a difference."

"And pray tell what is that?" asked Blunck, like he cared.

Barbarosa's white El Dorado slowed and stopped on the shoulder of S.R. 419 just short of the Econlockhatchee River bridge. He lowered his electric seat and leaned back, then turned to Blunck, who looked like a mortician in his drab, black suit. "You really don't get it, do you? This is an ecosystem." Barbarosa's right hand paraded a half-ash cigaret in front of the steering wheel. "It's the Virgin Mary, never been forked; God au natural'. Been like this for hundreds of years. Animals live in those trees; birds, bugs, maybe even fish and I – I can end it. I can make it not be anymore. And then I get to put what *I* want there. That's power, Blunck, what the Bible calls 'opinion over the earth.'"

To ease pressure on a ripe carbuncle, the doughy, Crisco-skinned lawyer leaned against the passenger door. "And you came all the way from Maryland to do it," he pointed out, farting insignificantly. "What's the matter? No virgins between there and here?"

"It's so forking easy here. The politicians are lining up to sell out. I could be one of the Five Horsemen of the Acropolis and they'd line up for autographs." The developer paused for effect.

The ignorant fork, Blunck thought, inhaling Marlboro. He leaned over and swept ash off his customer's pleated brown slacks and polo shirt, in the process shaking ash onto his own pants. Barbarosa cracked the window enough to flick his cigaret onto the road, then extended his right hand into the glove compartment for another one.

Discomfort returned to Blunck's buttock and he raised himself slightly into an attentive pose. "You get any resistance, all you've got to do …"

"— is threaten to take my plague and go home. Next day they're so scared they're all trying to pluck my cork at once."

"Stop it. You're making me jealous." The lawyer laughed uneasily.

Barbarosa lit a Camel. "Don't worry, Tom. You're my favorite corkplucker. Anyway, I just wanted you to see what you're fighting for."

Blunck became thoughtful. "If you don't mind me saying it, one of the greatest things about you is, you don't care that you're coming in here forking these people up. At these public hearings you can feel the hatred they have for you. But you don't let it worry you. You know what you want to do and you're doing it."

Vincent Barbarosa stared through the carcinogenic haze and into Blunck's watery, hazel eyes. "It's because they're nobody. They're nothin'."

The stretched skin parted and a gray volcano erupted in the lawyer's briefs, signifying relief.

Barbarosa sat back and drummed his fingers on each other. "Let me ask you something, Blunck."

The lawyer nodded with a little dread.

"Why did you say 'forking'?"

"That's just the way I talk," Blunck stammered.

"You can say the other word if you want to?"

"Yeah, sure."

"Okay," Barbarosa dropped the subject sadly.[1]

---

[1]Human: most intelligent thing on the planet; status based on capacity to recognize environmental degradation as an achievement. Probably alone in needing to achieve beyond its fellow inhabitants. Also only one that smokes camels, made easy by the opposable thumb.

Tom Levine

The Cadillac's drive wheel sprayed gravel turning around as Vincent Barbarosa aimed it back to town. Almost directly below him under the bridge, Mary Barbarosa prepared for the first time to slide down Doc Stiles' firepole. She was hovering at the zenith as Stiles felt his hands on the firm, grapefruit-style breasts trembling with anticipation under her shirt. Like charmed pencil erasers, her nipples grew plump and out between his fingers and he was awash in wonder that such a woman could be stimulated by his skinny little elf-like self. Shampoo-ad blonde hair lifting lightly in the breeze was ignited by morning sun, splashing a halo effect around red sofa-cushion lips and shimmering blue eyes. "Before we do this, I suppose I should tell you," she said sweetly, swishing angel-food pubic hair around the end of the pole, "I have active herpes. Should I stop?"

He watched her lips massage the words as if lips were something sublime he had heard of in fables, never before seen. He was enraptured that her breath carried sounds just for him through that undulating portal. Doc was incapable of caring if she had bubonic plague. "I guess I don't believe you. No way they've got herpes in Heaven."

"You know, Doc," Mary noted, sliding down, "you have a crummy truck," alluding to the passenger side window that couldn't roll up. "Do you think maybe it's never going to rain?" She was establishing a rhythm. "Or don't you mind getting wet?"

Doc started singing in his mind The Suwannee River.

"The only reason I'm with you like this in this heap of scrap metal you call a vehicle," she said, speaking in time with her hips, "is it's as far as I can get from my real life. I hope you're okay with that."

Looking at the Econlockhatchee River, Mrs. Barbarosa accelerated the beat and her captive switched to Camptown Races. "That line you had out with a big float on it?" she cooed, "The float just went under."

"No way," Stiles nearly sang, glad for a distraction - "There's no fish on Cloud Nine."

"Let me check. It could be a big one." Before Doc could object, she had slid up his pole and sprang out of the truck wearing only a white

20

T-shirt. On the riverbank the developer's wife bent over and grabbed Doc's other rod, closed the bail and set the hook. "Oh, my God. There's something on here," she yelled, struggling to hold on. "It's huge."

Doc fell out the car, also wearing only a shirt, and staggered to the scene, rapidly returning to earth. He saw the bend in the fishing rod and heard the drag whining. "Okay. Good. Now give me the rod."

"Not on your life, buster." Mary looked down briefly. "You've already got one."

Doc began responding to fishing instincts. He started jumping around shouting instructions, his forgotten rod see-sawing in front of him. Noting Stiles' groin, a passing armadillo allowed that it never had seen anyone get so excited over fishin'.

"What do you think it is?" Mary shouted.

"I don't know, but it's big. Keep him away from those snags over there."

"I know what I'm doing. You think I never caught a fish before?"

So it went, unknown to each other only hours before, together now on the bank of the Econlockhatchee, battling a monster.

"Watch out! He's heading for the bridge!" warned an alarmed Stiles.

"I know. I can't stop him." Mary backed to her right, toned legs trying to gain ground on the unstoppable force, her hard buttocks clenched. Just before the bridge, the mighty fish lunged for safety, wrapped the line around a piling and broke contact with higher life forms.

"Shit!" she shrieked as the fishing rod sprang back to attention.

Doc stepped over to console the vanquished battler and as he did, his other rod also returned to attention. "Hey. You did all you could. He was just too big." He eased his helpmate to a patch of grass. "Let me try and make it all better."

"I'm not in the mood now," she pouted. "I feel like crying. If I could have even just seen what it was."

21

Panicking, Doc said, "It was probably a gar. They're almost impossible to catch. Come on back to the truck and we'll talk about it."

"Doc, do you mind if we just sit here and talk now?"

Suddenly feeling inappropriate, Doc tried to hide his manhood under his button-down shirt. Why, he condemned himself, did I have to put that stupid line out?

Sitting on the bank dangling her perfect toes in the tannic stream, long T-shirt pulled down as a seat, Mary spoke softly. "I'm married, you know."

"You already told me your name."

"No. I mean I have a husband."

"Is that what you meant by active herpes?" the man of the nineties asked sensitively.

"More like inactive. Most of the time you don't know it's there but it's always in the background waiting to ?##* you up."

"Hmmmm. You don't really have herpes, do you?"

Mary shook her head, slightly amused and pointed at the place where the stream narrowed and returned to the forest. "They're going to destroy all this, you know."

"All what?" replied the preoccupied man with little interest. "And who?"

"My husband and other greedy, selfish, money grubbers. You know. The people who run the world. Vincent's company wants to fill in the swamp and put a city out here."

"Right here?" asked Doc, not taking Mary seriously.

"Upstream actually. But right here won't really exist anymore. This will be like some bridge in the middle of Orlando."

She was starting to feel a little sad.

"I knew it!" Doc stated positively. "Angels don't have assholes. You had to marry one."

Mary brightened. "Anyway, it's here today, for me to go slumming. And you're here, aren't you. I'm glad you brought me here. But now you'd better bring me back."

Doc gazed at his companion as a strange sensation built up inside him. He kissed Mary tenderly on the cheek, then leapt to his feet. "Shit!" he yelled and jumped into the river. "Those damn ants crawled up my butt."

As Doc Stiles reluctantly guided his truck back up to the road, a canoe-carrying Volvo followed a Honda Civic down on the other side of the bridge because the day still was young.

3

anking on the Orange County Commission's policy of approving anything on a grand enough scale, Barbarosa Development Inc. had proposed a "planned unit development" called Havalawn. Sprawling over ten thousand acres of wilderness at the Econlockhatchee River's headwaters, it would be started in the fall.

Laid out as a New England town, it would mix residential and business and, most authentic of all, mostly New Englanders would live there. Houses would be packed tightly in rows to maximize Barbarosa's profit, so it was being touted as "traditional." Since the targeted area lacked infrastructure, the developer needed the county commissioners to extend the "urban service boundary" with its sewer pipes and utility connections.

A public hearing had been scheduled so the public could hear what the county commission was going to do. It would be the first use of the new county commission auditorium, denoted outside by a red, white and blue neon sign proclaiming DEMOCRACY WORLD.

After the ribbon cutting, the meeting began with an apparently infinite cavalcade of politician credit-giving and taking for construction of the building, attended by the usual catastrophically boring speeches featuring self aggrandizement in the form of humility. The audience were trapped in their seats by optimism which constantly dictated, "Surely to God this is the last one."

At the height of the ordeal County Watch Representative Lloyd Bruell, recently weakened by a cold, caught a fatal blood clot to the brain; two janitors trying to interrupt the relatively benign monotony of their job, became hypnotized into believing they were broom handles and glided out the room, for some reason squawking like the eerily amphibious tawny frogmouth of the Australian outback; and an elderly gentleman who had wandered in looking for Walgreen's died of old age while waiting to ask directions.

Veterans of these crucibles had brought books to read. Commissioner Liz Mango, who had campaigned for a series of tedium alerts to be posted outside, ranging from yellow to red depending on its projected severity and duration, shook her head sadly as the casualties were carried out.

Following the opening ceremonies, the show proceeded predictably. Engineers and planners presented a mind-numbing depth of graphs, charts and displays to build momentum and project the inevitability of their goal. Because of the high stakes and widespread public opposition to this plan, the developer then addressed the ruling body in person.

Thirty-two sheltered and friendless years old, tanned with impeccably styled black hair, Vincent Barbarosa was comely enough straight on though his profile seemed a compelling argument for The Descent of Man from Bulldogs. He was enhanced by pinky rings, cuff links and Rolex. While speaking, he was fascinated by the segmented wall mural behind the commissioners. Set among palmettos and sand was a fisticuffs between a middle-aged Fidel Castro in army fatigues and Mickey Mouse draped in the Florida flag. In the final stage, Mickey knocked Fidel's head clean off and it flew through the sunny day, landing in parking area Pluto F where it was run over by a shuttle bus driven by Goofy. The climax was in "DYNAMATION" and visitors could actually work a lever to raise and lower the bus, squishing anew the vanquished dictator's brain which oozed a colorless, disappearing, Marxist gel. Concentrating, Barbarosa finished:

"I am an environme'talist," he declared, answered by general coughing, laughing and gagging throughout the room. "I'm as much an environme'talist as anyone here. No one has more concern than I do for Florida's fu…, er, fragile ecosystems. We understand the concerns of the residents of Central Florida. We share them. Believe me, we want this to work, not for ourselves but for the benefit of all Floridians. We have opened the door to a new tomorrow. Do you have the courage to walk through?" He smiled at fifty-something County Chairman Betty Baxter who was leaning over grinning like a star-struck groupy. "Thank you." Barbarosa resisted the urge to walk to the mural and work the bus.

During the intermission preceding the rebuttal period, the opponents of the proposal gathered to discuss their disgust. Except Mortecai Cohen. Wearing his orange HELP KEEP FLORIDA BEAUTIFUL - SHOOT A DEVELOPER T-shirt, he reached out and stood among the developer's people. They didn't take it the right way and abandoned their little caucus. Then, exhibiting the injured feelings of a rejected puppy, he followed them around.

A reporter from Rollins College Radio WPRK was interviewing Gertrude Buttmaster, stately middle aged commissioner whose district was the Spanish speaking and black areas on the west side of Orlando.

"Mrs. Buttmaster, how do you feel about Havalawn?"

"Well, let me axe you this young lady," Gertrude said, her shiny green pantsuit dangerously close to the diminutive blonde, "How many of my constituents does you thinks is going to be moving in there?"

"I'm talking about the environmental impact. There are several known gopher tortoise communities on the property."

Suddenly Gertrude was interested. "Gopher turtles you say? Now them is good eatin'." The commissioner was distracted, planning a food gathering family outing for the coming Saturday.

"They're endangered."

"You got *that* right."

The reporter paused for a moment. "What about the wetlands?" she asked as in a dream.

Buttmaster stabbed her in the eyes with a lifetime of scorn. "Wetlands is white man's business, lady. The only wetlands I knows about is when the sewers backs up around Willie Mays Drive. When's the great city of Orlando going to give *me* some new pipes?"

The meeting was reconvened. Supplicants including housewives, homeowners, and nature lovers spoke in favor of preserving the headwater area. Betty Baxter and the lesser commissioners politely accepted this verbal homage to their power and grandeur.

Mortecai Cohen had fixed his van to drive to the meeting, though he wasn't quite sure what he had done under the hood that worked. Still in the afterglow of his blow against the jet-skiers three days earlier, he had intended to leave the speaking to the experts. As usual he became inspired by a developer's presentation and the commission's loving acceptance of it. He finally rose from the audience and approached the pulpit, considering potential improvements for the mural.

"I'm Mortecai Cohen, 513 South Asphalt Road, Orlando. I only live here, so disregard everything you're about to hear."

Relative tact never having persuaded anyone in the past, Cohen had recently abandoned it and simply granted himself the pleasure of speaking his mind.

"I'd like to ask Mr. Barbarosa what an environme'talist is, but I'm afraid we already know, all too well." The crowd burst into laughter at the puzzled developer. "I guess our highly engaged developer meant to say he's an environ*men*talist but he couldn't handle the mental part. If Mr. Barbarosa is an environmentalist may I suggest that Attila the Hun was a fun guy?"

Commission Chairman Betty Baxter's jaw dropped with the weight of an inexpressible admonition. "Mr. Cohen!!" she managed finally.

"Betty, why do you get upset every time I make a slightly disparaging remark toward some stinking developer, but you don't mind that someone is trying to further ruin the lives of your constituents and steal the future from their children? And why are you listening to Mr. Barbarosa brag about his lousy subdivision? We're not going to live there. We don't care if Havalawn is so fine that God Himself slides down out of heaven and starts vacationing there; which He won't do because He'll think it's garbage. Why do you think He put trees there anyway? Just to hold down the ground until some developer with a better idea can bulldoze them?"

"Mister Cohen, we must weigh both sides equally."

"Who's the wise guy?" Barbarosa asked Blunck.

"Don't you remember? That's the guy who broke up your town hall meeting."

"Ha! He keeps jumpin' in the pool but he still don't make a splash."

"It's not your job to be judges," Cohen continued. "You're supposed to defend the interests of the people who live here. Why does the greed of a handful of wealthy low-lifes equal the heartfelt concerns of thousands of regular voters? Because voters only vote once every four years but developers pay on a regular basis?"

Barbarosa chuckled knowingly until Blunck elbowed him.

Jake Lessup had made a modest fortune as a small-scale developer, building and selling mini-storage facilities. He now turned his time toward defense of the Econlockhatchee River. In the last row Lessup yawned and slid down in his seat.

"Development will come," Baxter predicted from on high. "We feel fortunate to have a developer with Barbarosa's deep pockets and reputation for quality. Mr. Barbarosa has cooperated and worked very closely with us on this."

"It's in his interest to cooperate. Right now we've got God's standard and that's how we'd like to keep it. (applause from the partisan crowd) Here's an example of Barbarosa's quality. The dufus they hired for an attorney doesn't have the sense to grow hair on top of his head. [2]

"Just remember. If you pass this, you'd better soak Barbarosa for as much as you can, because you'll be out of a job come next election. Thank you for your time and top quality condescension." Cohen glared

---

[2] This is the unfortunate condition of developer lawyers. It is unknown if baldness turned these men against Mother Nature or if God hurled this plague upon them for squandering their educations.

at the developer, who was leaning over listening to Tom Blunck. "As for you, Barbarosa, you need your ass kicked and these are just the feet to do it. But I'm sure you're too much of an environme'talist to accept a challenge."

No longer aware of Cohen, Barbarosa said something to Blunck that the attorney felt obliged to snicker at.

"Mr. Cohen!" cried an appalled Baxter one last time, exciting earpiercing feedback from her microphone.

Cohen stepped down to hearty applause.

Representing the Sierra Club, the petite yet well endowed Amelia Niceones made an eloquent and angry appeal based on the right of nature to remain natural. With this she misjudged the commissioners who never would know the Econlockhatchee beyond the fleeting view while driving across a bridge.

Commissioner Hairwarp leaned her mouth over to Baxter's ear. "Nutty as a fruit cake." The chairwoman nodded agreement.

Niceones was applauded as she stepped down.

The president of the Audubon Society spoke on behalf of the endangered red balloon-headed woodpecker. This is the only creature known to fly backwards with any degree of skill at all, often with the aspect and duration of a released balloon. Oddly, it was inadequate for the humans to argue out of self-interest for their own habitat. They needed to include this fragile, obscure bird for legitimacy.

A chubby, round faced man in black pants and badly tucked in long sleeved white shirt ascended the dais. Having safely found his way there, he removed and pocketed his thick, black rimmed glasses.

"Hello. I'm Peter Pickels, president of the Homeowners' Association at Squashed Turtle Crossing, which backs up to the proposed west boundary of Havalawn. We think Havalawn is a fine idea. We'd just like to know a few things like how high the walls are going to be and if our clotheslines are going to be a problem for our new neighbors."

Baxter almost choked on her spit, she was so eager to respond. "Mr. Pickels, let me tell you how refreshing it is to get someone up there with positive input."

The developer was granted the last word so a parade of Barbarosa's testimonials concluded the meeting, highlighted by a hick who unaccountably appeared at every meeting concerning this river, with the sole purpose of making insulting remarks like it's muddy and most the time his dog walks across it without getting his belly wet; and Gene Urbansky, proudly proclaimed the "Father of Florida's Growth Management", who seemed to believe Havalawn was a great idea.

Short senior citizen redhead Miriam Canblaster stood up and hollered in her aristocratic southern accent, "Who's some of your other bastards? Charles Manson and Richard Dahmer?"

Commissioner Baxter glanced sharply at Cohen as if he were an evil influence.

Came time for the vote and the fight led by Commissioner Mango was shockingly close. She had managed to convince two novice commissioners that a "Yea" vote on Havalawn would abort their budding careers. It was a tie coming to Gertrude Buttmaster, whose vote would determine whether or not a high-density city would be dropped onto the pristine headwaters of the Econlockhatchee River. Earlier in the meeting a state biologist had pointed out the development inevitably would flood. The city of Orlando and Orange County would have to mop up with money that might have gone to inner city projects; so some felt she would drive the nail to kill Havalawn.

The defenders of the river were hoping to win for none of the right reasons. For them a lot was riding on Mrs. Buttmaster; not only the river but their faith in democracy. Amelia Niceones fidgeted in her seat. Jake Lessup sat calmly fatalistic as if he already knew the outcome. Mortecai Cohen filled with dread. He did not wish to be sucked into the battle he knew must follow if Buttmaster sided with Barbarosa.

Gertrude began to speak and all suspended breathing. She framed her coming remarks by fawning over Gene Urbansky for his groundbreaking leadership. She acknowledged the Audubon Society's concerns by alerting them to the fact that "there's plenty of peckerheads to go around." She considered herself quite a character and this elicited her obligatory laugh for the meeting. Then Buttmaster summed up with pluck, "If the first woman hadn't a wore high heels, then nobody'd be wearin' 'em today. We got to try sumptin' new. I vote 'yes'."

Heartbreak in the air was palpable as the defeated warriors began filing out the room like a troupe of clowns with their noses shot off. Mortecai Cohen strode across the aisle to the developer's side, then walked through a row to where Barbarosa was standing, just giving fate a chance. Loitering behind the backslapping winners, he noticed at his feet a large, overstuffed notebook. Hoping it might contain embarrassing if not incriminating information on Barbarosa Development, he put out a foot to slide the bonanza to him. He was suddenly face to face with Vincent Barbarosa. For a moment their eyes fought like same-pole magnets; then the developer's gaze dropped and he bent to pick up his papers. Cohen stood on the cover with his full weight. Barbarosa straightened back up.

"Get off it," he said.

"Get off what?" Cohen asked innocently.

Suddenly Cohen was surrounded by dark suits. "This guy giving you some trouble, Vince?" a large, swarthy man asked, unbuttoning his coat as the man behind him popped his knuckles.

"That's not a very nice T-shirt you're wearing," a third suit pointed out. "You're not encouraging people to shoot Vinnie here, are you?"

Cohen drilled him with his deep blue stare. "You should see what my underwear says."

Jake Lessup walked up with the Democracy World sheriff's deputy. "What's this all about?" the deputy accused Cohen due to his casual attire.

"These creeps are trying to steal your habitat," he said, pushing through the crowd. "Ask them."

Shaking and filled with arrogant fury, telling himself Cohen was unworthy of his wrath, Barbarosa retrieved his prize from the floor and turned and walked for the door, stepping on his own shoe.

"Mr. Cohen - did you speak?"

Mortecai turned to see a smoking, bleached apparition staring at him through Pepsi bottle bottom lenses. "Nah. I never say anything. What'd you fall asleep again, Lessup?"

"No, I was awake."

"Great, ain't it? The Econ goes down because of high heel shoes. Who'da thought it?"

"Did you hear? Orlando's got the number one growth rate in the country," Jake Lessup jabbed.

"The boys downtown must be creamin' themselves over that one. What an honor. And they call it growth. Grow is what a plant does. It's a good thing."

"Cancer's a growth."

"Yeah, you're right," Mortecai admitted. "They're being honest after all."

"And still they want more. Our wells are salt water intruded, toxins are seeping into the aquifer and the lakes are full of mercury but we need more people here," Lessup added cheerfully.

"The government doesn't like wells anyway. Too independent. They want everybody drinking that official water. How about that Jeb Exclamation Point?" Cohen struck back. "Yep. Old George took Jeb aside, put his wormy arm around his shoulder and said, "You aren't planning anything for the next four years, are you boy? How about being governor of Florida so we can get going on that offshore drilling?"

"I don't want to be governor of Florida, Paw," Jeb whined. "Why can't Neil do it?"

"Neil's all used up, son. I'm counting on you."

"How about Old Stupid?" Lessup interjected.

"No, he has to be governor of Texas."

"But don't the folks there care that I've got my head up my ass?" Jeb continued, scratching the top of his head with one finger.

"Heck no, boy. They're mostly Northerners anyway. They expect that."

Cohen crossed his eyes. "Alright, Paw. I guess I'll be Governor of Florida."

"And he just may be," Lessup finished gravely. "With all these northern numbskulls voting here now, anything can happen."

Jake dropped his Winston to the floor and crushed it thoughtfully with his shoe. "Listen, Cohen. You're a good talker and you could be an ally. But right now you're just pissing into the wind and it's getting all over everybody else."

"What do you mean? I got a round of applause."

"They were embarrassed for you. We all know who the commission works for. And the fact that they think they're fooling us could be our only edge. I'm not saying you caused the vote, but you made the assholes feel better about it. You've got to stop taking this thing personally."

"It *is* personal. He made it that way."

"Look. These people have a vast plan in mind and we only get to see a little bit at a time. When we fight we have to win. Over and over again. They only have to win once and it's game over. And they never stop coming back. Today they finally got east Orange County."

Lessup knocked a new smoke from its box and lit up. "Let me give you some advice, Cohen. The Lone Ranger routine only works on teevee. You have to be perceived as representing other people. Give yourself a name - River Watchers or Friends of the Econ, something corny the media can get ahold of. Until you do that, you're just some isolated malcontent. And be careful." He exited ahead of a wispy trail and then he was gone.

"No. We are not leaving. You built this place. It is our home. Our children know the area and can play safely. They have no right to take it away from us."

"But they're coming. You know that. It is their destiny. You know what happened before. You were stubborn then, too. I built that place and those children also knew the area. Everyone else had left but we stayed; because they didn't have the right, you said. And then came the giant yellow monsters. Remember?" Mrs. Rabbit was trembling with the memory. "We gathered the children and we all huddled in the hole while the ground shook and the trees fell and the giant things walked over us, back and forth. I thought we would be crushed. If I had not made such a strong hole, we would have been. I do not want to feel that again. Please, Mr. Rabbit. Let us leave now with everyone else."

Mr. Rabbit was standing, ears twitching, trying to define some vague disturbance of the air. "But where will we go? Always they find us. Just when we settle in and the children know all the bushes and holes and the favorite perches of the owls and hawks, they find us."

"Maybe this will be enough for them. We could move east again. Maybe they will not come," said Mrs. Rabbit.

"Some rabbits return after the yellow monsters have left and they live among the humans. Would you like to do that? We could go back to the last place and see how it is."

Mrs. Rabbit fiddled with a dandelion. "No. Let others do it if they like. I do not want my children growing up like that, living or dying at their whim; eating their garbage, surrounded by cats and dogs. The end of living and the beginning of survival. No. Only when they have it all and there is no further place to go." Mrs. Rabbit paused to compose herself because she was about to propose a very big thing. "You know when we were young how we often spoke of The Big Place and how fine it would be to live there, beyond the threat of the humans?"

"Of course. The fabled place where The River begins. But every niche there is filled. Surely."

"Maybe not. Some of our neighbors are going there. They say a spirit of tolerance has been adopted. The residents do not demand large territories to themselves. Many live in warrens. If we went there, we would finally be home."

The roar of a diesel engine starting up could be heard in the distance. "Leave. You must leave now, Mrs. Rabbit," cried a red tailed hawk flying overhead and then landing on a branch of a pine tree. "Take your brood and run for it."

"Now we cannot go," cried Mrs. Rabbit. "We are trapped."

"No. You will go. Take the children and go to The Big Place." The roar of the machinery was closer. Mr. Rabbit dashed into the open and the hawk dived. Mrs. Rabbit chased her children ahead of her. "Run!" she commanded. "Do not look back. Your father is not there."

4

Lo! Cohen heard the words of the Lessup and on that day did the Lone Ranger die. From his grave was wrought upon the earth not a club or a lobbying group; no, from the dust of renewal was come in Cohen's old frame house, a religion; and from this, hoped Cohen, a tax break. But more importantly, "Wait 'til I tell Violet about this."

Pastor Cohen participated with little zeal in the seven day week and so observed the Sabbath when the mood struck him. The following Saturday Ray Macon impatiently stood in bare feet and cut-offs through the first service of the Holy Crap Church of the Coupon Redeemer. It was another perfect spring day and he just wanted to get fishing. "This is the last time I do this," he warned, exuding urgency with his refusal to sit on an egg crate. "I didn't get out of the house so I could stand around here."

"Just shut up and hang on. This'll only take a minute. Besides, I think you'll find it timely."

Under backyard oaks Cohen ranged up lean and tan behind the pulpit, an empty URANUS Colostomy Bags box. Below his broad forehead and black eyebrows, two startling blue pools bathed his world in sea and sky. Speaking, smiling and drinking migrated across his long, elastic face like kaleidoscope designs, all betraying grim undertones in those days.

"Holy Crap, brethren," the baritone boomed, "as Good God Almighty has deigned to spill a bucket of heaven's atmosphere on us this morning, the service will be short that we may take full advantage. We shall now read the Gospel according to Cohen."

Ray's belch was so loud a frightened squirrel fell off its branch. Feet scrambling and fluffy tail switching frantically, it plummeted between the men and thudded sideways on a patch of sand. Before the stunned rodent could get its footing, Mortecai's cat, Juice, clamped his jaws around its neck and sped off.

Cohen was devastated. "Goddammit, Ray. Look what you did. What a great initiation for a church devoted to Mother Nature."

But Ray was beyond caring. It just happened to strike him as funnier than anything he'd ever hoped to see. He staggered, then collapsed to the ground, paralyzed by an ecstasy of humor that nearly transcended the corporeal plane.

Curled on his side, Ray was gasping for air between moans of happiness.

"I thought you wanted to get going," Cohen said pensively.

Ray joyfully wiped tears from his eyes and started recovering. He stood, trying to say something, but then his throat made a crying sound and he relapsed, whimpering against an oak tree. Cohen concentrated on a jet contrail.

Straining mightily to hold his features in check, Ray faced Cohen seriously. "Guess I've still got it," he managed to squeak out.

"You know, you're the one in such an all-fired hurry to go fishing."

"Alright, alright," Ray said, composing himself. "Go ahead."

"You're sure?"

Ray nodded cautiously.

Cohen began his religious career:

"The native Floridiot lives with a mild version of the sense of loss the native Americans felt, the essential difference being the Floridiot is invited to participate in the destruction. He is allowed to remain and witness it. Everyday his home habitat is less, degraded or restricted. He cannot go places he used to. They're not worth going to anymore. His eyes are constantly pained by the sight of beauty and harmony shoveled under and replaced by concrete, Northerners, walls and NO TRESPASSING signs. Clear lakes fertilized, rivers canalized, forests malled, beaches overshadowed by condominia; all under the auspices of the local representatives of the people. But which people? He attends public hearings to watch his government defend his home against the onslaught, only to see that the government is a necessary conspirator. Some folks go home, shrug their shoulders and say, "Well, we tried." A few others get angry. I feel like my hands have been tied behind my back while someone slapped my face. Day after day. Year after year. Today I free my hands.

"Let us pray. Good God Almighty, me and Ray are about to embark on a crusade. Please guide our hands, sharpen our eyesight, make our sugar as damaging to its victims as the sugar industry is damaging to the Neverglades. Could be a fine irony, don't you think? And if you think of it, drop me off a bag of big money.

Amen."

"We'll talk about it. Now, if we don't get out of here, I'm going without you."

Ray and Mortecai agreed completely on the value of saving Florida from improvement, the difference being Mortecai's determination to do it. Cohen believed the populace would join in once he began, and vanquish the developers through sheer numbers. He worked on Ray while they fished and was happily surprised that he didn't require a lot of convincing. For sure the random nature of the attack appealed to him, but maybe some part of Ray just couldn't abide the smell of chickenshit.

Taking on their first machine was a big step. They targeted an offending backhoe ditching the edge of a field just beyond the city limits. Cohen had bought a quart jar of Karo Syrup and Macon a quart of beer. Fortified by Schlitz, Ray picked him up Saturday night. They parked across the street, ran over and dove behind the hoe. There they lay, nervous and happy as they donned their gardening gloves.

Feeling around, Mortecai found the gas cap, located flat atop the fender. He reached up and removed it. With audacity that surprised Mortecai, Ray stood and poured in the syrup, too fast. It bubbled out. Mortecai was even more impressed that Ray waited to add the rest slowly, making sure to finish the jar. Unfortunately, syrup coating the area around the gas cap was a dead giveaway, which would lead to a simple draining of the gas tank to neutralize their effort.

"Shit. This stuff won't come off," Mortecai remarked, rubbing with his glove as Ray watched a pair of lightning bugs twinkle through light mist floating over the grass.

"Maybe it'll rain," Ray offered weakly.

In spite of the sticky clue, the strike force shook hands euphorically and ran, crouching, back to the car. That night in bed at almost the same moment, Ray and Mortecai thought they heard distant thunder. As they tried to wish it closer, the thunder began to rumble. Soon they smiled as a drenching cloudburst broke loose. Cohen considered it a benediction.

Two days that week Ray drove by the improved backhoe, hoping to see it grinding to a halt in mid dig. Instead, the machine carried on as if it liked sweets. He told Cohen to get granular sugar next time.

As luck would have it, Ray was a salesman for Chemical Springs Bottled Water, giving him legitimate access to construction site trailers. He was driving onto an expanse of loose sand that a short time prior had been a pretty woods. Its new incarnation would be an apartment complex called Deer Run. Finding himself alone in the trailer, he noted Rusty Springs bottled water already in place. More inclined toward spontaneous acts of self-satisfaction than grand schemes with an ultimate goal, Ray tipped up the jug and urinated in it, saving some golden rain for the Gatorade he knew would be in the fridge. "Enjoy," he said, exiting the aluminum door.[3]

---

[3]Unknown to just about everybody is Bladderhorn, Patron Saint of Creative Urinating. He is a minor player, left over from the middle ages. In the purging of outdated saints from serious worldwide influence, he was simply overlooked, much like the Havasupai Indians of Arizona. A terrestrial deity, he smiled lovingly from the roof of the trailer upon one of his favorite disciples.

That evening Ray and Mortecai were bass fishing in Orlando's Lake Roadwater, the familiar urban aroma of pennyroyal filling their nostrils, the occasional car whizzing by behind them.

"Deer Used To Run, eh?" said Mortecai, casting a black and silver Culprit worm. "How much stuff is out there?"

"Lots. Bulldozers, loaders, graders. Raccoon suckers, squirrel grinders, possum pulverisers."

"I've been thinking about using sand. That way you don't have to carry anything. Must be the reason God put sand on construction sites."

"Think he's dropping a hint, eh?" Ray was getting inspired. "You could put that in the oil, too." He cleaned some exotic aquatic weed from his Hula Popper and tossed it straight out.

"Alright. Think you can get out of the house Sunday night? All you have to do is drop me off."

"Not likely. I can't be doing this all the time."

"I know. You've got a fambly."

Ray grinned slightly. "I find them. You do them."

"Oh, yeah. That's fair."

Sunday night few headlights traced the unlighted road that someday would lead to Deer Run. A family of raccoons watched from the moon-shadow as a Honda Civic whirred by. The father was trying to understand the "death space" that shot up and down the stinky land-divider; why sometimes it came and killed the animals and sometimes it held back and spared them. But it was beyond him.

"Just get in there and do it quick. I don't want Daisy wondering where I am." Ray took another slug from his quart of Old Milwaukee.

"I don't even know where anything is yet," Cohen protested.

They passed a big fenced lot of Caterpillar heavy equipment for sale. "Would you look at that?" said Ray. "The reinforcements are already waiting. You've got some chance of beating them."

"Turn around, Ray."

"What?"

"Why wait for 'em to get on site? Let's stop 'em here."

"Jesus." Ray finished the bottle.

Mortecai followed his crescent wrench, funnel, trowel, five bags of sugar in a Publix bag and can of WD-40 over the ten foot fence, then donned his rubber gloves. "If a security guard is in there," he reasoned, "I should be able to outrun him." Ray drove to a small dive they had passed a few miles back, to develop his alibi.

Cohen easily found the gas tanks of five identical bulldozers and dispensed a bag of sugar to each; then he hunted for the oil port, finding it behind an unlocked side panel. He scooped sand with his trowel, then slowly funnelled it to the oil, washing it down with WD-40 to remove any traces. The more he did, the more relaxed he felt about it. Over the next hour, he sanded the oil of twenty-two assorted wheeled machines, feeling a rare and splendid sense of accomplishment. As he looked for something else to do, the familiar sound of Ray's wounded Civic approached. He followed his stuff back over the fence.

"Man, I'd like to see these Caterpillars when they metamorphose," Mortecai said.

"That's a great bar back there. Big women," Ray said as he turned the car around.

"What about the apartments?"

"It's either The Dew Drop Out or home. Lots of good second hand smoke..."

"I am kinda thirsty."

Ray swerved to miss a large raccoon loping hesitantly across the road and nearly hit its mate.

5

ALL DENOMINATIONS WELCOME

to the

Holy Crap Church of the Coupon Redeemer

Featuring: just squeezed orange juice
and a different home-made sermon every
time, likely but not guaranteed to cure
warts, pimples, gout, ignorance, Christianity and
thirst.

Deity: Good God Almighty
Idol: Mother Nature

Guaranteed Death Afterlife!!!

SATURDAYS: 9 am or later   513 S. Asphalt Rd.

Orlando

All coupons respected

FREE!FREE!FREE!!!!

oc Stiles had parked his junkyard-yellow pickup by First Aquapedestrian Church, one of the biggest downtown palaces of worship, then crossed over to Mickeyola Park to feed the ducks.

Cohen felt hopeful about the old Chevy workhorse as he slid a flyer between cracked windshield and wiper. The hyper Stiles seemed to live on the brink of being surprised, so nothing ever totally surprised him. He read the notice and was sure he would attend at least one service. A native Orlandoan six years his junior, he turned out to be exactly what Mortecai Cohen was looking for.

Cohen greeted his new parishioner at the door with a glass of orange juice, then enlisted Juice the cat to lead him to an egg crate around back.

Behind a newly emptied URANUS box Pastor Cohen flung a terrible grimace upon his audience of one before thundering on: "It is written that tempests shall fall upon Florida, sweeping first down one coast and up the next and then once more for good measure, carrying away all condominia and state park ticket booths. Deep sinkholes shall yawn beneath the government buildings in Tallahassee and all of downtown Orlando. Very deep. DisneyWorld will disappear overnight in a colossal cloud of prehistoric termite flatulence. Torrential rain will burst the Rodman Dam, freeing the Oklawaha. The Kissimmee River will flood back into its rightful path, bursting all locks along the way. Giant cows from space will eat the Lake Okeechobee levee and then fly away again and lo! We will be cleansed."

The pastor threw back a slug of juice. "Let us pray:

Good God Almighty in the sky
We don't want our state to die
And to this end we have a goal.
Come on Good God, we'd like to see

43

What you can really do with a sinkhole
Miracles are what we need
So our faith can carry ya.
Could you please return to us
some good old time malaria?
We just want to live our lives.
Don't you know it's true?
Hear our prayers. Return our state!
We all depend on you."

Cohen rubbed his belly, slapped his forehead and grabbed a foot while reciting "In the name of the Otter, the Sun and the Holy Coast, Amen.

"Meeting's over. You may all go now. And remember - you can play in the gardens of desire only if you bring something to cut the barbed wire."

Doc Stiles shook the Pastor's hand. "Great sermon. Now what's this all about?"

A public hearing was scheduled for two weeks from the last one, concerning another subdivision proposed by Barbarosa Development, this one at the confluence of the Big and Little Econlockhatchee Rivers, to be called Two Rivers.

"It's time the Holy Crap Church went on a crusade," Mortecai said to himself as he read about the proposal in the Orlando [4]Goofy Gazette legal announcements, "but how will it be?" Driving down Interstate-4

---

[4] The local daily always *seemed* to be published by Goofy so locals came to call it the Goofy Gazette. For all practical purposes, this became its name and will be the one adhered to in this book. Goofy, of course, was the vile legacy of a fifth dimensional cartoon window that opened briefly between Warner Brothers and Disney. Elmer Fudd had sneaked through and impregnated Pluto Pup, establishing the path that later led to the birth of our president.

later that day, he noticed a blank billboard. Pulling off at the Longwood exit, he went looking for access on a dirt road that paralleled the highway.

Cohen felt the key to getting away with unauthorized billboard painting would be to do it boldly, like he was authorized. He returned at rush hour and stood before his canvas, excited about this new outlet of expression. He tossed his can of black spray paint up onto the built-in scaffold and then, gaining the initial foothold on the electric box, scaled the posts of the billboard using the cross braces behind it.

"Shit," he said, finishing the first letter too small. He got the hang of it after that, starting each subsequent symbol on tippy toes. With a sense of impending doom, he continued spraying his message as the traffic crawled by fifty yards away.

"Man, this takes a long-ass time," he thought, as he learned visibility required spraying wide letters with a few coats. At the third letter Cohen noticed a boy of about twelve looking up at him.

"What are you doing?"

Mortecai replied, "I'm painting a message."

"Oh," said the child and ran off toward a house.

A few minutes later the boy returned with a blonde, sparsely bearded biker who crossed his tattooed arms across his Harley muscle shirt and watched the writer.

"Howdy," Mortecai greeted with dread.

The biker gave the faintest impression of nodding gravely.

"What's up?" Cohen asked, eager to end the suspense.

The interested biker remained noncommittal. "Just watching."

Soon a crowd had gathered at the foot of the billboard, from kids to weathered, over-the-hill bikers all silently looking, waiting to see the message revealed. The word "SAVE" was followed by "the" as silence reigned. Followed by E-C-O-N. He completed the "N" and the crowd broke into cheers and applause. As he continued to paint "from Barbarosa, plus the meeting date," he heard the original biker say, "That guy has balls," considering the source, the finest compliment Mortecai ever had received.

Mortecai saw the original boy run back to his house and return momentarily with a can of spray paint. When all the kids and the able adults climbed the billboard to paint their initials, Mortecai thought he must be having a wonderful dream and resisted the temptation to leap off the platform and fly away. He felt like hugging everybody. In a relaxed euphoria he completed his advertisement, feeling the safety of numbers, the gratification of hope and the power of the media.

"Not gonna cry, are you?" the original biker asked from the ground.

"Not today," Mortecai answered.

As the meeting time drew nearer, the message was whitewashed many times by Dambig Sign Company, only to reappear mysteriously. The company placed a watchman by the sign on random nights, never considering the work might be done in the day. It was almost a blinking signboard and they were stupefied. Sometimes the reappearances were a happy mystery to Cohen. When he called the sign company and explained his motives to the manager, the whitewashing stopped. Mortecai's plan of raising an environmental army seemed to be coming true.

For the first time in history the general public was aware of a Seminole County Commission public hearing. By seven-thirty Tuesday night, the usual antagonists were ready to do battle bolstered by a steady stream of five hundred regular citizens who never before had participated, many arriving on motorcycles; also a junior high school civics class there to witness democracy in action. They all read the notice and left: Meeting Postponed.

"They wear you down, Doc," Mortecai said, kicking a Sprite can across the parking lot. "They'll keep canceling until nobody comes. Then they'll hold their meeting."

"Where in the blue Hell of a Goofy dwarf do they come off pulling crap like that?"

"That's alright. We don't have to play fair either. I represent a church."

At four a.m. the next morning, Cohen and Stiles parked at the Howard Johnson's, then walked across the street and squirted Super-Glue into the keyholes of each of the twenty-one doors on the building where Barbarosa Development rented its office.

Universal Studios, who had rights to Cohen's canvas, suddenly asserted them with EBOLA and within a week, there were no blank billboards on Interstate-4. Barbarosa Development bided their time and concentrated on Havalawn.

An Alligator's Story

Orlando Police Department. How may we help you?"

Man from Brownditch, Ohio: "You're not going to believe this, but there's a crocodile in my lake. A fricking huge crocodile."

"Has it done anything illegal?" asked the voice on the phone.

"Really. This is not a crank call. There is a real live breathing crocodile out here. It was lying on my goddamn dock like it owned it or something."

"Many of our city lakes are equipped with lifelike polyurethane crocodiles. Are you sure that isn't what you saw?"

"Do polyurethane crocodiles dive into the water and then swim away?" asked the terrified homeowner.

"No, they don't. I'd say we are almost certainly dealing with an alligator here. Do I understand that you would like to charge it with trespassing?"

"This is not a joke," screamed the new resident of the subtropics. "I live practically in downtown Orlando and there's a fricking dinosaur in my lake. If you're not going to believe me, let me speak to your superior."

"As you wish sir, but I do think you have a case for a restraining order."

"Hello, this is Sergeant Whatsitabout. What's it about?"

"Sergeant, I know it sounds crazy, but there was a fricking alligator in my yard."

"Well now, this is worse than I thought," said the interested Sergeant. "Think carefully before you answer this question. Are you sure it was fricking? Because that's very important."

Silence

"Sir? Are you still thinking?" asked the patient policeman.

"Am I going to have to go out there and shoot the thing myself? Is that the way it's going to be?"

"What sector do you live in, sir?"

"What do you mean, 'What sector?' I live on Lake #$!king Putridia and I paid plenty for the privilege. I'd like to think I can walk around my yard without getting eaten by some relic from the Stone Age. Shit! We don't have this problem where I come from."

"Lucky for you, sir, Lake *#$^ing Putridia is located in Tomorrowland, the only part of town where civilian shooting of nuisance beasts is allowed. Do you have a ray gun? Because that's the only catch. You must use a futuristic weapon. I suppose a phazer would do in a pinch. Do you have a phazer, sir? Sir?"

"Damn! I lost him."

The information room of the OPD exploded with laughter. "Oh, that was classic, wasn't it?" wheezed Sergeant Whatsitabout. Wiping away tears with his sleeve, he ordered, "Benny. Call Fish and Game. We've got a gator for them."

To be continued…

6

Ray Macon quit the cutthroat bottled water racket for an equally competitive but higher paying telemarketing agency where his native resourcefulness quickly distinguished him. But he had to sacrifice being outside and mobile. His workmates, none of whose appearances would have helped them in the business world, wondered at Ray forfeiting his looks on the phone. In a swivel chair in his cubicle he lost almost all his days and some of his nights talking to voices without faces, dedicated to making ends meet, the difficulty being they were opposite ends of the same line. Daisy was there for the kids when they came home from school and she kept the pets alive and cooked delicious meals to keep Ray coming home. Sometimes he went back to work as his only guilt free, legitimate excuse to be out of the house. Suffering from family health insurance payments and the state crackdown on unpaid student loans, he never had more than two or three dollars to call his own. More devastating, Ray Macon was growing his first gut.

This, Ray knew, was not life but life squandered. From the lost world inhabited by young, single Ray Macon, a day-long train clattered outside his office building. Every morning it brought a sparkling new, unique opportunity to live, and every day he failed to hop on. But he heard the strong, inviting horn as it approached like the Hallelujah Chorus sung by a flat-car full of buff virgins, bursting with the joy of opportunities on the way; then the sharp change as it plaintively sang of things leaving. As phone call after phone call dragged him deeper into the morass of his job, he could hear the pitch gradually alter to a

Tom Levine

desperate wail, a dirge and finally to a faint cry of premature burial. Then it was time to stand up and go home.

Equally resourceful and delusional, Ray continued searching for a reason to live and making the most of the piddling little he found. He noticed that the world has a measure of fair play, the concrete usurpers of his boyhood rural wonderland offering themselves up in the night for some small recompense. Ray derived greater satisfaction from wrecking new construction than trying to prevent it.

Inebriated Ray would stomp without warning up the wooden steps of Mortecai's porch and rattle the sticking screen door or simply walk into the house and lift him, sleeping, from bed. There was no asking Mortecai such a stupid question like did he want to go out. Cohen would awake already caught in the irresistible current of destiny, strangely being stood up in the arms of the monster he had made, facing the reckless goodwill in those deep-set green eyes that hinted at the rare knowledge of unlimited possibilities out there. Like a sociological experiment gone awry, Macon was briefly on the loose, no damn time to slumber.

While Cohen kept watch, Ray heaved rocks through model home windows, obliterated FOR SALE signs and bashed sledgehammer holes into pretentious subdivision walls. One night Mortecai blue-spray painted FIRST PRIZE across the front of a Parade of Homes model in Majestic Cove while Ray eliminated a window, frame and all, with a hunk of concrete he'd found nearby. The man-made rock then delighted Ray by bouncing ambitiously across the plush carpet and busting open an interior wall. Life had become bearable.

50

7

t Ann Hinga's Fish House and Tavern Mortecai encountered
Violet Chance, as he had hoped to. She seemed greatly
impressed by his establishing a church glorifying Mother Nature.
The even-slower-than-usual season for her business had begun and she
agreed to accompany Cohen on a float trip down the Econlockhatchee
River.

"This is an unbelievable chance for you," Ray told him. "The fact
that she's going means two remarkable things: she trusts you and she
may not be one-hundred percent opposed to having sex with you some
day. You don't want to change either of those things on this trip."

"I think it's going to be great," Mortecai assured him. "How can
we go wrong?"

Pastor Cohen presented an abbreviated but, he hoped, power-
packed sermon: "Some places are suited to become urban centers and
some are not. If we must have big cities, let them grow in already bleak
places. It was rotten luck that Disney came here and made a city out of a
town like Orlando. Surrounded by noxious fumes and assorted sensory
insults, the 'I heart New Yorkers' will soon feel right at home here and
be happy. Bless 'em! They're so easily satisfied.

"It is a trick of developers and other idollartors to link
overcrowding of humanity and the destruction of nature with the
forward movement of time. Hence the catch phrases, 'You can't stop
progress' and 'You can't turn back the clock,' designed to make us
believe the vandalism they call development is as inevitable as the future
itself. Striving for clean air, good water and green fields is not longing
for the past and when it is, how lousy life will be. We simply wish to

carry these good things into the future with us and it is not only our right but our duty to do just that."

Violet did appreciate the words but chose not to show it. She clapped wildly, stamping her feet and whistling. "Yahoo! Mortecai for mayor! Cohen for commissioner!"

"Please! Please! You're not supposed to applaud a sermon. Usher," Mortecai beckoned to his oblivious orange cat. "Quell the crowd."

"Wow, Cohen. Where do you get that stuff?" asked Violet.

He bowed to an aged and yellowed stuffed flounder grimly perched in a plastic chair behind him. "Since you asked," said the wounded pastor, "it came from the source of all wisdom, The Immortal Sole."

"Jesus Christ. Now can we get going?" Ray implored, like he could die at any moment if he didn't start fishing.

It was the best of times. It was the worst of times to go camping. It was the end of May. They took Mortecai's ten foot magnesium jon boat, to be propelled with wooden paddles. The green, lightweight craft had bench seats in the stern, middle and bow with leg room and storage space between. They brought an ice chest for the keeping of prepared food, and fishing tackle for recreation and obtaining new food; standard camping stuff including separate rolls of Eco-Asswipe and two tents, that number stipulated by Violet.

Taking an errant shot at appearing more planet friendly, Mortecai packed no insect repellant. "There won't be any bugs out there," he stated with authority. "It's only May. That stuff's nasty anyway. Hurts the air. Trust me."

Mortecai decided to put in at the farthest upstream bridge though he'd never been on that infant part of the river. He thought he had some idea how far it was to the next bridge but that was as the anhinga flies.

The river snakes, weaves, goes back the other way and has more bends in it than a Mercedes dealership.

Ray dropped them off with Mortecai's van, then zoomed to Mosquito Lagoon to wade for sea-trout and redfish. At the bridge was a trailer park where Cohen and Chance decided to launch.

The park manager walked over. "You're putting in here? Now?" He was stupefied. "Nobody's going down now. River's too low. Had a big storm blew lots of trees over. Ain't been cleared out yet."

"Yeah, well that's why we're goin'," replied the pioneer with lack of bravado, looking to see if his partner was impressed.

"Mosquitoes'll be settin' the table for you two. They's fierce out there," he elaborated.

Violet looked at Mortecai. "We didn't bring any repellent."

"What?!? You can't go in there without bug spray. Let me sell you a can."

"No, thanks," Mortecai said.

He took Violet aside. "Hey, don't worry about it, partner. People are always telling you not to do things. If you listened to people, you'd never get out of bed. I've always found that the worse everybody tells you something's gonna be, the better it turns out. He probably just wants to sell us some Off. The Indians didn't use it."

"We're not Indians, Cohen."

"Don't worry. It's too early in the year for bugs. Besides, that stuff makes the mosquitoes dizzy. I can't believe you'd use it."

"Tourists," the park manager said to himself.

With that unique happiness felt by adventurers who give themselves over to a river, Cohen and Chance slid and bumped the boat through a narrow space between cypress trunks over hard roots onto red water that would carry them through a shadowy wilderness. Wearing baggy shorts and a light white cotton shirt, Violet slid onto the middle seat and faced forward as Mortecai held the boat close. Clad in shorts and purple t-shirt, he stepped in front of the back seat as they pushed off from the root lined bank. They left time shattered and meaningless behind them for it cannot keep up with a downstream floating boat. Violet and Mortecai were free. The woman of his desire swiveled around briefly to drill Mortecai with black, gypsy eyes from her off-white porcelain face and his gaze collapsed to his paddle. The next three days would be forever counted among the most horrendous of their lives.

The root beer river was about fifteen feet wide at that point and mostly shallow enough to show its rippled sand bottom through the surprisingly transparent black water. Though late morning, little light penetrated the canopy as the boaters glided into an unimaginable nether world, Mortecai trying desperately to stop picturing his companion naked. They had not gone fifty yards when a deep hole beckoned. Surprisingly cold, the river felt great as they floated and splashed in it. Then they should have turned back.

Mortecai and Violet were about to present themselves like a windfall Thanksgiving dinner, two bags of blood floating downstream through a galaxy of tiny, starved vampires, their body heat and scent loudly clanging the dinner bell. From up and down the narrow ribbon of water and throughout the dark forest, clouds of mosquitoes were answering.

Mosquitoes are a misery. One deer fly can be a misery. A swarm of deer flies is a living Hell. Forward motion is a help against these plagues as are unoccupied hands. As is insect repellent. A few boat lengths beyond their swimming hole, the intrepid duo met its first obstruction. For the entire day and the next and the next they would average twenty yards of open water before the next portage, often requiring emptying the vessel, dragging it over, under, around and through some trees, then reloading the boat so they could do it again. And again, endlessly for scant reward. Occasionally they scrunched into the bottom of the boat to glide under fallen trees. These obstacles are a nuisance and nothing more, even a challenge to a boater's wits; simply part of a barely navigable river. They hold far greater significance for people madly trying to outdistance misery in a living Hell.

"Yeah, Cohen. You know what you're talking about alright. There's not a goddam bug out here, is there? You're one of those #!☹!ing goddam naturalists, aren't you?" Violet was trying to cuss out Mortecai while swinging her paddle around her head. "Shit! There's another tree! Ow!" Violet hit herself in the head. "I'm going to kill you, Mortecai. Let's just turn around."

"This won't last, Violet," Mortecai assured, pulling his shirt over his head, then pulling it rapidly back down to cover the greater area of skin. "The farther we get, the less trees there'll be, the sun'll pour in and the river will open up so there won't be as many bugs." He coughed on a mosquito. "And it'll be paradise. This little bit will just help us appreciate it even more."

"You better be right."

Mosquitoes would be swallowed at a rate of about one per fifteen words.

Optimism is a deadly vice of gigantic proportions lodged into the human psyche by Satan. It is the enemy of reality. We see a bad situation and optimism prevents us extrapolating from that. Instead we think, "Oh, it's bound to get better." So we plunge into the thicket, sure that it will thin, denied the aerial view that would show us the true, unacceptable horror of our lot. Perhaps optimism is good for prison escapees, who have no choice but to plod on. The rest of us are not well served. It poisons our judgment.

The upper reach of the Econlockhatchee winds through an enchanted world of cypress castles and gnome hideaways. Sometimes a giant cypress tree stands midstream forcing the black water around and through its legs astride a space almost wide enough for a jon boat. Then perhaps it moves on. Who knows? Some very loud, unexplainable sounds are heard on this river at night.

At sunset deerflies return to Hades to refuel. By complete dark, the hordes of mosquitoes have retreated, leaving behind a few token individuals. With a smudge fire and some luck two friends can sit out and enjoy their splendid surroundings, cook something, have a civil conversation. "If we ever live through this, Mortecai, I'm going to kill you."

Mortecai placed another greenish palmetto frond to keep the smoldering embers smothered. "Oh, come on. Tomorrow's bound to be better."

Violet stopped breathing and shut her eyes as the smoke column tilted into her face.

"I may kill you even if we don't live through this," she said as soon as she could.

Mortecai stood up, walked to the boat and rummaged through the ice chest. He tossed Violet a granola bar.

"Great, Mortecai. Save nature by not bringing insect repellent, but buy individually plastic-wrapped granola bars. Do you have any idea how wasteful this is?"

Mortecai sighed. "Did you get a chance to notice those amazing trees?"

"Yes, they're very beautiful. Whenever I had a second to look. I'm determined to get something good out of this."

"I guess it would have been a lot better with insect repellent," the explorer admitted.

"No shirt, Shitlock. How far to the next bridge so we can get out of here?"

Terrific, Mortecai thought as his heart sank. "I don't know. It can't be far now."

Thunder rumbled and lightning bleached the blackness like a demented cosmic flashbulb. As if born from that burst of light, biting black flies inexplicably attacked the campers.

Exasperated, Violet stood up. "Good night, Dan'l. You sure were right. What do other people know?"

Mercifully the storms were much show and little rain. Once inside their tents, the trip held no terrors for the voyagers. Violet enjoyed the blissful sleep of the snug camper. Mortecai lay awake half the night lashing himself for not starting the trip farther downstream, Ray's words haunting him. "If only the river will open up before the bridge," he fervently hoped.

It was impossible to tell if the boaters were feeding the same insects or if they were servicing new ones along the way but the second day varied from the first in two distinct ways: it was much longer and the inevitable accident occurred. When people are frantically getting in and out of a boat 150 times a day from slick banks, eyes peering out from a cloud of biting insects, somebody is going to put one foot in the boat, the boat will move away from the bank and she will tumble into the river banging her shin on the top side of the boat. And she might cry if she had time.

The river did not open out and obstacles were no less frequent. Optimism no longer playing a role, they were desperately fighting downstream.

Redbreast beds were visible in the sandy shallows along the bank and after making camp Mortecai caught one of the spawning sunfish and fried it for dinner. Like one Fig Newton, it tasted excellent but didn't go very far.

"So Mortecai - tell me again why we couldn't start this trip downstream where we could have actually enjoyed it."

"If you must know, I felt you needed to build some character." Mortecai looked at Violet approvingly. "I think it's working."

There was a monster splash in the river, the kind that happen only at night and are too loud to bear logical explanation.

"Did you hear that?" an awe struck Mortecai asked rhetorically.

Violet nodded, feeling slightly scared. "So tell me what you're going to do when they put all this inside a city."

"You sure know how to take the pleasure out of an outing."

"Yeah, but where are you going to take women to torture them?"

"That's one reason we're out here. You got to enjoy things while you have them. Personally, I don't believe in spoiling the present worrying about the future."

"I know what you mean. I'd sure hate to ruin this experience."

"Glad you feel that way."

The stream's perversities did not abate on the third day but Violet and Mortecai began to feel expert in the art of overcoming obstacles.

"Alright, Violet, you get out. I think I can push it under that log." Violet exited the boat and Mortecai went to the front where, bracing on the log, he pushed the boat down so it slipped under the obstacle. Mortecai had done this many times already to avoid unloading the boat and dragging it around. It was a tight fit and he walked to the back of the boat pushing it along with his feet. Lying down to slide himself under, he became jammed between boat and log, completely helpless and for practical purposes paralyzed. To free himself he needed Violet's help.

"Why the hell should I?"

"Because you need the boat to get out of here," Mortecai answered in muffled tones.

"Alright, I'll do it. Leaving you here to die horribly, covered in deerflies and mosquitoes, while appealing, isn't the same as killing you myself." Violet swung the boat around, freeing Mortecai, more expert yet.

They continued haltingly downriver, Cohen wielding paddle over his savior's head to fluster the deerflies, the stream a meandering train wreck of trees. The insect bait were not sure the low water level made things worse. If it were higher, they could glide over certain snags but couldn't duck under other ones. They passed mysterious deep bends where giant catfish taunted from the bottom and lovely sandy coves where they would have loved to swim and refresh their sweltering bodies, cool their itches; but they had to move on or be plundered, keep working toward the clear, open waterway logic told them had to lay ahead. Maybe beyond the next bend.

That night they camped on a high, grassy bank overlooking a sandbar trailing off into a deep bend. With abundant Spanish moss and palm fronds in the area, they built an effective smudge fire. The biting black flies did not make another appearance and Mortecai and Violet were enjoying the evening's light show, not in the sky but as it soaked palmettos, trees and river in electric illumination, taking momentary photos that seemed to develop in the memory, then disappear.

"This is the life, isn't it?" ventured Mortecai as he watched a banded water snake slither down the sandbar and into some floating branches.

"It's very character building," Violet added with a twinkle in her remaining eye. "I think you've improved. How about a kiss?"

"Where?" he asked, trying to be cool.

"Oh, I think there's a place just below my nose that doesn't hurt. How about there?"

"Is there a catch to this?"

"That depends on how good the kiss is."

Daybreak found the pair splashing about in the mid depth of the sandbar, where they played away the waning end of the night. They had become one, joined while in Mother Nature's irresistible grasp. Unable to plumb the river's darkness, to understand the denizens lurking there, they explored each other and found it a gratifying excursion filled with mystery and lore. They became keepers of a great secret.

As they opened to each other, the passage opened to its visitors. The change they fought for began, as a duo drifted into a new day. The river widened slightly, revealing miraculous eighty yard stretches of relatively clear passage. They reached a sunny cove where they whiled away much of the morning swimming and sitting on logs suspended just below the surface. A power line crossed the river there and two gangly county workers drove down the maintenance track to the river to kill the work day.

Each party was equally surprised to encounter the other. Mortecai asked did they have an extra can of insect repellent and Elliot Yeats produced a partly used can of BUGS-B-GONE.

"Okay," said Mortecai, flourishing the can. "Now we have insect repellent. Are you happy?"

"You folks come here often?" Elliot asked.

"First time. How about you?"

"Uh, yeah, we come here all the...How'd you get here?" asked the county spokesman.

"We put in upstream. Mighty nice out here," said Mortecai.

"You ain't been *campin'*!" Booger Pilsbury figured out.

"Yeah," Violet put in.

"You ain't sceered to be out there at night?" He looked at Violet, straining in vain to view her erect nipples through the red water. "You don't mind bein' out there with all them snakes and alley-gators?" he asked, bewildered.

"Shit!" said the jungle woman. "I don't know what we'd eat if it wasn't for them things."

He shot a look of indictment at Cohen. "Man, I wouldn't bring any woman of mine out here."

"I probably wouldn't either," said Mortecai.

And so it went. First contact with the supreme species in three days. Time to hook back up with the current.

Only the joys of the Econlockhatchee lay in store for the battered travelers. Thus began the stretch Mortecai knew, loved and needed to be whole. Whenever he was away, this place called him back. Though he had walked and run barefoot its trails, crawled through palmetto thickets where there were no trails, waded its shallows and swum into its depths, still it withheld a treasure trove of secrets from him. The mysteries kept him coming back, not to solve them, but to wonder at them. When the river was low and clear, it held secrets only in the deep holes; but mysteries abounded in the shallows where their clues were visible; like the migrations of gar, forging ever upstream, never down. In fine spirits Mortecai and Violet floated to the confluence of the Econlockhatchee with its main tributary. There is a bridge just downstream and a modern miracle, a telephone, a mile away.

"I won't blame you if you want to call it quits, Violet. I can see some advantages to it myself," said one weary boater to another.

"Oh, man. A nice soft bed tonight, a salad bar at Quincy's. Just imagine it, Mort. Someday. But not today, I think. Come on. The best is yet to come, as they say."

"You're alright, partner," Mortecai declared with admiration.

The remaining days of their float require no record except to say it was blissful. The river became open and sunny, affording numerous sugar sand playgrounds where they chased each other and wrassled, with midstream diving logs of all shapes and angles nearby. Annoying insects winged into a distant memory. Fishing was excellent and the two occupants of Eden feasted twice a day on bass and far more frequently on apples. On a few nights Violet caught a brown bullhead or two for breakfast. They glided past deers, hogs and turkeys, often holding or tying to mid-stream vines in order to linger. Sometimes they saw themselves seated on the bank together oblivious to the passing jon boat. In no hurry to leave, they remained for a day or two at each camp. Gradually the forest disappeared, the river widened and deepened, curving less and becoming vulnerable to boats from the St. John's River and they knew they had floated too far. Mortecai and Violet kept going then for there was no further reason to tarry. They drifted into the St. John's, landed and found a telephone.

8

Two honeymooners from Japan were cruising at thirty-five thousand feet over Alabama en route to Florida and DisneyWorld. They had requested martinis in Disney monogrammed cups with Minnie Mouse umbrellas so their souvenir collection could begin. They each brought twenty-five rolls of Fujicolor for their one-week stay and were practicing smiling. They were very happy to be over America.

"Your smile looks excellent," said the man in Japanese. "Imagine us in front of all these famous places."

"Imagine you in my heart," she responded.

Blessed with an overpopulation of taste buds demanding satisfaction, jammed onto his tongue and all over the inside of his cheeks as if they had been breeding in there, Doc Stiles' mouth was an extreme pleasure dome. And these weren't ordinary taste buds. They were taste Buds. The marvelous first slug of bubbly Budweiser draft into his craven mouth is what he was waiting for. It would be in a realm of its own and all subsequent slugs together could not equal it, if it were done right.

Anticipation had run its course to the moment of truth. He slid his fingers around the handle and lifted the heavy mug evenly, poking his nose into the perfect head to breathe the bouquet and preview the next step. The olfactory assault was all he could have hoped for, practically tasting it nasally, maybe a few taste Buds having started a colony up there. Then he put the thick, cold, downward curve of glass to his lower lip, tipping it slightly to release a sample as the upper lip clamped down on the rim, then slowly opened the flood gate as the bottom of the mug elevated, pouring it in, pushing his tongue up in the flood to distribute the bubbles, the frenzied, tiny explosions of Arctic 4th of July, the pride and joy of Annheuser Busch dancing all over his oral trampoline as it flowed toward the eagerly waiting throat, the vulgar swallowing as indispensable to the effect as the murder climaxing a bullfight.

Ray Macon and Mortecai Cohen were staring at Doc with a blend of derision and awe. They were seated with him at a wooden corner table surrounded by the antique fishing tackle, buoys, black and white fish photos, rubber sharks and other memorabilia and angling decor of Ann Hinga's Fishhouse and Tavern. Shadrack and the Shiners were taking a well deserved break.

"You know, Stiles," Cohen said, "if God ever saw you drink a beer, it'd be a mortal sin."

"He did once; sat right across the table from me and watched."

"And?"

"He's cool with it. Actually went and got himself one."

"That's God for you. He probably remade himself in your image. I watch you drink a beer and I feel like dumping mine out and going home. They oughtta at least charge you extra."

"Stop whining about it, Cohen, and get yourself some taste buds."

"There's people don't get as much out of their whole life as you get out of a damn dollar beer."

"Okay, Cohen. I appreciate that. But what's the caper? What'd you get me down here for?"

Cohen leaned forward and dropped his voice. "All right. Barbarosa Development has got to go. Unfortunately, it looks like it's up to us to do it."

"Death to' em. Death to all of 'em," sentenced Stiles and lifted his mug to the sentiment.

"Reveritt!" Ray said with gusto, exciting the momentary interest of some nearby drinkers.

"If only Disney hadn't come here we wouldn't have any of this crap happening," Stiles moaned. "Why couldn't St. Louis have panned out?"

"Face it. We don't live in a place that remains recognizable from day to day like Iowa or Hell or something. Disney did come here and the one thing that could focus the world's attention on us happened," hammered Cohen. "You and me, we get ideas, they stay right there in our head. Walt Disney got ideas, they rained down all over the planet like he was God."

"And the stench is spreading like a nuclear fart from the asshole of the earth," added Ray in his usual metaphorical way.

"I'll stink to that." Cohen lifted his mug.

"What kills me is nobody cares. They just sit there and let it happen to 'em," said Stiles, disgusted.

"You know why, don't you," said Cohen. "It's the traffic lights. The government's insidious way of training people to obey arbitrary authority."

"That's not it, Cohen. People are just sheep. We've been playing follow the leader since we were kids. Shoot. The only reason people go ahead and die is everybody else is doing it."

"Just another fad, huh?" Ray said, twisting the end of his thick moustache.

"Sure," added Cohen. "I see it. If you were the only one had to die, you'd protest, probably call Channel Nine."

Ray had long since abandoned his efforts to be socially acceptable, seeing little to be gained by it in the state of matrimony. It was an unsustainable condition anyway. He was naturally reticent and far too social while chemically improved. When mingling with upwardly mobile people, Ray preferred to just get it over with, and his companions' repulsive journey into philosophy supplied the urgency. Suddenly one of his power-packed, concentrated belches roared from its diaphragm launching pad, reconfiguring the bones of his inner ear and practically shattering his head as it surged through that constricted passage-way. It was mid range in tone with no vibrato and emerged as a sonic battering ram to atomize any esoteric discussions, expose anyone's assumptions about the divine creation of man and possibly push over a wall. A black hooker crossing her legs at the corner of the bar screamed instinctively as a lion flashed in her head, and an entire fashion caucus lowered its cigarets to look at Ray with infinite disdain, not unnoticed by him. The thirty-one year old bartender, who had aspired in his youth to the New York Ballet and a life among the culturally refined, never had acknowledged the loss of his dream. Stripped of denial in the power and clarity of Macon's inhuman blast, he saw at last the enormity of his detour from that innocent goal. The bar rag dropped from his hand and he walked lifelessly into the kitchen where he sat on the grimy rubber floormat and turned off the world.

Mortecai waved the wine list, since Ray's gaseous expulsions painted the air brown regardless of their point of exit.

"You want proof?" Mortecai continued. "How many times have you seen somebody sit at a red light with no traffic in sight? Maybe you do it. Ray does. He does it at four in the morning. That's training, the kind of obedience the government is hoping for." Cohen slugged down some frosty Bud and warmed to his subject as Ray rotated slightly in his chair, then leaned to one side and squeezed out a sound like ripping the fabric of space down the middle.

Cohen knew the sound well and pushed out his chair in a panic and fled the room with Doc close behind.

Ray smiled hopefully as he tracked the progress of his fetid cloud by the tables evacuated in its path. He glowed within as it floated into the fashion caucus, making them disperse amid exclamations like "Oh...my...God!"

A few minutes later Cohen and Stiles returned to the relatively abandoned section of the tavern. "Nice one, Ray. Now as I was saying, in the beginning, traffic lights were never meant to be an absolute authority. Just an arbitrator in case two cars approached an intersection simultaneous."

"Or at the same time."

"Yeah. But over the years people abdicated their free will, living scared. 'Ooh. Maybe there's a cop somewhere.' Once you train people to do what a light tells them, the rest is easy. 'Trust in your government. We're looking out for you.'"

"Well, I think a bluebird shits in the eye of a tomahawk," countered Ray.

Stiles cast a perplexed look at Ray and chuckled softly. "You know, Cohen, you really are full of it." Doc reverently lifted his mug to Mortecai.

"What's a traffic light?" thought a palmetto bug pining for closing on the underside of the counter.

Out of habit Doc scanned the crowd for women. "Where's Ray off to?"

"He's prob'ly gonna urinate behind a cigaret machine or something. Long range planning makes him nervous. You just gotta catch him when he's in the mood. Or drunk. I always feel safe doing stuff with Ray when he's sober 'cause he's so amazingly cautious."

"He covers all the bases?"

"I know that if he's doing it, there must be absolutely no way we're in danger. But he'll do anything after a few cans of courage and that can be scary. You want to catch him somewhere between paranoid and fearless.

"Sounds too tricky."

Cohen nodded grimly. "Ray does have a certain style to him, though. This one night we were at the Popped Blowfish over in Canaveral. We're leavin' and there's this shiny new, white Cadillac of all things in the parking lot. Well, Ray's an artist, you know, and he recognized an incomplete picture. So he bends down and bear-hugs this giant coquina boulder out of the landscaping, staggers over and gently sets it on the hood of the car."

Doc grinned at the image. "That is totally bizarre."

"Yep, it was a beautiful thing. I don't even think he scratched the paint."

The bartender emerged from the kitchen and walked around to the outside of the bar. He touched the rail with one extended hand and bent his knees in a manner more graceful than anyone who saw him ever had seen. Several customers whistled and applauded and begged for more. His life back on track, he returned to work with a gladdened heart.

Approaching Florida in Delta First Class, two young newlyweds looked into each others' eyes where they locked gazes, then brought them down lovingly to their stack of badly translated tourism brochures. Their parents had toiled almost ceaselessly in Tokyo office jobs to afford them this spectacular wedding present. They were happier than a Kamikaze pilot on Surrender Day.

"You are the biggest attraction of all," said the woman in Japanese.

"No," said the man. "You are all of Disney World and I am only poor Ocean World."

His bride was leafing through their brochures. "No," she said in a frightening manner, making of her hand a perfect replica, "You are Alligator Land. Chomp! Chomp!"

They both laughed and fell further in love.

"You worked construction in the seventies, didn't you?" Doc continued. "Got a little blood on your hands."

"No blood, just chlorophyll. Well, except the time Ray staple-gunned his hand to a stud."

"Ouch!" Doc winced and took a long slug.

"We knew not what we did. Didn't see the big picture... you never got into that?"

"Shoot, no. Air Force, man."

"Bomb the crap out of helpless people, eh?"

"I wish. Never got off the ground. Crashed too many simulators."

Mortecai ordered two drafts from the shorts and Hawaiian shirted waitress and returned to the seventies. "Construction was unbelievable in those days. They couldn't have too many hammers goin'. Get five jobs in one day if you wanted to. Me and Ray used to overstate our qualifications to get the big carpenter bucks."

"They took your word for it?"

"You just had to show up with at least a twenty-three ounce hammer. When they'd finally figure out we didn't know a soffet from a sofa and fire us, we'd go fishing, then walk on someplace else the next day. One job, they put me in charge of a guy who actually knew what he was doing, installing windows. I'd stand off to the side watching him, trying to figure it out so I could tell him what to do. I never made it. Or you could hide in plain sight. One guy used to pick up a two-by-four in the morning and walk around with it on his shoulder all day."

"Now it's starting to remind me of the Air force," Stiles said, struck by the same threads that run through vastly different human enterprises.

"The contractors weren't much better. And the subcontractors! God almighty. Things that hadn't seen the light of day in years crawlin' out the swamps to run jobs. It was something alright." Mortecai smiled in disbelief. "One job we were on, they didn't want to pay the crane operator all day, so they had him lift all the roof trusses at once. He'd drop 'em on one end of a building and move on to the next one. Two guys would pick 'em up one at a time and run 'em across. One time he didn't swing 'em high enough and they slammed into the building, knocked it lopsided and shook one guy clean off."

"Damn, Sam. Was he okay?"

"Yeah. Luckily I was stoned like everybody else. Landed on a scrap pile and didn't feel a thing. When I stood up, some wood came with me, though. Had a piece of plywood on my shoulder and a one by six on my hip. Couldn't see drivin' to the hospital like that, so the foreman pulled 'em off. It was only a six penny on the plywood, but that sixteen on the one-by seemed like it was two feet long comin' out."

Doc winced. "I'm glad I missed that whole experience. You get some tetanus shots?"

"Too painful- they were clean nails. Me and Ray did take the rest of the day off and went to the coast, though. Lots of those places stood empty for years, they overbuilt so much."

"You remember how cheap apartments were?" Doc recalled with awe.

"And first month's rent free. Yeah, those were the days to be a renter."

"Those were the days, period." Doc took a satisfying hit of Bud Draft, swished it around his mouth, rasped "Ahhh!" and slammed down his empty mug. Then he quickly scanned the yuppy throng before returning his gaze to Cohen. "Beeper" was to the male patrons as make-up was to the females, Ann Hinga's known for its long lines to the ladies room. Mortecai liked this place for its ambience, Ray for the high ceiling and relatively smoke free atmosphere which minimized drive-time airing out his clothes before domestic reentry, and Doc just liked draft beer.

"Well, I wanted us to have a three way discussion of this thing, but I guess that's out. What I want to do is go after Barbarosa now. I don't want it to get to the point where we're trying to stop 'em at the river."

"Kill 'em," said Ray smiling, reappeared with a fresh pre-owned beer for himself and an ash tray full of urine which he casually placed on the bar by a pack of Virginia Slims and a temporarily vacated stool. "Just kill 'em. They don't deserve to live. Set an example."

"Nobody'd miss 'em, that's for sure," agreed Stiles. "Their families would probably thank us."

"Who you gonna kill?" the waitress asked Ray with a smile as she deposited the new frosty mugs in front of Cohen and Stiles.

"Goatbusters!" Ray replied happily, grinning at his tablemates.

"Good grief, she's flirting with Ray," Cohen said, feeling the injustice.

An out of shape weight lifter, coat open to let out his belly approached the waitress, complaining that somebody took his beer. "I'll get you another one," she said, winking at Ray as she turned to the bar.

"He's married!" Mortecai yelled, shaking his head. He turned back to Doc.

"Anyway, I don't know about actually killing 'em," said Mortecai, "although one or two and the rest would probably get the idea. We could threaten their lives. That's one thing everybody understands. It transcends County Commission meetings, money, everything."

"Yeah," Doc said. "Put their asses on the line and suddenly Frog Piss Landing isn't so urgently needed after all."

Ray was becoming animated. "Look! Look! She's back."

"Who's back?" Cohen said, following his friend's excited gaze to the answer.

"Ray just pissed in an ashtray and put it next to that beautiful woman," Cohen explained. "He'll be happy the rest of the night waiting for her to douse it in there."

An astonished look grew on Doc's face. "Alright, Ray," he finally said, "cleaning up the air."

"No. This is what's left of getting lucky for Ray."

"Anyway, I don't know if threats are a good idea if you're not willing to carry through on them," Mortecai continued. "Ray seems to think I'm a prime suspect for just about everything."

"I proved it to you. Daisy hands me the paper and says, 'Here's an article about Mort'. If she can tell then anybody can. You're just a lot more obvious than you think." Ray finished his warmish beer then started looking around for another while watching for his victim to light up.

"Lessup says it's the mob. Don't know if I want to play that game with them," said Mortecai.

"So Ray," said Stiles, doodling in his mug frost, "Cohen says your wife doesn't have a clue about what you do."

"The man leads two separate and distink lives."

"It's the best way," said Ray. "Some people are just better off not knowing certain things. You'll understand if you ever get married."

"No. I understand," said Stiles. "I had a goldfish once, never had any idea what I did after I left the room. And that's the way I liked it. Better for him, better for me."

"The really ironic part is, like that news item. Ray was in on that, too. She's married to him and never suspected him. Daisy apparently knows me better than she knows her husband."

"She's doing it. She's doing it," Ray whispered loudly. As the three watched, the businesswoman slid out a Virginia slim, put it in her mouth, tilted back her head with anticipation and lit up.

"It's only a matter of time now," Ray continued his account, nearly bursting with suspense.

The nicotine delivery system went several times to her lips and each time she broadcast the residue upward as if fumigating the ceiling. She looked over the crowd with something in mind, her eyes hesitating almost imperceptibly on Ray. Then she laid her cigarette in the pool, shouldered her bag and left.

Ray was transported. "God, she didn't even notice," he whimpered through tears of catharsis.

"You can learn a lot about having fun in a bar from Ray," Cohen pointed out to Stiles.

"He is having the best time," Stiles admitted as Ray blissfully slid down his chair, his face frozen in hilarity. "He's not going to shit himself, is he?"

"Don't worry. This has happened before."

With no one else seated near the cigaret extinguisher, Stiles and Cohen sat in silence for a minute, dead in the water, each contemplating his own individual beer or lack of it, immersed in the gibberish of a hundred bar patrons. Ray returned to the top of the table but still the grin occasionally sprang back onto his face and tears returned to his eyes as he relived his recent glory.

Mortecai came to life. "I got an idea."

"Come on, Cohen," said Stiles. "You don't get ideas. You get hypotheses. Chapters pop into your head. But let's hear it if it isn't too long."

"Hell," said the pastor, "What are we sitting around here for? We've got manpower. We've got objectives. We have the night."

"We've been *drinking*," Ray added exuberantly.

"Let's wreck something! We can discuss it on the way."

Filling a mug with Bass Ale, the bartender watched Stiles and Cohen guzzle their dregs, slam down their mugs together and head for the door, Ray grabbing a half-full Tuborg Gold from a vacated table and mints from the cashier station.

"You always keep a sledge hammer in your car, Ray?" Doc asked in the parking lot.

"That's mine, actually," said Mortecai. "Better to have a sledge hammer and not need it than to want one .."

"...and shove a corn cob up your ass," Ray finished.

With so little resemblance to Alice and Ralph Kramden that it hardly bears mentioning, the Japanese honeymooners were holding hands as their jet broke out of some night clouds and prepared to land at Orlando Tourismatic Airport. They were trying to identify theme parks through the small cabin window, viewing with respect and awe what they assumed to be the lights of Disney World. Excitement glowed on their fresh faces.

"The place that I look forward to visiting most of all is not down there yet," said the man as his bride blushed.

EPCOT, Disney's **Experimental Prophylactic Community of Tomorrow**, had been constructed on the formerly rural Route 15A between Orlando and the small town of St. Cloud, encompassing two pristine lakes now off limits to ordinary Floridians. Known by locals as Masturbation, it was a venereal disease-free community. Blood test, physical examination and notarized affidavit of no priors were requisite for residence in the posh condom-iniums. Monthly repetitions were required with sworn affirmation of no unprotected sexual contact with an "outsider." Failure of any test meant immediate expulsion. Any citizen observing a cold sore on another was expected to report it. Only certified Disney employees made deliveries there and even the mail was left at the gate, for on site distribution. The maintenance contract included eight-hundred dollars a year for latex condoms, delivered monthly to every household. The waiting list was out to the moon.

On the road leading to EPCOT was an elaborately landscaped median strip. While their children went without school supplies, Orlando taxpayers gave $200,000 a year to maintain it. The entrance to the luxurious subdivision was heralded by a polished granite sign at the entrance. To Cohen and Macon, it was the stone representative of everything gone wrong, a monolithic slab in the face. About a foot thick and five feet by four, it offended Ray and Mortecai. Cohen had bought his sledgehammer for the express purpose of altering that monument to his satisfaction, having always entertained the highest regard for the destructive capabilities of such tools.

Fifteen minutes after leaving Ann Hinga's, the Civic shot south under the Bee-Line Highway and approached the target. Ray drove a mile past the sign, turned around and slowly returned. Traffic was not heavy on the two lane highway but he slowed to let every appearing set of headlights pass. Then he timed oncoming cars so the ambush could be mounted unobserved from the road. The guard house a hundred yards in was something that simply couldn't be helped.

Ray pulled over across the road, catty corner from the sign. "I get the first swing," he said, leering at Cohen.

As Cohen liked to encourage Ray's active participation, he was inclined to grant it. Besides, they were using his car. Ray opened the door to get out and Stiles handed him the hammer from the back seat. Starting across as Mortecai was exiting the other side, Ray saw headlights appear far down the road. He said, "Shit!" and jumped back into the car, leaving the demolition tool on the ground.

"Don't worry about it," said Mortecai. "Whoever it is ain't gonna care about what we're doing."

"Where'd all the traffic come from?" said Ray.

"It came from all the people living out here now," informed Mortecai. "Where do you think?"

Doc Stiles was disgusted. "Hey, listen guys. I'm psyched. If one of you candy asses isn't going to cream that sign, then give me the hammer. I'll crack that sucker in half."

"That hammer weighs more than you, Doc. I'll do it," said Cohen. "There's always gonna be someone coming."

The car passed, the unseen driver an unknowing temporary deterrent to vandalism. Ray picked up the weapon and ran, Mortecai right behind, Stiles staying with the car for contingencies.

"Hit it on the corner," Mortecai advised.

Just north of the Bee-Line several rental car agencies vied for the tourist stream. As a newlywed Japanese couple drove their shiny red rental car out onto America, under the Bee-Line and into their first 7-11, Mortecai gave Ray swinging room. He stood helplessly by as Ray lurched a few feet farther and went for satisfaction, leaning back and clobbering the middle with all his inebriation. Both men cringed when the impact of sledgehammer against the supremely hard, reflective surface perfectly mimicked a rifle shot, the ten pound hammer bouncing off like a super-ball.

"Jesus," Ray said. "Everybody for two miles heard that."

"And look," Mortecai said with wonder, "you didn't even scratch it."

Winding up for a second hit, a wiser Ray aimed for the corner. The report was muffled as some of the energy went into cracking granite.

"Let's get out of here."

"Gimme the hammer," Mortecai said as a new set of headlights approached from the north.

Macon was running for the car as Cohen swung. Mortecai waited in the shadows until the car passed, and then sprinted across. "Got it. Knocked the whole corner off," he reported jubilantly as a frantic Ray begged him to get in the car.

The Japanese bride was giggling at a Bride magazine written in English while her husband picked up a crossword puzzle book, smiled and returned it to the rack. "Coming on," he said in English. "We must buy our Amellican ice cleam number one."

"Alright!" said Stiles, high-fiving Cohen as Ray gunned the little engine for Orlando.

Mortecai turned to Ray. "See? No problemma. We're still free men."

Looking back, Stiles announced a vehicle pulling out of the entrance gate. In the rear view mirror, Ray saw something lighted on its roof and gunned the tiny engine. Doc thought it seemed like a cab but he wasn't sure.

The Bee-Line Highway overpass was two miles ahead, commonly driven by tourists between Cape Kennedy and DisneyWorld. Stiles monitored the pursuit vehicle and reported that it didn't seem to be gaining. He also saw Ray transmute into his paranoid frenzy escape mode anyway, accelerating the Civic beyond eighty miles per hour as they neared the Bee-Line. In the distance, Mortecai and Ray saw the little Toyota rental car pull cautiously out of the convenience store lot and onto the road. Ray continued to floor the throttle. The road temporarily expanded to four lanes under the highway and Ray was sure he could find one of them unoccupied; but the rental car moved into the escape lane. Ray swerved and the rental car swerved with him as if locked into his trajectory. He swerved back and so did the Toyota, driven by the now frantic tourist trying to elude Ray, but always in synch, like a mullet in front of a barracuda.

Mortecai really couldn't believe it when the awful crunch of metal came with all its ramifications and he felt the sick shock of a mission gone so quickly wrong by pure bad luck. Ray had cobras striking in his stomach, and his testicles had retracted so far he had eyeballs. His brain already was running the gamut of ways he could sacrifice Cohen to claim innocence; he had picked him up hitchhiking with a sledge hammer being his immediate choice.

In their first five minutes driving in Florida, the honeymooners were smashed into at eighty-six miles per hour and launched like a Cape Kennedy rocket across the intersection. Mortecai braced and took out Ray's glove compartment door with his foot and the rear view mirror with his forehead.

"Great driving, man," said Stiles, unhurt.

Hoping to shrink the depth of their trouble, Mortecai was out instantly, heaving his sledgehammer into the off-road shadows, then returning to the wrecked car to stand with Ray and Doc as the cab cruised slowly by viewing the accident. Ray felt the strange blend of relief and deep regret.

The bride seemed to be injured and stayed in the smashed rental car. Ray suspected he might be home free as soon as the Japanese man got out and spoke. "How many fast you go?" he accused.

"Looks like failure to yield right of way," Macon judged.

Ray was more confident when the highway patrolwoman arrived and asked if anyone was hurt. When informed that the Japanese woman had been sent to the hospital, she said, "Good." Clearly not "Good" because she would receive medical help, but "Good" because she required it. She practically gave Ray a medal for his participation in the case.

"I'd never get one like that," Cohen bemoaned.

"Me neither," said Stiles. "I'd probably get a Jap cop still sore about the war."

Ray felt a little bad about injuring the woman, quickly allayed by

Mortecai. "Don't worry. She's probably writing a haiku about it already. 'We drove, crash-boom.'"

Ray's car still was drivable. Guided by one headlight, the trio returned to town celebrating the marring of the sign, a strike heavily laden with symbolism. The humor of immediately dispatching a pair of Japanese tourists, unlikely victims of Macon's fevered imagination, was not lost on them and they described the event with many hilarious haikus. As they looked to projects to come, Ray already had begun his retreat.

9

Reclining in opposite ends of the hammock, they rocked gently, the west rope creaking where it was tied around a porch beam. "I'm sick of this penny-ante crap. It's time to go for the throat," Mortecai said, sucking on a home-made orange juice popsicle.

"So what is it, Mort? Is it the thrill? Life isn't exciting enough without that old getaway feeling?"

The terrorist passed the delightful confection to Violet, stretched his arms out straight, then locked hands behind his head and burped softly. "I've asked myself that question a few times. Like why do I have to go out and do this? Out of this whole city, why do me, Ray and Doc have to be the ones? And why am I the instigator? Why do I get mad about all this stuff?"

Cohen watched Violet slowly lick all around the popsicle. "I used to be part of corporate America," she said between licks, "and I can tell you it's better to fight them from the ground up. Raising consciousness in the community, showing people alternative ways to live. You're trying to get rid of a noxious weed by pruning it."

"Sure, it'd be easier to recycle, eat organic fruit and let all the rest of this slide. You might not believe it but I don't like the risks. And I hate confrontations. It's just that the idea of backing down is even worse."

"Backing down from what? Nobody's challenging you. You won't lose face if you let them have their stupid monument." Violet twiddled his armpit with her big toe.

"That's just it. I think I would. I picture 'em sitting around saying, 'Got another one by Cohen today. He's no trouble.' I guess it's a territory thing, plain and simple. It's my turf and I don't want these shitheads messing with it."

"So while you're out marking your territory, you make the rest of us look like a bunch of nuts, too."

"You could look at it the other way. Instead of 'What's with me?' how about 'What's with everybody else?' Why do you sit back and let everything happen?"

"We're just ordinary, everyday people, Don Quixote. Trying to get by as best we can."

"Like Ray, I guess."

"Well, not exactly." Violet laid the denuded popsicle stick on the floor.

Cohen pushed on the rail with his hand, rocking the hammock. "You know, I was thinking the other day. What was it like before anybody had written any good songs? What if you felt like singing? What if everybody in the world felt like singing and no songs. Some early songwriter comes by the cave with some songs - what the people wouldn't give for them. Suppose Pavarotti was born back then. This incredible instrument in his body and no outlet. There he stands in his bear cloth, much skinnier of course, just blasting out notes, his heart bursting with frustration."

"Yes?"

"What about Mozart? Where would he be if somebody hadn't bothered inventing the piano and the violin?"

"Dead."

"Nope."

"Selling songs to Cave Man Pavarotti?"

"Nope. Digging ditches to a beat, that's where."

"Dig it, man."

"Think about it - all those thousands of Mozarts down through the ages - out there killing mastodons - we don't hear a peep from them."

"Good. Because one Mozart was plenty. What you've got me pissed off about now is all the Manilows."

"It's kind of like that." The hammock stopped rocking. "I don't think Cave Man Pavarotti gave a shit about singing."

"Really."

"It's the thrill, isn't it?"

"I don't know. Why don't you ask Pavarotti?"

Violet wondered, a little uncomfortably, which epoch her partner was best designed for as she watched him snatch a ping-pong ball from the floor with his toes, toss it in the air and catch it with his armpit.

"Yeah, that's the kind of luck Ray's always had." Cohen plucked the ball from his pit and balanced it on the back of his hand. "Comes away from everything unscathed. The rental company's insurance'll pay for the car. Meanwhile I got a sore neck and leg. Didn't hurt my head though. I'm kinda proud of that."

"Ooh. You probably need some attention, huh?" Violet said.

"Badly," moaned the victim.

"So who's this Doc Stiles character?" Violet asked, rubbing Mortecai's neck.

"Basically an unemployed Munchkin waiting for that big remake. He's got the right spirit, that's the main thing, but I was surprised. I used to know people he knew a long time ago, we played tennis once or twice and he struck me as kind of a cool Barney Fife. So he reads my flyer and shows up one morning, turns out he loves to go camping and canoeing and he's mad as Hell. And his schedule is as flexible as mine, which is good. Aaah. Right there. That's good, too."

"What does he do?"

"Used to sell vacuum cleaners. Now he has one of those pressure washers. Goes around and talks people into getting things cleaned. He's got the only job I've seen might be better than mine."

"Oh, Mort. Nothing could be better than selling colostomy bags."

Mortecai sighed with satisfaction. "Speaking of that, when are you going to start stocking them?"

"I'd rather attack the problem on the dietary end."

"Sure. Put me out of business."

"What about Ray? You two are such good friends and so different."

"Vive la difference! Basically, about the time Nixon's oil crisis knocked out the construction boom, Ray met the love of his life cruising the Stake 'n Shake and I went traveling. I never found true love. See how we have grown apart."

"How ironic. Three salesmen. The scum of the earth trying to save the planet."

"Even scum needs a suitable habitat to live. Anyway we're just trying to save our own little bit of heaven."

"It sounds like you guys could use a good driver."

"Sorry. Men are screwing things up, it's up to men to unscrew 'em. Besides, you're already saving the world from ordinary toilet paper. I think that's great."

Violet scanned the deserted street. "Okay. So maybe you need a good screw driver." She leaned over and sent her fingers through Cohen's curls. "Have you ever done it in a hammock?"

"Done what? Hey! Cut that out," the pastor pleaded. "We're on the front porch."

"So?"

"So it's broad daylight."

"I'm a broad. Must be time for me."

The lusty woman removed her pants, rendering Mortecai helpless to resist. As she mounted him, two large Negroes mounted the stairs at the other end of the porch. The floor creaked and Violet jerked to one side to look behind her, spinning the hammock which dumped two half-naked people onto the floor.

"Hello. What can I do for you?" asked Pastor Cohen from halfway under Violet.

"Well," said the woman, "We just wanted to know if you're saved or not."

"Do you suppose we could discuss that at a later time?" asked Violet.

"Oh, I think now would be a fine time," said the woman, laughing. "But we'll let you put some clothes on first."

Violet begged Mortecai with the need in her eyes. He looked at her and shrugged helplessly. "Okay," he said, "but I'm going to try to save you, too."

"Try to keep it short," Violet advised.

While their guests looked away, Mortecai and Violet pulled shorts back on. "I get to go first," said Mortecai, "because this is my church."

Cohen sat on the porch railing while Violet reclined back stiffly in the hammock. "I heard you folks believe that sooner or later all the sheep that ain't in your flock are gonna get converted into mutton and you all are going to be left here to enjoy planet earth by yourselves. Is that true?"

Jacob Moseby nodded slowly. "I've never heard it put quite that way, but yes, I suppose so. Many will stay here for eternity. The soul is the body, so when He resurrects one, the other follows."

"Is it just people who are here when the big foot comes down, or every Jehovah's Witness that ever lived?"

"Those who already died are kept in God's memory until the time comes. He knows every star, every grain of sand on the beach, so it isn't hard for Him."

"Okay. If it was me and I had that kind of information, I'd keep it to myself. The idea of being here with a drastically cut down human population is mighty appealing. But you are less selfish than that, so my condom's off to you and I thank you for your concern for my future. And Violet's. I do surely like the idea of heaven on earth better than heaven on some cloud with a bunch of harp playing Baptists. I'd rather be able to go fishin' sometimes, take a swim, play baseball..."

"Have sex," Violet interjected.

"Am I correct in assuming there ain't gonna be no cops or government left to help the survivors?" asked Mortecai.

"We certainly hope not," answered the man.

"Alright. And I see there's a lot of black Witnesses, so there'll still be somebody to do the menial labor."

Mortecai's guests laughed uncomfortably. "Oh, fo' sho'," said the woman.

"Okay, I'm in," said Mortecai. "Now this is where my church comes in. Your heaven is deteriorating on a daily basis. If the big foot doesn't come down soon, you might as well float up in the sky with all the unsaved losers, because this place won't be worth hanging around for. My church is dedicated to rescuing Mother Nature who, as powerful as she is, can manage no better than a stumbling retreat, like Superman faced with a steadily advancing army of kryptonite clad warriors. She needs our help. We need yours. If you're not willing to preserve your own future instead of just trying to expand your circle of friends in the hereafter, then you'll deserve the mercury infested, eroded, salt water intruded home that you'll inherit. The updated translation is: 'The meek shall inherit a degraded earth.'"

"I think you've hit it," Violet came to life. "It's a pyramid scheme. They can't wait for all these people they recruit and all their recruits to walk up to them in the hereafter and shake their hand off and say, "Thanks, man. You were right after all. Anything I can do for you over the next million years or so, let me know. Now I think I'll go have sex. But wait a minute. That would be necrophilia. Well, guess I'll go fishin'. Or play baseball. Huh, Pastor Cohen?"

"It's not that," Philodendron Moseby objected. "We're spreading the word out of love for our fellow man."

"Maybe," Violet continued, "but you just better make sure you save somebody before you die, Mort, because the last one in's going to have to spend about a billion years paying off his debt with no help. About the time you get where you can enjoy death, the planet will probably fall into the sun." She curled into a spasm of laughter.

Mortecai looked at Violet with raised eyebrow. "Clearly the divil has got ahold of her brain," he offered in an abominable Irish brogue.

"Well," said Jacob Moseby, "what do you propose we do to prove our good intentions?"

"Glad you asked," Cohen pre-empted Chance, still catching her breath. "Very simply, all living wild things are holy and we must care for them. Their enemies are easily identified. Quite often they are yellow and have big wheels or half tracks. When operating, they have morons attached to them. They look evil. If every Jehovah's Witness would personally wreck just one such fiend, the tide would turn our way. You have the manpower. We have the know-how. Join our church to save your own."

Mortecai could see the witnesses were temporarily derailed. "Call me an evandalist," he offered. "Now how about some orange juice? Not that crap you get in the store; just-squeezed fruit stolen."

"Oh, yes, that's the best kind," Jacob said in the deep, rich voice of a man who clearly had known great orange juice in his day. "Thank you."

"Is this man on the level?" Philodendron asked Violet as Mortecai disappeared into the house to ream oranges.

"Oh, no," Violet assured her, "but he's serious."

"Are you saved?" Mrs. Moseby asked Violet.

"I believe in God, if that's what you mean."

"And is this man your pastor?" Jacob inquired with a wry smile.

"No, our relationship is purely secular."

Back with a couple of chairs and Flintstones glasses of vibrantly orange juice, Cohen offered a toast to Ballou, Patron Saint of the Econlockhatchee River. The Moseby's tested their drinks gratefully. "Yes, that is real good," Philodendron said, sitting down.

"Are you talking about destroying earth moving equipment?" she asked.

"Nope. Just rendering it immobile."

"But what right do you have to…immobilize someone's machine? The people who own them have a lot of money invested. What about them?"

"We have our lives invested in this good green earth. It's not my fault if they've made a bad investment."

"I suppose they have insurance," said Jacob, taking a satisfying hit of juice.

"Exactly. And we don't. Some developer wrecks my favorite river, where's my compensation?"

"But you don't own the river," Philodendron persisted.

"It is illegal, of course," Violet noted as Juice the Cat hopped onto the hammock and started kneading her belly.

"I suppose that depends on whose law you're talking about," Jacob said thoughtfully.

"She's talking about the law that can put your butt in jail," Philodendron clarified.

Jacob chuckled. "Are there any other branches of your denomination?"

"Nope. This is the only known one. But we're growing."

"Why the church aspect? You don't need to make a religion out of caring for the bounty that God gave us. That's everybody's responsibility."

Cohen poured down some juice, impressed by its sweetness. "I think this is a heretofore undiscovered branch of Buddhism or something. Got sacred cowpies and everything. We believe our conduit back to grace will be through our relationship with the planet."

Cohen glanced shyly at Violet to view her approval of his enlightened posture. She smiled patiently.

"As a society we have broken faith with nature by crapping into a communal pool when we are supposed to enrich the earth with what we eat, completing the circle of life. This is also bad for people, setting from birth the pattern of irresponsible behavior and substituting this unnatural connection to every other butt in the city. Modern man is robbed of the one, fundamental act he is asked to perform autonomously. With a foundation like that, no wonder nothing else works. So we encourage people to dig a hole in the yard and do your part. And, of course, use Eco-Asswipe, the world's most helpful anal hygiene paper, when you're done."

"Interesting concept," Jacob tried to find something nice to say. "I've read about farmers in India personally fertilizing their crops."

"Exactly."

"What about people living in apartments," disgusted Philodendron said.

"I suppose they don't get to do it. That could be the incentive to become a home owner."

"Yes, I'm sure many people will be inspired to increase their income so they don't have to use the toilet. Does your religion have any moral standards?" she asked.

"We believe it's a sin to spend a beautiful day indoors," Cohen rhapsodized on. "That's turning your back on a divine gift to do what you think is more important, like going to work or something. And we worship Good God Almighty instead of Plain God Almighty, who, judging by a lot of his followers, I suspect of actually being El Diablo."

As Jacob started his next question, a jet aimed for Orlando Inner City Airport drowned his voice in its roar. Cohen raised his hand in time-out as all smiled in the uncomfortable suspension of speech.

"That was very loud," Mrs. Moseby said as the sonic violation moved on to another neighborhood.

"Also illegal," Mortecai pointed out. "but as long as it brings people here, economic law prevails."

Jacob was surveying the rustic porch. "What is the significance of the candles under that big flounder on the wall?"

"You have much to learn," Violet instructed dramatically. "That's not just any flounder. It is The Immortal Sole, the vessel through which Mother Nature speaks to Pastor Cohen."

"Oh, I see."

"Speaking of that," Philodendron picked up, "what about *your* immortal soul, Mr. ...."

"Pastor Mortecai Cohen."

"Pastor Cohen. What do you believe concerning that?"

"Well, I ..."

"Pastor Cohen teaches us that the soul is deodorant Good God Almighty in his infinite wisdom sprays upon everything," Violet interjected, "because we really stink when it leaves."

The pastor beamed upon Violet. "For that you get to be an apostle."

"It's also a tax dodge," Cohen continued. "After the Persian Gulf Massacre I decided it's the moral obligation of everyone not to pay taxes, like churches. I used to think they were just getting away with something by being tax exempt, but now I realize it's a moral stand so obvious most everybody misses it."

"Folks grow up learning they're supposed to pay taxes," Philodendron said. "It's a hard habit to break."

"People try in small ways to avoid taxation, which is called cheating," Pastor Cohen went on, "but that word presumes a moral obligation to pay in the first place. The religious population apparently lacks the faith to flat-out refuse. By paying taxes, people fund an organization over whose actions they have no control. That is irresponsible. Churches are indeed the moral treasury of our society and I am embracing their example."

"You don't think Jesus would do it?" Jacob asked.

"Mark Twain said you can't be a patriot and a Christian," Cohen responded. "I think he was right."

Jacob took a long slug of his wonderful drink and smiled warmly enough to melt butter. "Folks complain about paying taxes and then they line up to pay that voluntary lottery tax," he said. "The government's slick. They take all they can and then get people to give the rest."

"Pastor, yours was the easiest soul we ever saved," said the woman, "but we've got a lot more to talk about. What is the name of your church, by the way?"

"Holy Crap Church of the Coupon Redeemer."

Jacob Moseby almost spat out his juice. Cohen found a flyer on the floor and handed it to him.

The woman stood and took Mortecai's hand. "Ya'll can take your clothes off again. But we'll be in touch."

"Jacob, you know what he said about the menial labor?" Philodendron Moseby asked as they crossed the driveway.

"Yes," he said gravely. "Wouldn't it be something if it's a white man's paradise, too?"

Violet said, "That's one way to get rid of them," as she and Mortecai watched the hefty figures progress up the street.

"Yeah. But I wanted them to stay."

"Mort, do you think you'd ever actually sabotage a bulldozer?"

Cohen hesitated. "I'd like to think I would."

Mother Nature looked like she'd just plain had enough. She was angry. Miniature tornadoes were swirling around her and lightning was cracking over her head and flashing between her legs. She was beginning to have an adverse effect on the ozone layer. She had a grievance.

"Yo! God! Monsieur Almighty. Mister Dammit!"

"What on earth do you want, Mother Nature?"

"At least You got the planet right."

"It's not easy, you know. From where I sit they all look the same."

"Well, let me tell You something. From ground level most of them are real flops. The way You go about things, it's a miracle there's anything here either."

"That's what they say," God the Australian Aborigine boomed proudly.

"They're either too close to the sun or too far away. And what was that tenth one for? What was that all about?"

"Well, I hadn't quite finished."

"And while I'm at it, Captain Creation, what happened to putting them all in a ring in that nice life-friendly 90,000,000 mile range? I was supposed to get a solar system to look after, not one measley planet where every last thing is based on carbon."

God closed his eyes and turned his head half away, then rotated back and glared at Mother Nature with the freezer-burn of a million lifeless moons. "Did you just call me *Captain Creation*? Because I am the creator of the solar system, such as it is. I'm *God*!" he blasted, temporarily disrupting the ether. "Where do you get this stuff?"

"Look. Just because your people things worship you, don't get a big head. I've seen morons make better solar systems. Let me get to the point. The reason I called is, I'm fighting a losing battle down here. Right now I'm counting on three salesmen to pull my fat out of the fire in Florida and one of them is trying to recruit the Jehovah's Witnesses, for Christ's sake!"

"Watch that!" God warned, a few stars temporarily blinking out. "Maybe you need to improve your methods."

"You're the one who had to invent humans because You were lonely or something. Had to make them in your image, eh! I told You. 'Use a better model. Something that might fit in.' But You said, 'No. I'm lonely.' So what we got is a bunch of tiny 'Gods' running around screaming 'We have dominion over the earth. Everything's here for us. We're freaking special!!' And finally, 'Screw Mother Nature.'"

God was morphing into a Neanderthal named Dan. "Did you say salesmen? Things are bad, aren't they?"

For her part, Mother Nature stayed the same. She always looked like an exaggerated Dolly Partin. It was God's will.

"Look. For a long time, people did okay, I'll grant You that. But then You had to have Your Europeans. You thought they were cute. *Germans*?!? What were You thinking? The last couple hundred years, Phew! That was another one of your great ideas. 'I'll just hide the oil here where they'll never find it'. I happen to think they've run their course."

"Well, they'll never find my little doomsday devices I built into the atoms. That's for sure."

Mother Nature just stared at him. "You really haven't been paying close attention, have you? A couple billion years before You convert it into a star and they've already started the countdown."

God yawned. "One or two here and there. They should see what happens when every atom goes at once. Now that's some pop."

"At the rate Your humans are going, they won't be around much longer anyway. What do You say You take them all back now so we can get on with life?"

"Let me think about it, Big Mama. Maybe I'll bring on a rupture or something."

"Rapture. The word is rapture."

"Whatever you say, dear. But you know I can't bring them all up. I told those Jehovah's Witnesses they could stay."

"Oh, for the love of ....sod! Why do You always have to make these promises?"

"Guess I'm just a big Softy."

"Well, I can live with that, Guy in the Sky. Say, whatcha doin' later on?"

It would be unseemly to report further details of this conversation. Suffice it to say that God does not seem to be considering sending the type of help that Cohen, Stiles and Macon are looking for.

10

The winds of change are as steady as the winds of worn out wiggle worm farts.
Cinderella's Castle is a hoodoo household in a racquetball world.
"Timber!" cried the spotted owl as his alder came crashing down on the economy of the forest leeches...Whoo?

"Alright. Let's talk about 'wetlands mitigation.' It's an unmitigated lie. Another way destruction is allowed under the guise of conservation. Developers get to destroy wetlands as long as they agree to build artificial ones somewhere. The catch is that wetlands are where they are for a reason. So all these fake ones fail but by then, the damage is done, which is the idea. An environmental engineer told me the other day that they make better wetlands than the original ones. Said how they keep water in them all the time and when the plants die, they get right in there and replace them with new ones. How can you talk to someone like that? How about the Airport Authority hiring a bounty hunter to shoot deers around the airport. Paying him a hundred dollars a body. It's all because one of these trouble making deers might step out on a runway one day. Great solution to the problem, huh?

92

"How about Ronny Layton, just wants to keep farming sod like his family's done for generations. Loves all their land and wants to keep it natural, doesn't want to sell to the airport authority. Tough. His land has been condemned and taken. 'Right of imminent ptomaine' or something. Got to build yet another runway, kill more deer, get more tourists here; all in the public good.

"Now let's touch on another problem. Seems they can't build a subdivision anymore without its own golf course. Can't get people to come down and live here without a golf course in their back yard, can we? They just wouldn't come. When I think about it, what a poor thing my life is. Got no golf course. Hell. I don't even golf. Some four thousand golf courses in the country and I think Florida's got most of them. But that doesn't stop the St. John's Water Management District from granting commercial well permits to water them. They've never denied a permit yet."

"What a way to save the state. Just stop issuing permits."

"Exactly, Brother Stiles. But it would take a constitutional amendment and the opposition from the forces of evil would be overwhelming."

"So it would actually take an act of God."

"May I continue?"

Stiles nodded.

"Anyone needing that much space for his hobby is an irresponsible glutton with no regard for non-golfing life. It's bad enough that forests are destroyed to accommodate the goddam houses but then a further swath of habitat is murdered and the aquifer drained so a handful of lazy, fat ass, club wielding turds can persecute a tiny white ball until it finally escapes into a hole. Can there be a more colossal waste of time and life than this asinine game? And these people actually think, God bless 'em, that they're engaging in a sport. Where is the combat? The opponent? The loser? Who do you beat? The hole?

"'Ah hah! Found you at last, hiding there in the ground. Under that flag. Eat this!'

93

"There's this amazing world all around them and they choose to be *'golfers,'*" Cohen ranted on. "Got to be on a 'golf course,' even, be*lieve* it or not, returning to the same holes, no doubt easier to find the second time. They do it in groups to impress each other with their ability to endure tedium."

Cohen leaned forward in his chair and softened his voice. "And, Stiles, I kid you not, when they're not golfing, they're *thinking* about it. They watch other people doing it on teevee. They read magazines about it and look at pictures of guys in brand new clothes holding golf clubs. And you know what?"

"Okay, I'll bite. What?"

"These guys in the magazines - they never, *ever* wear shorts. I believe the whole stupid game is just a scam by the fashion industry to sell more cloth. 'Be a golfer - look like this.'

"The grass ought to be chemically treated to sterilize these weirdos for the good of the gene pool. And the developer gets away with claiming it as *green space!*"

"Kinda getting it all off your chest this evening, huh, Cohen?" Doc flicked his used-up tooth pick over the porch railing.

"They shouldn't have done it by the Econ."

"You left, Dad. Things happen. You weren't here so they couldn't ask permission."

"I'm back now."

"Big tournament there tomorrow."

"You have the canisters full of Round Up?"

"Round Up? That's kid's stuff. I've got the real thing, Bud. We're gonna kill the grass all the way to China. But this time it's your turn to drive."

Doc transferred his weapons of grass destruction to the van. At ten o'clock that night, he and Pastor Cohen set out for the Twin Rivers golf course, recently installed near the meeting of the Big and Little Econlockhatchee Rivers.

As they rumbled through the night on the once isolated two lane road, Doc viewed with disgust the regularly spaced apartment complexes and the endless gauntlet of walled subdivisions, invariably named after what no longer lived there. The sign at each entrance was a trophy: Deer Run, Otter Creek, The Pines, Eagle's Landing …bitter echoes of the past. "So Cohen - how'd you get into selling colostomy bags?"

"Ain't lookin' to go into competition with me, are you?"

"Don't worry. Vacuum cleaner bags was bad enough."

"Well, there I was at the doctor's office and a guy comes in sellin' 'em. I thought, I bet that's a field with a lot of room in it. I never forgot it. When the building boom ended, I found a source for the things in The Taiwan Exporter."

"Somehow I can't see you getting on a coat and tie and calling on medical buildings."

"That's the other guys. They work for medical supply companies and get dressed up and do it all official like that. Me, I buy 'em wholesale and sell 'em where I can - side of the road, gas stations…even set up at the flea market sometimes."

"Trust you to take the luster off colostomy bags, Cohen."

"It's a great product, really, with the huge mark-up. Medicare doesn't cover it 'cause they're not 'durable'." Cohen swerved to miss a large black lump of fur in his lane.

"Jeez. What was that?" Doc asked.

Cohen just shook his head. "You don't hear about it but there's a real problem with muggers stealing people's bags, and I don't mean purses. I was talkin' to one old lady who'd been bagged, as they call it. She said she was hopin' the old guy was after somethin' else. It's insulting."

"Ooh, God," Doc recoiled. "Stop before I throw up all over your dashboard."

"Well, just imagine what it's like to be out of bags. It gives 'running out' a whole new meaning. And I haven't even touched on the homeless problem... I sell 'em discount and people flock to me. The only drawback is the limited demographics; so I'm working on marketing ideas to get the rest of the public." Cohen turned right onto a darker two lane road. "Like selling them as a hedge against inflation. 'Invest in the future. They'll only be more expensive later.'"

"How about this? 'Free colostomy with every purchase.'"

"Now you're talkin', Doc. Most people only get one, so it's not like they'd take unreasonable advantage." Cohen wheeled right again onto a road flanked by new walled subdivisions. "I've been thinkin' about Disney themes, too, like instead of colostomy bags, call 'em 'Goofy bags'. Little picture on the side."

"That'll pull in the kids."

"Exactly."

Doc's brain was on fire. "Here's a slogan for the macho men: 'Don't be a fag. Shit in a bag.'"

"How about this? We hook in a promotion with those beef ads. I sell 'em to Winn Dixie and they tape one to every steak."

Doc nodded approval. "That'll stimulate sales. Good for them, good for you. Sky's the limit, really. How about a billboard: 'Don't be a party pooper!'"

Mortecai smiled at Doc. "Or 'Don't poop out.'"

"That'd hit home. And just think of the pictures - a couple making out in the corner..."

"Hold it, Doc. Now you're going beyond the boundaries of taste."

"Alright, but man! Can you just feel this think tank thing happening?"

"We've got to do this more often, Doc." The muted shapes of trees reappeared like fugitives along the road, then Cohen pulled off onto a dirt track that ended at the river. "I'm gonna ride this wave 'til WalMart hops on and flattens it out."

June doesn't get dark until about ten o'clock. This makes it a relatively poor month for creative maintenance, the cover of darkness withholding itself until it is too late for a pedestrian not to excite suspicion. Cohen parked the van under the 419 bridge at 10:45, their target across the Econlockhatchee. The two ground maintenance volunteers were standing beside Cohen's van, its utility truck orange sides subdued by the half moonlight to a kinder hue. Two customized scuba tanks with hoses were at their feet and a spade leaned against the van.

"Okay, Doc. Do we ford or cross the bridge?"

"I don't know, Cohen. You're the man. I'd just as soon stay dry."

Cohen stepped from the bridge's shadow and scanned the length of the concrete guard rail. "We'll look awful funny running across the bridge with these things."

"There's no cars out here this time of night. Let's go."

"All right, but watch it suddenly become I-4."

They dragged the heavy load of herbicide up the concrete embankment to the bridge and, seeing no approaching headlights, stepped over the rail and started across. At about a third of the way a hint of discovery appeared in the distance.

"Start running, Doc."

"We better be ready to throw these things over."

"We can't do that. Anyway, there's no law against possessing this stuff," Mortecai puffed. "Maybe we can't stand seein' weeds growin' in the road."

Before they reached the end of the span, a small car was upon them. "Quick. Take a leak." With the tanks jammed between their legs and the wall, Stiles and Cohen presented an innocent silhouette to the disinterested driver.

Relieved as rabbits to be off the bridge, they quickly crossed the thin line of trees that were spared to buffer the golf course from the road. They emerged onto a fairway.

Cohen grimaced at his heavy weapon. "Dammit, Stiles. You were supposed to hire caddies."

"I did. They just didn't show."

"That's the sort of thing that's wrong with this country."

"Quit complaining. We can drag them from here."

The tall and short figures proceeded toward the vague outline of a flag in the half-lit distance, like upright slugs leaving a shiny trail in the dewy grass.

"Doc, did you know these golf players are so fit that when they have golf contests, they can't use wheelchairs?"

"Yeah?"

"It's a rule. No cripples allowed. You have to prove you can actually walk the course."

"So if we make it tonight, we could be one of them."

"Kind of scary."

"Hey, Cohen. We could start an underground golf magazine, with one-legged guys wearing shorts."

"Or old clothes, like maybe they went there after work. How about pictures of hobos taking a swing?"

"Yeah. Call it *Golf Bum*. They live in the trees and come out at night. And instead of a ball, they'd use potatoes. It's exciting because they can't cook supper until everybody gets one in."

"I feel that think-tank fillin' up again, Doc. You know, they never have kids in those magazines either."

"Supports your theory about the cloth. And probably no midgets."

"Which leaves you out. And speaking of that, no Putt-Putt golf."

"That's because it's challenging." Doc shifted his tank to the other hand. "How about women?"

"Rarely, 'cause women get to wear shorts sometimes, to show they're not really serious."

"I think we're onto something, Cohen."

Their enjoyment of the cool evening mitigated only by aching triceps, the vandals found themselves in a quandary when they finally reached a green.

"What the Hell do we write, Doc? F#!K YOU?"

"Nah. Something profound. This should be a learning experience."

"F18K GOLFERS? Man. This is a problem. Why didn't we think about it before?"

Suddenly Doc performed a tiny dance, like he'd been slightly electrocuted. "*I* know! *I* know! Let's just number the holes. Help 'em out a little bit."

Cohen's teeth slowly displaced the bottom half of his face. "Yeah. I like it. But we don't know what holes they are."

"That's alright. If we get it wrong, it'll make the game more interesting."

"You think so, Doc? It might piss 'em off."

"To make it up to them, let's make the holes bigger."

"Yeah. That way everybody'll have a better score and then they'll be happy. You go ahead and do that."

The pastor and his congregation set about encircling the cups in giant figures of dying Bermuda grass so that future wayfarers would know exactly where they were; more or less. And they made the holes themselves much wider. Their load became lighter and the outing an unadulterated pleasure, such are the rewards of helping people.

Returning to the van at 2 a.m. with dirty spade and empty containers, Mortecai and Doc were in a meditative mood. Doc made an observation. "You know, there's gonna be some interesting putting strategies out there tomorrow."

The next morning Doc Stiles listened as Mike Signout of WDUM - AM reported, somewhat skeptically, that there would be no putting strategies of any kind that weekend at the Twin Rivers Golf Tournament, officially cancelled due to some unforeseeable plague of nematodes and moles. No one was allowed in, for fear of contamination.

11

As the Bic disposable blazed a smooth, lightly tan trail through foam on his cheek, Doc Stiles contemplated the interplay between sex, romance and mudfish. He had dreamed he was standing naked, chest deep in a lake and Mary Barbarosa, mushroom-white rump poking through the surface, rivulets streaming down her electric skin, was swimming toward him from a drifting boat. He could feel her through the water. Closer and closer she came, her flaxen hair, miraculously dry, shining in the moon-light. He ached for her arrival. After seemingly endless strokes, the magnificent woman stood before him. As Doc prolonged and savored the moment before touching, a mudfish swam between them and swallowed his turgid dick. After a brief thrashing the valued appendage was torn off by the strong jaws and numerous small teeth.

Sex and romance were out of the dream then, leaving only the mudfish. Doc dove after the unromantic denizen and found himself underwater surrounded by a school of dick smoking red-tailed tarpon. Mary was riding one of them. Judging that her tarpon must be smoking on his dick, he swam over and asked for her help. Immediately she dug her heels into the great fish's sides and the dick flew into Doc's hands, when he found that he had no use for it as he already had two. He woke up just then and was thankful for it.

It was eight o'clock and Doc had some free time. He tried to admire his skinny torso in the two x two mirror above the bathroom sink, flattening flexed bicep against ribs for a widening effect. Doc shook his head incredulously. "What a waste. This body should never sleep alone."

Pulling on shorts, smiley face with bullet-hole in the forehead T-shirt and two brand new white sneakers, he was off to Lake Mickeyola with a bag of bread to feed the fish. He biked slowly along on his old one speed, almost too big for him.

Doc found the thirty-pound Russian amurs in their usual cove by the life-size Walt Disney topiary on the East side of Lake Mickeyola. As fry these fish had been tossed by state "conservation" agencies into many Orlando lakes ostensibly to rid them of exotic weeds; but their true purpose was to become a nuisance in their own right which would have to be dealt with, in the usual self perpetuating way insuring these agencies a purpose in the future. Already this ploy had succeeded. The Asian fish were seen as a threat to native aquatic plant life and the same agencies which introduced them were employed developing a method of eradication.

Refusing to yield to the gargantuan foreigners, a few feisty sunfish battled through surface scum for the doughy substance Stiles had cast upon the urban water. One large, colorful male bluegill, dorsal fin spread wide above his alert body, pectoral fins pushing water alternately, confidently held position. "Make way for the nuculer sub? I don't think so," he signaled with his lateral lines.

"I've seen some cigar butts before, but this is ridiculous," sent a smaller male shellcracker.

An amur mumbubbled something in Spanish (the amurs all having learned rudimentary Spanish before arriving in Florida) as a small female bluegill darted in front of its mouth and snatched some Wonderpan.

"Ha! Ha! You stupid Russian big piece of otter shit!" the big bluegill taunted just before the mouth of a six pound bass closed over him.

Observing the murder, Doc made a mental note to return with fishing pole.

Mary Barbarosa flashed across Doc's entire being and he felt the need to ride his bike some more, fast.

Mary O'hara had studied to be a registered nurse like her aunt who raised her. Her aunt encouraged her because as a nurse she could be self reliant, in a trade with a constant demand. As illness knows no social borders, Mary understood that nursing also could be a shortcut to a life of ease for her and, eventually, her aunt.

With this in mind, Miss O'hara opted for private-duty work. She was twenty-four and wished a change of scene, trading her home state of Delaware for Maryland. Mary's first job and her last was for wealthy developer Ravioli Barbarosa.

Barbarosa had made his fortune leveling sections of Mother Nature's domain and improving them with malls, most of which were built on speculation and stood empty for years. During the six months he required to die from phlebitis, he became infatuated with his lovely nurse, angel of mercy; for she commonly conjured that image in men's imaginations. She, on the other hand found him to be a charmless, disgusting old lecher, and eligible. She was very kind to him and hoped to arrive in his will without matrimony. She would have considered a proposal, as consummation easily could have been avoided.

When their only child Vincent was seven, Ravioli Barbarosa's wife broke her vagina in a macabre skiing accident, rendering it incompetent at its more valued function. Within two years her husband had taken to calling her Pretzel Pussy to the exclusion of nearly all other terms of endearment. By Vincent's tenth birthday he had seen his mother for the last time.

At twenty-nine years old, Vincent Barbarosa was not altogether unattractive, and Mary O'hara was touched by the devotion he showed his father by visiting dutifully, and valiantly fighting back grief. She also was touched by Vincent's inheritance. Mary saw him at his best and spread this impression to life in general. She let herself fall in love and he recognized a woman who would give the man on her arm the look of success; the very look an ambitious young man needs. And besides, his father had wanted her desperately, hadn't he? Four months after phlebitis finished the man who had brought them together, Vincent and Mary were married and Mary O'hara was no more.

Vincent really didn't need ambition because he inherited his father's wealth and business; but he had it anyway, though it took a different form from his father's. His father had destroyed much but that was his means to success. Already wealthy by default, Vincent saw destruction as the end: destruction of nature, of people's lives, of people's homes, of anything at all, really, as long as it testified to his power. He had taken no small pride in destroying Mary O'hara, nurse, angel of mercy, by forbidding her to work; out of love, he had said; obliterating all future solace she might have given, the lives she might have saved, the smiles she would have inspired, the satisfaction she would have felt. By marrying her, he had erased the happiness another man would have known in her arms, and his secret vasectomy cancelled the children she might have borne. Indeed his wife was a goldmine of satisfaction.

Doc rapidly finished pressure-washing the big Winn-Dixie sign on Colonial Drive. Much to Stiles' ongoing astonishment, Mrs. Barbarosa had used his phone number. They agreed to meet at Blueveiny's Canadian Pub on Church Street. "Let's wear disguises," Mary had proposed.

"Bond. Doc Bond," he rendered in his vintage Scottish. "But how will I know you?"

"No underwear. How about you?"

"The same." Doc blushed slightly on the phone.

Mary was doubtful. "Could take a long time to find you. Better try something else."

"Okay. Underwear."

"Fine," the angel had said. "That will be much quicker."

Doc lived in an old downtown neighborhood, an upstairs studio, all louver windows on the north and east sides away from the street. No kitchen but that wasn't a problem. It encouraged cooking outside on the landing. There was a big open space and a cozy area for a bed under some east windows. A ceiling fan in the big space and a floor fan near the bed were sufficient for exquisite comfort. Behind the house was an old garage no longer connected to a driveway, where he housed his pressure-washing equipment.

As he cold showered the day off, Doc imagined Mary in his lair, on his bed under the window, under the stars, under him. He cared nothing about her husband or anything else. He would bring her there that night for the first time. By seven o'clock Doc was constantly erect and he felt like a volcano trying not to erupt. He had swept the studio, showered again, strategically placed candles, put the champagne on ice and tried in vain to think of baseball. Nothing left but to hike to the bar. He'd be a little early, but it would be pretty cool sitting there with half a beer when she radiated in and saw him, he bursting into laughter as she floated straight over. "Light your lollypop?" he'd ask in his best Bogart.

By eight-thirty Doc Stiles had watched four and a half Bud drafts come and go. By the end of the fourth glass, he had overcome his disappointment and started introducing himself to the unattended women in the bar.

Mary Barbarosa had expected Vincent to hold the 7 o'clock meeting without her at the office downtown, a bull session concerning Havalawn. But important "investors" would be there and he decided instead to wine and dine them at the Rat and Son Hotel. For this he had to bring along something sure to impress them: his wife. The developer hardly needed her, as he was in rare form at the meeting. "Gentlemen, I give you the headwaters of the Econalahootchee River. I give you Havalawn…"

Doc Stiles headed to the upstairs bar for breathing room. From the top of the stairs he scanned the throng below one last time. Not there, he wrote off his date and headed to the darts lane.

As the tragic Stiles turned away, a lovely blonde woman entered through the front door accompanied by a bored man. Her radiant glow was picked up by Stiles' mating instinct and he turned back around. The Barbarosas surveyed the crowd back to back, the woman seeking something in particular, the man nothing in general. Mary took her husband's arm and walked straight to the man who was bounding down the stairs with a brand new erection and no consideration of anyone in his path. Soon Doc was approaching Mary, in his mind, through a field of flowers.

"Look, Vince." she pulled him around. "Here's the pressure-washing man."

"Hi." The developer lit a Camel and erased the head of his wife, her devastated friend residing below the cloud, then turned to renew his survey of the crowd.

"Did I miss something?" he said to Mary, still looking away, "Or is anyone who forking looks like Mickey Rooney a friend of yours?"

Without waiting for a reply, Vincent Barbarosa pushed his way to the bathroom.

The one man band struck up, Irish tenor Cahir O'doherty exposing once and for all in song, the damning inadequacy of mermaids. Doc and Mary stood together awkwardly, pretending to care. The former Mary

O'hara saw her husband returning from the toilet, grabbed by a State Representative and sucked into his admiring entourage.

"I think we can squeeze in a quick kiss," she said.

Hope reignited in Stiles' breast. "Uh, sure," he said.

Just as Doc was balancing on his tippy toes, Vincent Barbarosa left the legislator's circle with the promise of returning with his charming wife. Mary saw him approach and turned away from Doc.

"Still hanging out with Mickey Rooney, I see."

"Stiles. Document Andrew Stiles, Bozo," Stiles corrected.

Leaning back with one eyebrow arched over his most deprecating look, Barbarosa focused on the diminutive man. "You're standing there like that calling me Bozo?" he finally managed with great astonishment.

"What's the matter. Cotton candy in your ears?"

Something about this person bothered Vincent in an indefinable way but it was the lack of respect that irked him the most, and here was someone just the right size to take into the alley and pummel.

"Let's go," he said to Mary. "I've got some real people for you to meet."

Mary looked sadly back at Doc as she was whisked away like a beautiful bag of dog food.

"Well, there he is in the flesh," mused Doc, his erection destroyed once and for all as he started the long walk home. Thunder rumbled in the distance. Except for a few big raindrops, a storm had passed north of downtown.

12

What is the most wonderful sound in the world?
Cat burps
What makes you happy all the year 'round?
Cat burps
What does an alligator do after he has eaten your pet?

More of *An Alligator's Story*

A flock of irate blue jays was dive bombing a cat. Looking to all the world like an object of unjust persecution, the fluffy tabby skulked along the gutter, melting into the line where curb meets asphalt. Undaunted, the jays tormented this criminal by birth until, with a purr of relief, she gained the refuge of a storm drain leading into Lake Putridia.

The feline never had been in a storm drain before, never having had a reason. Curious, she hopped to a lower ledge which ran the length of the pipe.

"Where the ✗ ☞ ✗ ☜ that sombitch go?" sputtered the flock of jays in relative unison.

The perplexed birds ascended to the branches of a laurel oak above the storm drain, for deduction. After a minute a jay known as Einstein blurted, "She descended the mother#*!#ing hole!"

The jays all swooped down and landed around the opening, peering into it with one eye and then the other. "Bird's Eye Peas and Corn! Einstein's got it!"

"What the Hell do we do now, Einstein?" demanded everyone at once. "Shut up! I'm talking," said every jay. Blue jays being, if nothing else, polite, silence prevailed.

"Well," said the brainy bird, cocking his head to make it work, "we could attack this problem from many directions." He paused for effect. "But I say let's just fill in the goddam hole!"

Such a squawking and activity among blue jays, you never have seen. Immediately they went to picking every acorn they could get their beaks around with an uproar of inane chatter and random cussing so loud that a young fellow walking past with his pants hanging from the bottom of his ass couldn't hear his boombox.

From the bowels of the city the cat heard all this commotion. The acorns clattering into the storm drain, many bouncing to the bottom where they splashed into the stagnant rain water, confirmed the cat's suspicions about the lower level. "Yes, I'll just stay high and dry," she thought, exploring further. "Wouldn't it be something if all the rats and mice in the world were in here?"

Suddenly a shadowy form rocketed from the blackness below and fell back, splashing monstrously with the tabby clutched in the side of its mouth. The alligator chomped its meal back and forth twice to break the bones before swallowing. This is the essence of symbiosis and the first account of such a relationship between alligators and blue jays, an alliance formed in the city. Out of town they are unknown to each other.

The flock of jays mounted the attack until the oaks in the neighborhood had been stripped of enough fruit to ensure the birds a starvation diet until the next crop. No progress was evident and they lost interest, retiring to their nests for a much needed rest, many grumbling disparaging remarks about Einstein. A thunderous belch rose from under the street.

The cat hadn't been entirely wrong about that storm drain leading to a bonanza of rats and mice. Being a pretty good cat, she went to cat heaven and was surrounded by vermin. Bad vermin of course. These creatures were not in heaven, further evidence that one man's heaven can be another man's hell. Cat Heaven boasts other residents. Many dead jet-skiers go there. Although normally he is not, a jet-skier may be many things in life. For Judgment purposes he is a jet skier, that being the defining trait. Half of these people are sent to Cat Heaven where they are a great boon to the cats who love to watch them go around and around.

Although we have little information about it, Cat Hell is quite another story. Symbiosists claim there is no exclusive Cat Hell. They just go to Dog Heaven. Call it what you will, it is generally agreed that the rest of the dead jet-skiers go there and to the delight of the dogs, drag cats around and around.

Once two adventurous and really stupid dead cats grew bored after nine thousand years of the pleasures of Cat Heaven. They determined to vacation on earth. Their names were Heavenly Ben and Heavenly Jerry.

The feline glory train was unguarded so they casually hopped into the back and awaited the next pick-up run. Soon they were skimming over highways scooping up the souls of the good cats that lay freshly squished and steaming below them, zooming by veterinary clinics where souls are conveniently bagged and hung from a hook by the back door; through medical testing labs where, having lived in Hell, all the animals are Heaven bound, and then they cruised aimlessly and picked up scattered souls.

"Where should we get off?" Ben asked as he scoured the tip of his tail.

"Right here," said Jerry. So they sprang off and half a second after landing they changed into real cats that had been dead for nine thousand years. Their vacation lasted a couple years, such as it was. Then they went to Cat Hell; or Dog Heaven.

13

rlando really exists only in the minds of people who live there, a highly restricted playing field at best. It has no meaning for the bricks under the asphalt street where Mortecai Cohen's house fronts. In fact the bricks probably don't even think of themselves as bricks, much less part of a larger picture. Their personal identity may still be that of clay or straw; just that plain. If clay even thinks at all. The trees don't give a damn, much less the blue jays. Orlando, Central Florida, Bum#$!#, Egypt - it's all the same to them.

In 1910 a three room house was built on a dirt road in Jernigan, Florida. Its floors, ceilings and walls are heart of pine, its joists, rafters and roof, cypress. There is not a sheet of drywall, plywood or flake board about the place. The small floor-level fireplace on the south wall is capable of chasing the occupants outside to cool off on the coldest night this latitude can dish up, even though by the second half of the century four rooms had been added, putting the fireplace in the middle. The front porch, without which any address is a lesser entity, cannot be dated. The house perches atop blocks with no sub-floor, enabling air cooling from below. Solid wooden walls and ceilings ventilated by floor to ceiling casement windows blend in nicely under oak trees. Thus intelligently built and situated, it can be made comfortable in summer with ceiling fans. It is near a deep spring fed lake in which no natural law regulates the number of cooling dips one may take on a scorching day or sweltering night. With the sunshine and breeze, rain or cold wind invading this house as they do, as certain brands of thunder shake it more violently than others, in this house a person feels the vitality of being outside, sheltered but not isolated from the weather. It is topped by a hip roof, not the most popular roof in Homestead, but after Andrew, the only roof.

By 1994 ownership of this simple model of efficiency had fallen to a northerner, Mortecai Cohen. Yes, even he came from New York, at the age of nine, ever grateful for the move. In his mind was a critical difference between people who emigrated B.D. and A.D.; the adventurous folks who found an old house to live in and carved out a place for themselves, and the later crowd who would stay in Kalamazoo if not for the tidy walled central air conditioned subdivisions and ready made jobs waiting for them. It was a logical suggestion he had made to politicians pretending to seek solutions to Florida's problems that they willfully created: "Raise building codes state-wide to a standard that precludes the need for air-conditioning. Then make air conditioning illegal in new construction. There's your growth problem solved." No one ever ran with it.

"Hey, Mort," said Violet, just returned from a walk with Juice the cat, "what's that thing in the middle of Lake Gasoila?"

"Is this a joke?"

"No. There's some weird thing out there; looks like a space probe or something."

"I really don't have the slightest idea, although there was a strange light in the sky last night."

"I'm serious," said Violet. "Whatever it is, it can't be good."

"Alright, I'll look into it."

The next morning Mortecai phoned City Hall World to learn about the strange object floating in the middle of Lake Gasoila. They referred him to the Parks Department which referred him to Streets and Drainage which advised him to call the Florida Game and Fresh Water Fish Commission. There he struck pay dirt.

"It's a turkey feeder mounted on pontoons," a woman with a debilitating Minnesota accent told him.

"Are you going to put some little turkey boats out there so they can get to the feeder?" Cohen asked.

"It's been adapted to feed fish."

"Oh, my God," said the concerned citizen. "Are the fish starving?"

"No, sir. The fish aren't starving," she patronized him. "It's part of a program to eliminate problem fish."

"Problem fish, eh?" Mortecai considered. "And I thought it was kids today making all the trouble."

The spokesperson exuded silence.

"Listen. I can hardly understand what you're saying. Are you from Russia or someplace?"

"I live in Kissimmee," she drawled.

"Okay, I'm with you. So what are we gonna do? Feed 'em until they explode?"

"No, sir," she said petulantly, peeking under a slice of bread to check the amount of mustard in her sandwich. "We use regular fish pellets for six weeks to get the fish used to eating them. Then we switch to poison."

"But how do you keep the nice fish from eating the poison?"

"We don't. We reclaim the lake and start over again," she said, reading the official guidelines.

"Kill 'em all, let Cod sort 'em out, eh?"

"Sir," she said, wishing to get to her snack, "we have to remove the grass carp this way. They've started destroying the native plants."

"You mean the Russian amurs, don't you? Those expensive fish you people put there in the first place?"

"Look. I was in Frostbite Falls when they did that."

"Hey, wait a minute. It's Russian fish, you've got a Russian accent. What's going on here?"

"Would you like the number for the state department?"

"Oh, sure. You mean that number that blows up my phone when I dial it? No thanks. I've heard enough."

"Excellent. Good bye."

Mortecai called Violet at home. "You know your floating space probe?"

"Yes?"

"You were right. It's part of an alien plot to take over the United Nations. The Holy Crap Church must stop them. Are you up to it?"

"You bet. But why me?"

"This one's your baby. See you tonight."

It was the kind of heat soaked, molasses humid, thick evening that could melt your legs together, the day's inferno sealed tight by pendulous clouds sagging claustrophobically overhead like puss squeezed from the eye of God.

The swelter was but little relieved by Mortecai's ceiling fans. At ten-thirty that night, he in pink flamingo bathing suit and Violet in no underwear and her lightest cotton ensemble followed Juice the orange cat over two blocks and down the hill to Lake Gasoila. Mortecai was armed with a two inch pocket machete and Violet a crescent wrench and two screwdrivers, flat and Philips head. Violet sat on the concrete storm drain enclosure, oozing sweat that could not evaporate. Houses across the street were quiet save a chorus of air conditioners humming their environmental dirge. Nobody was outside so Mortecai walked to the edge of the pond where he hesitated.

"Do I really have to go in there?" he whined to Violet.

"It's just polluted, Mort. That doesn't bother you."

"This better make me an eco-hero. I want songs and poems about me printed on Eco-Asswipe."

Stepping in, he immediately sank to his knees in the corrupted mud bottom. He pushed his legs through the silt to deeper water. Though Mortecai dreaded immersing himself in this road runoff, he couldn't help enjoying its coolness. When the water reached neck deep, he felt undetectable in the moonless night, swimming head out, forty yards to the feeder. On the bank, Juice meticulously cleaned his belly.

With the calm finality of a candle snuffing out, the neighborhood houses became uniformly quiet and dim, the result of a utilities brownout, one of a strategic series orchestrated by the Orlando Utilities Commission to demonstrate the need for further power plant construction.

A door opened, throwing forth only desperation instead of the usual shaft of incandescence painting the immediate night. One skeleton lightly draped in skin and cloth, then another bent away from the small house. Slowly, cautiously, leg bones inched them toward the lake. The lifelong companions swapped moral and physical support along the way. They were locked into this dance, determined to keep each other functioning, as the breath in one affirmed the life in the other.

The turkey feeder was a cylindrical can about four feet high with a lid on top. As a fish feeder it was elevated three feet more by three aluminum legs attached to Styrofoam floats. Two ropes disappeared into the depths where concrete blocks held them to the bottom.

"This is pretty simple," Mortecai thought, as he cut one rope then swam around the feeder and cut the other. With hands on the floats he started swimming and pushing the contraption to shore. Halfway in, the defender of innocent fish spotted the ancient couple shuffling miserably by the lake, turning to goo as they went, appearing to drip wearily into the very sidewalk. They stopped and spoke to Violet, apparently out being walked by her cat.

"I can live without the lights," the old gent explained in a wavering voice, "but not the air. They need to get that new plant built."

It was the kind of opening Violet got up for in the morning, but she let it go. "Sooner the better," she said.

"You know, I can't tell if fanning myself with this newspaper is worth heating myself up to do it," the old lady stated her dilemma. Her husband ignored the invitation.

Mortecai stopped, blocking his face with the feeder. The couple soon needed to move on to create some movement of air around them, however slight. Instantly, the inexplicably powered fish feeder resumed swimming in. Violet met Mortecai on the bank.

"Under different circumstances," the frog man said, "I'd a sold 'em some colostomy bags."

"Well, let's get this thing out of here," Violet said, just before discovering it was too heavy to lift.

"You know, I think you've come over to the dark side."

"I'm only here to bring you back."

Mortecai held up the blade screwdriver dramatically. "Die, turkey feeder!" he sentenced quietly.

As the final screw disengaged the legs, the weight of the fish pellets tipped the feeder, pushing off the lid, and an all-you-fish-can-eat special spilled into the lake.

"Looks like it's just fish pellets after all," Violet noted.

Having completed his ablutions, Juice impatiently meowed at his workers to pick up the pace. Each with a hand on the bottom and a hand on the top of the canister, Mortecai and Violet trotted behind Juice who led the way to Lake Roadwater along one of the few remaining dirt roads in Orlando.

At the lake the cat remained on shore as the winded, sweat-soaked couple carried their cargo through extensive shallows to water deep enough to cover it. Before leaving the decommissioned poisoner, Violet opened a door at its base and removed two big Ray-o-Vac lantern batteries.

"A lot of people," Mortecai said, "just go to K-Mart."

"Spoils of war," Violet pointed out.

The next morning the saboteurs returned with rod and reel and breadballs to the scene of a feeding frenzy. Every fish in the lake who could swim, fly or catch a cab was within eight feet of shore gorging on pellets. Mortecai immediately tied into a big one. After a dogged battle he landed a seven pound Russian amur.

"Wow! That's a big one," Violet stated, rather impressed.

"What should we do with him?"

"Put him back of course."

"But this fish is a menace. Suppose he's not satisfied just eating all the native plants in the lake. Suppose he takes over the world. Then what?"

"I think he'd be a benevolent ruler. Let him go."

"God dammit, just put me back in the ☺☠👎❽ing water," said the amur in Spanish.

"What'd you say?" Violet asked Mortecai. "Did you say something?"

"Nope. You hearing things?"

"Somebody said these things are good to eat," said Mortecai. "You sure you don't want to try it?"

"Sacre Bleu!" thought the amur in Spanish.

"Yes, I'm sure. Put the poor thing back in before it has a heart attack."

"Yeah, it doesn't look any good. Just looks like a giant shiner." Cohen shook his head. "Man, if I'd caught one of these when I was a kid... I'd a thought I had the world record shiner. I'd a got it mounted."

To the relief of the frantic fish, Mortecai set it back in the water and it couldn't get away fast enough. "Strictly eating native plants from now on," the amur swore to itself.

14

It is amazing how well hidden is the Econlockhatchee River basin from outer space; amazing to those who know it, who might expect its wonders to be somehow apparent in the satellite photos. Viewpoint can be everything. The river's charms are unavailable to space travelers, developers and politicians. Would that they all were space travelers. Good for us, good for our perception of them, whose ignorance would be laundered by perspective.

County Commissioner Liz Mango had beseeched Tallahassee to no avail, the Department of Community Affairs crumbling before her eyes. The election was in a month and television sets were full of manipulative, subliminal appeals, "crime" the time honored whipping boy. Crime swam in with the population flood but no one proposed stemming that as a deterrent, politicians preferring the traditional punishment side of the issue. Beyond that, Mango was running for County Chairwoman, a position she claimed would serve as a bully pulpit for her and a wedge against Havalawn. Destruction could begin as early as October.

Mortecai Cohen and Jake Lessup had intersected at a yard sale. "Betty Baxter almost failed to put it through," Cohen argued. "If Gertrude Buttmustard had just sprained her ankle in high heels, Havalawn falls. So if Baxter had that hard a time putting it through, why should Liz be able to stop it just because she's chairman?"

"Nothing is left to chance. Baxter knew Gertie was going their way." Lessup absently inspected an art deco lamp. "I'm working on the Mango campaign. It's the best shot we've got."

"No. We're the best shot we've got. I'm not letting it go in, Jake. I can't. And we need to stop it before it gets out there."

"Oh, Barbarosa has to go down. They must go down," Lessup agreed. "Maybe a computer virus. I need to check with a friend. In the meantime, give me your number again. I'll be in touch."

Lessup fought for the Econlockhatchee by lobbying Tallahassee. A bit cloak and dagger, he felt his legitimate image jeopardized by being seen with Cohen.

"Just let me know the timetable," Cohen said as Lessup headed for his car. "I want to know when the first grain of sand is going to be disturbed."

Mortecai purchased *The Ink Spots Greatest Hits* for fifty cents.

15

"Why bother?" Pastor Cohen mumbled to his pillow. "The entire assemblage is right here."

"What about Brother Stiles?" asked Violet.

"He's probably off cleaning buildings somewhere. So it's just you, me and the cat on the end of the bed and I'm not that sure about the bed."

"Come on, Mort. Your pulpit awaits you. Suppose the IRS sends a snoop around today. Anyway I'm dying to hear your latest load of bullshit."

"I keep telling you. It's a sermon, Violet; not the disgusting outpouring of a bull's butthole. There's a difference. But I do happen to have some pretty good stuff ready."

Juice the cat seated Violet on an egg crate and Pastor Cohen took his place behind a soggy URANUS box that had been left out in the rain. "Since we have on hand today some exquisite fresh stolen Valencia oranges, this is our sacrament. Sacrament to excrement. Amen." Cohen took a meaningful slug of juice. He leveled his pelagic gaze at the woman of his life and a swell rode through her as she met it.

"So did you hear about this guy who was in jail for three years and just before he was gonna be let out, he wrote to his woman that he didn't blame her if she didn't want him anymore, but if he was the luckiest man in the world and she did want him back, then please to tie a yellow gibbon around the old oak tree?"

"Yes, I heard about that, Mort," Violet yelled from the multitudes.

"It's *Pastor* Mort to you and I'll thank you to remember that heckling a man of the cloth is very bad form."

"Man of the loin cloth..."

After a sharp glance at Violet, the pastor returned to his story. "The woman gets the letter and opens it with trembling hands 'cause it's the first she's heard from her true love ever since he went in stir. She's waited for him all this time not even knowing if he wanted her and her happiness is unbounded when she reads what he has written. Not surprisingly she assumes he meant ribbon, so on the appointed day she ties a hundred yellow ribbons on the old oak tree.

"The convict boards the bus with his heart in his mouth. The nearer he gets to his home town, the more hearts he gets in his mouth and by the time he crosses the city limits, he has about five hearts in his mouth and one that shot up into his brain. Well, he sees all these yellow ribbons on the tree and he's got everybody else on the bus lookin' too, and nobody sees a single yellow gibbon. There he sits on the Greyhound Bus, broken hearted which was a terrible mess in his case. The bus stops and he doesn't get off. He rides on to live a life of loneliness and lost love. One day after about fifteen years it hits him out of the blue that maybe she couldn't get a yellow gibbon so she put up the ribbons instead."

Cohen suspended speech as a distant rumble approached. Then it ceased and a truck door creaked loudly open. Soon Doc Stiles was walking briskly into the back yard. Juice seated him next to Violet.

"What did I miss?"

Violet turned to Doc. "Oh man, it was great. All about this guy with a mouth full of exploding hearts and everything."

Cohen sighed and continued. "Is a ribbon a gibbon? I don't think so. That is the moral of the story. Now let's talk about other words that aren't what they aren't: doctors and lawyers have no customers. They have patients and clients instead, like it's unseemly for them to be motivated by profit, Hypocritic Oath and all. Real estate salesmen are "agents." When something has a euphemism for it, watch out.

"The worse a thing is, the more euphemisms it has. Except for conventional church services, death is the most feared consequence of life. So there's a galaxy of euphemisms to moderate it. An excellent one improves the killing of our pet by a veterinarian. With our clever trick he doesn't really kill it, does he? He puts Old Rhubarb to sleep. That sounds better and we feel better."

Violet raised slightly on her plastic seat and a methane calamity ripped free of her anus. The congregation was temporarily dispersed.

"God damn, Violet. How lady-like," Mortecai said, certain illusions dashed. "Too bad Ray's already married. What a team you two would make."

Slightly embarrassed but tickled with her timing, she sat there trying to suppress laughter as Doc returned to his egg crate. "Cohen - looks like you're dating Stinkerbell."

Violet had to get up and walk around the yard.

"I can wait as long as you can...I actually spent time writing this shit, you know," said Cohen, a bit hurt.

"You did not," Doc said incredulously.

"No. Really he did," said Violet, returning with moist eyes. "Believe it or not. I saw him."

You're both gonna go to New York when you die," Cohen warned.

"He means it," Violet said with a grave look at Doc.

"Well, we'd better calm down and listen to him then."

"These euphemisms are harmless enough, aren't they?" Cohen picked up. "County commissioner's a euphemism for disturbingly sleazy windbag. If you use a euphemism long enough, it loses its effect and no longer mitigates the distrust generated by the individual scumbags.

"How about 'develop'? Nice word isn't it? It denotes the mindless destruction of Florida. But development sounds much better. It enables our politicians to welcome and encourage disaster. Developers are the visionaries who lead our home to its full potential – of degradation. They only kill the land and water; put it to sleep so to speak. Let me ask you this: How come before the land is destroyed, it's called unspoiled, but after it's been spoiled, it's developed?

"Here's an example for the history books: 'Apathetic fools who presided over the destruction of their home, formerly one of the finest places on earth'. Aw, come on. Let's call ourselves Floridians instead. Sounds better, doesn't it? Makes us feel better.

"Let us close our eyes for a moment and ask St. Ballou to guide the minds and hearts of Floridians everywhere, to become more than euphemisms."

Violet and Doc closed their eyes. Violet fell into a fit of ecstasy, wailing for St. Ballou to come down and help them, before Juice returned her to her seat.

Pastor Cohen continued: "If you doubt we are at war, listen to this. At the Orlando Defo Center three years ago Barbarosa Development Corporation made their 'by invitation' presentation of their plans to put a New England style city on the upper Econ. Though not invited, me and Ray attended. Vincent Barbarosa and his snobby Miami architect Poodlepig Morgenstroo spent two hours telling us how we don't know how to live around here. Got parking lots and we drive around in cars and stuff. From the audience I politely stated my opinion and asked a question or two. Although it had been billed as a 'town hall meeting', Barbarosa refused to answer and folded his tent. All this caught the attention of Morgenstroo. He came over to us, over the objections, he said, of Barbarosa, who told him, 'Don't talk to them. They're nobody. They're nothing. Fork 'em.'

Morgenstroo doesn't even like Barbarosa. He just has this concept he's dying to see come to life and he's using Barbarosa to do it. He doesn't care *where* it is. In his eagerness to show us he was the good guy, Morgenstroo let us in on the contempt in which we are held by developers; we who only happen to be the people who live here. It sounds like war to me."

A powerful belch resounded from the house, heralding the chiseled features of Ray Macon in the back doorway. "Yep. It's just like he says it was. I was there." An alarming fart followed. "I need to take a shit somewhere."

"How about your house?" Mortecai suggested, too late. Ray already had retreated to the nearest bathroom.

"Is it finally over?" said Doc, "because you and me need to talk."

"'Fork 'em?' Ooooooh. What a meany. I'm outta here," Violet said, kissing Mortecai on the cheek without slowing down.

"Alright Stiles, let's go throw the football."

Hungover and still a little drunk from fishing all night at Sebastian Inlet, Ray needed time before going home. He went to sleep on the kitchen floor.

Cohen was facing Doc, football dropping out of his hand. "You ⚡✴♦☀◎ed Barbarosa's wife?... You?"

Doc was pacing in a small circle pounding his fist. "Yeah man. She told me about the guy but it didn't hit me who he was until now."

"How'd you manage that?" Mortecai asked, his view of life's possibilities suddenly expanding faster than the universe.

"I was pressure-washing her house. She looked incredible and seemed interested. I didn't know she was married, so I asked her if she wanted to go fishing. You know, try to get something going. Told her I knew this nice spot. Man, it was unbelievable."

A thunderstruck Cohen sat on the road as awe cascaded from his mouth. "I hate that guy. What's she like? Is she on our side? You didn't premature ejaculate or anything did you?"

"Darn near. But she's definitely not on his team."

Mortecai stood and laid hands on Stiles' shoulders. "You're Mata Hari now, Doc. Imagine the inside info she could provide. You have to bring her over to the cause."

"I'll try, Bud. I'll try," Doc said as he thought, *I just hope I see her again.*

Stiles picked up the football and uncorked one as Cohen went long, pulled in the ball at full stretch, then tripped over the curb and flew into a viburnum hedge.

"Man! Where'd those guys come from?" the quarterback asked.

Ignoring the roar of the crowd, the star end trotted back to earshot.

"So what's the plan, Cohen?"

"A campaign of harassment. We'll Super-Glue Barbarosa's offices closed, after hours to keep 'em out 'til they get the locks removed. Also we post flyers in phone booths offering a fifty dollar reward to anyone calling Barbarosa's 800 number and telling "why development is good for Central Florida" in fifty words or less."

"Sounds good, dad. Once they get in the office, their phones'll be all tied up with people wanting their fifty bucks."

"But today, Glen Sanderling is running for re-election to the Seminole County Commission on big developer bucks so let's add FOR SALE and SOLD to his campaign signs. Then we fill in that I-4 lottery billboard by Lake Monroe: "WHEN I WIN THE LOTTERY, I'M GOING TO BUY A _____. What do you think? County Commissioner?"

"Perfect." Stiles ran a short down-and-out and Cohen threw the ball behind him.

Southwest Florida was a lucrative market for the discount colostomy bag trade. Mortecai spent the week addressing this need in Port Charlotte where Barbarosa had another office. He sold so many that he donated a box of bags to a local soup kitchen. After five o'clock he decorated pay phones. After nine he Super-Glued locks and fished for snook, keeping two undersize ones for cooking at home. Doc Stiles pressure-washed two office complexes in Winter Park and six-year old Joey Fernandez' red wagon. He Super-Glued Barbarosa's downtown Orlando office twice and distributed flyers to thirty-five phone booths.

"What have you to report, Brother Stiles?"

"Barbarosa's going to be investing heavily in aspirin," Doc said, leaning on the rail tooth-picking. "And the Goofy Gazette ran our photo of the billboard. COOL-105 was telling everybody to drive by and look at it."

"Fantastic! Things are happenin'. No trouble?"

"Nah. How about you?"

"I'd say Barbarosa's been put on notice."

"Alright! We need to have a toast." Doc high-fived Cohen.

"Got just the thing."

Doc followed Mortecai to the refrigerator. "IBC in a frosted mug. You do know how to boogey, Cohen." He sniffed the bouquet, smiled, and downed his first slug with gusto.

Mortecai took a medium hit. "You know, Doc, you ought to get out there someday and just pre*tend* to sell colostomy bags. It's worth it for the looks you get."

"I can only imagine, Cohen. And that's how I'd like to keep it."

Cohen leaned against the plywood table near the kitchen and set his mug on last month's utility bill. "By God, it has its moments. Last week I was going office to office and I come to this big brick law firm. Up the stairs I go. The receptionist looks up real friendly from her desk 'cause she thinks I'm a client, acts like she knows exactly who I am. After the chit-chat she says, 'Is Mr. Biltmore expecting you?'"

"'Not unless he's clairvoyant,'" I said. "'I'm selling colostomy bags.'"

"She's still smiling 'cause she's not over the idea I might be a client. 'You're doing what?' she says and her eyelashes do this flutter thing."

"'Selling colostomy bags,'" says I, unzipping my drop-down sample display. "'Got 'em in an array of colors and sizes to match your output. How many do you want?'"

"She looks at me awhile, I swear to God, like I'm the Ninth Wonder of the World. Then suddenly she turns straight to ice. 'None,' she says."

"It was good salesmanship, anyway," Doc noted. "You never say 'if', always 'how many.'"

"Exactly. So I said, 'You buy insurance right? You don't use it, it's just in case, isn't it? Same with these. It's always good to have an emergency stash if you run out, 'cause I'm sure I don't have to tell you, when you need a colostomy bag, you *need* a colostomy bag.'

"Doc, have I got this girl's attention. She just keeps staring at me. Then she says, 'I don't *need* a colostomy bag.' So I use the 'They're Not for Me' close. I said, 'Christmas'll be here before you know it. Don't you have any friends or relatives that use 'em? They'll never be cheaper.'

"Somehow I lost her. She looks down at a book like I'm not there anymore. To be nice, I finish up with, 'I just don't want you wishing someday you'd got some from me, 'cause that way we both lose.' Without even the manners to look up she says, 'There's no soliciting in this office.' Sad ending, right? Wrong!

"Right then this old guy sitting in the waiting room puts down his magazine and says, 'How much you getting for them?'

"She's looking up again with her mouth open like the guy just crapped on the floor. I smiled at her, then took the order. Gave him my bulk price and he got a whole box. I walked up to the desk and said to her, 'You see it's a money maker. I'll give 'em to you wholesale, you dispense 'em right here from the office. Should I get you a starter display while I'm at the van?' but her jaw dropped another notch and her face kind of got paralyzed."

"I suppose the great thing is," Stiles conjectured, "if he lives through that lot, he'll be ordering more."

"You got it. There's only one way I ever lose a customer. Plus I'm looking into setting up a vending machine at his condo."

At the back of Rocket City Mortecai and Doc picked up the road to the coal power plants, which skirted the sentenced land. A power line corridor was the north boundary. There they began seeing signs of Barbarosa. The land was fenced off but they were relieved that nothing

126

had begun, the curse of optimism afflicting their judgment. Each man was very happy to think he might not have to risk his freedom after all.

"But if we need to," Cohen said, "we can use that corridor to get in."

"Hey, look at the rabbits," Doc said, always excited to see furry little bundles.

Doc stopped the truck and they stepped out. Two downstream rabbits bolted for bushes.

"That was a close one, Mr. Rabbit."

"No, we are safe here. See? Humans cannot come beyond the fence."

"I am so glad we came here," said Mrs. Rabbit as they hopped along under palmetto cover. "Aren't you?"

"Yes. It's a dream come true. It was your cleverness that brought us here. I wanted to stay and fight the yellow monsters."

Mrs. Rabbit shook out a few bunny poops. "Of course. You are very brave."

"But here there are no yellow monsters. This is better."

"It is good for the children to stay in one place," said Mrs. Rabbit. "Oh! I am so glad that hawk did not get you. We are happy now."

"Yes, I was too swift for him."

16

And what of Ray Macon? Did he confidently stalk the earth, head held high breathing the sweet fresh air of righteousness? Did he obey his natural impulses as one to be reckoned with? A man among men? A man among women? Or did he spoil and putrefy like a sun drenched fish in a clear plastic bag? In his view, Interstate - 4 was a sludgy pipeline sucking the entire northern United States and Ontario into his home town and he was spread-eagle at the receiving end.

Since launching the Japanese honeymooners, Macon had lost not his desire but his taste for revenge against the establishment, having glimpsed the abyss of society's scorn and wifely ridicule before learning it was only a taxi cab. If Mortecai Cohen had liberated Ray to strike back at his stolid enemies, the car wreck returned him to impotence in the face of progress and a life stained by pent-up anger and sorrow.

Gone were those occasional satisfying, beer induced nights of righteous vandalism. Now Ray simply endured, inundated by an inert army of occupation consigning the only home he had known to a hallowed place in memory. He could only sit and reminisce about his brief offensive that a Japanese tourist had taken away.

It was Tuesday night and Ray had worked from nine to seven, losing ground all day. Cancellations outnumbered sales two to one and he wished he'd never gone in. Moreover, he had sort of lost interest in continuing to live, it had seemed such a waste of time lately. He gave up and returned home to a delicious pot roast supper. The house had a cordial if cluttered feel and he drove the baby around the block twice to put her to sleep, then kissed her and laid her in the bassinet in his and Daisy's room. He lingered over her stillness and allowed his chest to warm with pity and love. Then on the couch Andrea and Laura sat either side of him and told about their day as Daisy brought him a steaming hot chocolate with mini-marshmallows in it. As always the girls marveled at what a beautiful father they had.

"Life's really not so bad," he thought, looking proudly upon his progeny and reaching his arms across their shoulders so they could snuggle in. But everyone was sleeping by ten o'clock. Ray himself dozed in front of the teevee and almost fell asleep but a voice deep within him, perhaps the vibrant boy he had grown out of, lodged in his guts ashamed of what he had become, insisted he needed more reward for his day of frustration. Ray sat up and walked deliberately to the kitchen where he found Captain Morgan. For the same reason a virtuous woman may let her judgment be seduced by alcohol, Ray put the Captain several times to his lips.

"That ought to do," he thought, coming to life as he walked outside. Ray slid into his Honda. On the way to Mortecai's house, Ray played steering wheel drum and sang along with Johnny Cougar on COOL Radio.

Farts so good...
Come on baby, won't ya fart so good.
Sometimes love... doesn't smell like it should,
ya know you...
Fart so good.

Ray smiled, glad that he'd gone out and embraced the world, shuddering to think how he'd almost missed this good time.

There was no van at Mortecai's, so Ray proceeded to Lou's Lounge and introduced Captain Morgan to Mr. Bud Weiser, regularly calling Cohen's empty house.

Fairly well lighted by a porno movie playing on a side wall and all the smoldering cigarets, the bar was filled with friendly chatter, human gasses, smoke and the sickly sweet aroma of vomit long ignored. At the nostalgic atmosphere Ray filled with a sort of quiet joy. From his barstool he was staring blankly at the open back door when a stout, fortyish and legless man, filled with the anticipation of a fun night at Lou's, arm powered his wheelchair up to top speed across the parking lot and slammed into the threshold. The wheelchair stopped but he didn't. The payload landed about twelve feet into the bar where he thrashed about on the floor like an upturned turtle until the barftender bear hugged and returned him to his catapult. Thus reinstated, the cheerful fellow carried on undaunted, like it was par for the course and maybe he did it every night trying to set a new distance record.

If God were trying to cheer Ray up, he couldn't have done more; but Ray didn't laugh. Sitting there like a fire hydrant on the moon, he ordered another beer and became contemplative. He sat there earnestly trying to contemplate something pleasant and failing that, anything at all. Like many working stiffs, Ray had innate creativity with no outlet. He pictured a movie he had wanted to produce for some time, about a pig-abusing hillbilly who gets sucked by a terrible whirlpool down to the ocean floor where he builds a giant domed habitat out of squid skin. He goes inside the dome and gives birth to pigs so he starts a pig farm. They keep multiplying and eventually overrun the place. Ray wanted to call it *Twenty-thousand Peagues Under the Sea*. The pigs dissolved into Germans. Reruns of *I Love Lucy* set in Munich in the thirties started flitting through Ray's head. Lucy constantly hid the Mertzes on ledges and under lampshades while Ricky tortured the Gestapo with his Cuban German. The Ricardos disappeared when Ray remembered the Deer Run apartment complex under construction. "They oughtta be up by now," his brain slurred.

"Mr. Weiser! Have you ever been on the high seas?" the captain bellowed.

"Why, Mr. Morgan..."

"Captain to you!"

"Yeah, yeah, *Captain* Morgan. You know me. We weathered many a storm together. Why only last month, when that loser went sailin' without a ship. We were there. Now that was funny."

"I remember you now, Weiser. You're not working for the Vichy are you?"

"Oh, sure. I'm workin' for the Vichy. And you're mother's a damdelion."

"Alright. You can sign on for this voyage. I don't know where that rummy Brennan is. This promises to be interesting, so step lively."

"Oh, sure. Aye, aye, Captain Crunch."

Ray liked fire. If you glimpsed him across a campfire - just right - as Mortecai Cohen had a couple times, flames flickering on the high, wide, tan cheeks of his savage grin, you knew, somehow fire liked him, too. Ray Macon's grin had traveled across the millennia to him, through saber-tooth tigers, ice ages, volcanoes and meteor impacts, from a time and place where dancing around a bonfire was the way of life, not dancing on the end of a corporate string; when a man could ☺✹♥◗ his horse if he wanted to, and feel damn good about it. The grin had led cannibal powered Polynesian war canoes into mayhem and it was carved onto the bowsprits of Viking ships, gleefully showing their crews where to plunder.

That sort of behavior slipped through the strainer of social evolution to show how far the human race could come; except the grin, being too wide, remained behind in the future. In Orlando, Florida, late twentieth century, there was no safe place for this amoral, ungoverned invitation to life without consequences; but it had tripped along through the ages to land among the meek and there it was, waiting in ambush on Ray Macon's face. When he poured alcohol into it, Ray the father, pussy-whipped husband and dutiful employee retreated into an uncertain tomorrow and the grin took charge.

In some western time zone canaries twittered and smiling families lounged together wrapped in love as they shared a television show. Dishwashers hummed and clattered cozily in the background, assuring all of their secure place in modern society. Traveling eastward, more homes were unlighted, their occupants tucked safely into bed under the soft blanket of night. In Orlando, Florida the Macon children had long since stuffed shiny clean faces into pillows to join all other children in their common dream world. Searching very carefully, we could locate their father lying in a ditch so scared and drunk he had thrown up all over himself. One hundred yards north of him hungry flames licked at the low clouds of an arriving storm front. Rivaling the flames were the festively flashing lights of fifteen Orlando police cars, eight sheriff's cars and ten ambulances and emergency rescue trucks. Beyond that were five fire trucks and more on the way. Ray's Honda Civic was parked a block from the construction site on a residential side street. Two Orlando police cars were parked behind it with four officers in their snazzy new blue uniforms looking it over and writing.

Framed of kiln-dried white pine, buildings that had been devouring the countryside for years looked as if they were meant to be ignited, begging to be lit, beautifully stacked and ventilated before the siding went on. They had taunted Ray, teased the pyromaniac within. These arrangements of exquisitely dry tinder were an experiment set up but never performed, a rocket on the launch pad waiting for a light. He yearned to know just how well they would burn. The grin never would have a better opportunity to let him find out. Ray had procured two empty gallon water jugs from a roadside trash pile and filled them with gasoline at the 7-11 at Bumby and Curry Ford. He purchased his first pack of cigarets and grabbed a few 7-11 match books.

"Give me some cigarets," Ray had said, cigarets having been all the same to him until then.

"What brand?" the clerk had asked.

Ray had to think. What kind of a man was he? Marlboro? Virginia Slims? Suddenly it came to him - cheap. "Generic."

Again the clerk pressed him. "Filter?"

Ray had to think again. "Nonfilter. Got to have that full taste."

"I know what you mean," the twenty-one year old dude related. "You gotta die sometime."

"Like a sting-ray stuck up the anus of a New York ape," Ray impressed on him, suddenly feeling a bond. He was surprised by the odd sensation of manliness and power that came as he reached for the pack. The phony's cool departure was marred but slightly by knocking over a rack of Auto Traders.

Thinking of nothing beyond viewing the glorious ignition from a safe distance and the fun of relating it all to Cohen the next day, filled with the fervor and indignation of the trampled native, Ray had given free reign to Captain Morgan and First Mate Weiser. He drove to the construction site in a fearless euphoria, pulled into a side street and parked his car. He popped the trunk and cut two lengths of cotton bait bucket rope and pocketed his cigarets and matches. As often happens when men are on the brink of a daring deed, he had to defecate. This was so quick that he pulled down his pants over the right-of-way grass, squatted and pulled them back up in one smooth motion. Then he grabbed his jugs of gasoline and ran joyfully onto the wounded land and into the nearest stick building, framed out perfectly, no siding or roof, only studs, rafters, braces and stairs. Soon, Ray knew, his job would be bearable again. He sprinkled some gas around, then soaked one rope and led it from a jug placed by a double door-stud, to a matchbook. He ran heedlessly through the loose sand to the adjacent structure and did the same. Then he lit a cigaret and placed the unlit end in the matchbook. Ray had known about the "cigaret fuse" since childhood, when some big kids used one to try to light a telephone pole. His heart began pounding like it was trying to get out. He sprinted madly back toward the first building and tripped on some loose re-bar, sprawling into the dirty sand. Scrambling up in a panic, his legs turning to rubber, he made it to his first jug. He fumbled with the cigaret pack, couldn't get one out, then ripped it apart and got a smoke. He lit it and threw down the match. Then something happened that was not supposed to happen until he was far away. With a whoosh that Macon never would forget because it was sweeping away his life, the front wall of the building burst into flame. The Captain, Mr. Weiser and the grin had departed. Ray Macon was alone and heart broken.

Suddenly a skulking, hunted vermin, his claim to a decent place in society forfeit, the telemarketer was afraid to run for his car, which he knew would be a police magnet. He could have fled with no more furious panic from Dr. Ruth Westheimer naked. "Jesus Christ, Jesus Christ, Jesus Christ," Ray's terrorized brain cried as confused legs tried to gain traction away from the car and the nightmare. Then his feet churned in mid-air. He came down in a ditch, tumbled in the tall grass near the bottom and rolled into a few inches of diesel-water. Flashing lights appeared from every direction and he crawled to the rim of the ditch to witness through a dewy spider web the capture of his escape vehicle. He watched with no pleasure the second building roar to life. Ray slid back down and tried to melt into the ditch bottom, crawling under weeds, piling branches on himself and wiggling into the wet sand. When he realized for an instant what he'd done and what he'd lost, his stomach convulsed into a carnival of wretching. After that he cursed Mortecai Cohen and rued the day they met. He even cursed his high school for bringing them together. Wind heralding an approaching thunderstorm blew the fire into a third building.

A rookie sheriff's deputy enthusiastically scouting the grounds for clues picked up Ray's trail. He called to his partner and they followed the helter-skelter footprints through sand to the ditch.

"He's probably long gone by now, if these prints do mean anything."

"No," said the rookie shining his light across the ditch. "See? No prints on the other side."

Regrettable actions are most agonizing in the immediate past, so close it seems you could almost take them back. Buried in the weeds directly below the two casual conversants, Ray Macon was fervently wishing he could rise from the couch and simply go to bed, trying with all his mental might to push himself back in time.

"Probably just some carpenter walked over here to take a leak."

"Speaking of that, I haven't gone in hours." The deputy unzipped with the roar of a jet taking off and completed Ray's misery.

"I don't think so," the rookie defended his hypothesis while shaking off the last golden drops. "Those prints are awful far apart for a guy walking."

"Maybe he had to go real bad. But let's check the ditch out."

The cops separated and took opposite directions, imposing their powerful beams on the urban wilderness of murky weeds, startling many frogs who leapt from shadow into the questionable sanctuary of the shallow mixture.

Mosquito ravaged and contaminated by cop piss, official vehicles everywhere, Ray remained part of the ditch for the next hour. He did not move when mosquitoes buzzed his ears and inserted siphons in his legs, arms, hands, neck and face, often at once and he did not scratch his skin, on fire with itching. Body and soul Ray focused on a possibility growing out of boundless despair - that his suffering might be the road to getting out of this; and for this he loved his suffering. Then he received once again a benediction from the heavens, the storm sweeping through like an army of opaque liquid brooms. In the camouflage of torrent Ray crawled along the ditch to an intersecting road, then slithered along below the shoulder of that road an eighth mile to the shallow swale along the highway. He stood for the first time in eons, it seemed and sprinted in the downpour to a Handy Way convenience store pay phone.

Almost afraid to search his pockets for change, he reached in and found quarters, bringing him hope. He rang Mortecai Cohen's still empty house.

Ray slipped unseen into the store rest room and locked the door. He counted off each second with the one-Mississippi method, memorizing for all time the placement of the sink, liquid soap dispenser, hand dryer, waste basket and extra toilet paper roll below the current one; counting the wall tiles, forcing himself to give Cohen a monstrously elongated fifteen minutes to come home. Macon's ears were pricked for the slightest approach, desperate that no one should rattle the door.

The corpulent Caucasian cashier returned from tidying frozen confections. "Oprah says if you're fat, it's because you put other people first," he said, breaking a packet of quarters on the edge of the register drawer.

"If you're fat," countered the robust black girl cashier, glugging some Yoo-Hoo, "it's because you put food in your mouth."

"But you don't have time to take care of yourself so you put on weight," he said, dumping in the coins.

"So where you find the time to eat so much when you out there doin' for ev'rybody?"

It was three o'clock in the morning; time to roll onto his left side pulling the sheet off Daisy and dream of giant bass. Instead Ray Macon emerged to the surprise of the store employees and went outside to call again.

"Whud he do, fall in?" said the girl, jerking with laughter.

The phone rang in Mortecai's house and this time Ray heard the sound of hope. He told Mortecai to look for him in the restroom. He did not re-enter the store unnoticed. When Ray headed back to the toilet, the portly white altruist picked up the phone and dialed 911.

17

S ensitive to such things, Ray had noticed the uneasy glances of the Handy Way clerks as he nonchalantly carried his mud-caked, dripping self back across their shiny floor. He locked himself in the restroom and sat back on the toilet, as if his proper use of the facility would waylay their fears. He was a rabbit, hidden. But what if his hiding place were discovered? He wanted to vomit again but dared not grant himself the luxury. What did they have on him anyway? He wasn't sure. If only he could erase the last couple hours of his miserable existence, he'd be happy to stay home the rest of his life. He could not go back for the car tonight. How would he explain it to Daisy? Ray remembered the looks on the store clerks' faces and his thoughts cleared. "They called. I know they called." Ray left his cage and retraced watery steps out of the store, not looking at anyone.

A block away, invisible in the shadow of the roadside culvert, Ray Macon lay shivering in the relenting rain, chilled more by the icicle through his heart than the weather. With an eye out for the orange van of Mortecai Cohen, he wasn't sure which road his friend would come up. Ray couldn't even think yet of getting away, for fear of the disappointment when he didn't. He wouldn't think of anything except the task at hand. There was no pleasure to be had in savoring his deed, the amazing conflagration. Not yet, he told himself. I won't even think about it yet. Just please, God, let me get out of this. Watching the side road, too late Ray saw an orange van limp by on the highway. It pulled into the Handy Way and Mortecai got out. As Ray stood to run to his friend, the first sheriff's car pulled in. As he lay down pushing back tears, the second one arrived.

Cohen went immediately to the restroom and finding it empty, forced himself to urinate. The portly clerk was saying, "The guy left. I guess maybe it was a false alarm. But he looked mighty suspicious. I mean, you know he must have done something."

"Did you see which way he went?" asked a deputy.

"Yes. When he left here, he turned left. I'd have followed him a ways if it wasn't raining."

In the store the officers concluded their interview and Mortecai bought a 3 Musketeers, concluding his, wondering what it was all about, what the fire trucks were doing down the street and starting to feel hormones rising on the back of his neck. As he stepped from the store, he scanned the area trying not to be obvious and noted the culvert.

Entering the rain, Mortecai approached a squad car. Jim rolled down his window slightly. "Can I do something for you?" he asked, meaning "What are you up to?"

"Well, I don't know if it's anything or not," Cohen drawled, "but I just saw two spooks runnin' across the highway up there like there was a sale on watermelons and Jesus is comin'. It looked like they had a couple of women's pocketbooks on 'em. They headed into that empty shopping center. Thought I heard somebody screaming, too."

"Could you identify them?"

"Thought I just did."

The lawman looked knowingly at Mortecai and thanked him. Then he informed the other car and they sped away to apprehend the wrong-doers.

Cohen drove out of the parking lot, pulled down the side road out of sight of the Handy Way clerks and stopped, leaving the engine running. He leaned over and pulled out the passenger door latch, opening the door a crack, then took out a map from the glove compartment and looked at it. Shortly, fingers appeared at the door bottom, pulling it open a little more and a shivering, scared rabbit squeezed in. "Get the hell out of here," it said needlessly, scrunching down on the floor.

Mortecai threw down the map and gunned the six cylinder.

At Violet's apartment Ray gave himself a total scrubdown in the luxuriantly hot shower, then traded his clothes for an ill fitting pair of her shorts. Mortecai transported everything to a dumpster a mile away.

"What about the rope? They can match it to your bait bucket rope in the car."

"I'll guarantee you there's nothing left of that," Ray said as if Cohen really hadn't been paying attention to events.

"Never can tell nowadays. The ashes might be all they need. Get rid of it."

"Wow! I go away for two days and you guys go nuts," Violet remarked.

They decided that Ray would claim his car quit and he walked to the Handy Way in the rain to call for a ride. "What was that fire all about?" Feeling as secure as they could hope for, Mortecai and Ray decided to go for the car. It was about six-thirty a.m. What to do about the looming threat, Daisy, and how to explain the loss of his clothes, Ray couldn't yet consider.

On a quick drive-by they looked up the side street where Ray had left his car, seeing no activity. In fact, they saw no car. On the second pass this observation was confirmed.

"You sure that's where you left it?"

Ray just eyed his friend from some distant purgatory. "They towed it."

At a different pay phone Ray reported the car stolen. Then they went by Mortecai's and got him a pair of male shorts. It was time for him to go home.

"I don't think I'll come in," Mortecai said in front of Ray's house. "Thanks."

Always there have been men who faced horrors beyond the pale of everyday existence: sailors who rode a mounting sea into the teeth of a typhoon, woodsmen whose last aspiration was blasted back into their faces by the rank breath of the grizzly bear straddling them, the heroes of mythology who confronted demons of unspeakable hideousness and catastrophic ferocity. In the wild history of the titan human spirit, no man ever had accepted his doom with less cheer than Ray Macon as he stood that morning at the bottom of the path to hearth and home.

Ray's beloved, not a frail woman at the least of times, was filling the doorway. Indeed, she seemed to inflate as she stood there, like a blowfish does to look more menacing. The door frames on either side appeared to press outward as timbers sagged. A frightened neighbor who had chanced to glimpse her face would relate in future years that snakes bristling from Daisy's head would have softened her aspect. The children were gathered around her as the prudent person sticks near the body of a madman swinging a baseball bat in close quarters. "You kids, go to your rooms," she said firmly. They were reluctant to move. "GO TO YOUR ROOMS!" In an instant they had vanished, dandelion fluff before a gale.

All fury and promise of destruction, Hurricane Daisy swirled on the small front porch of their fifties cinder block home, scattering toys, leaves and cats. She was a compact storm and Ray did not yet feel the fringe winds as he started his walk with the leaden weight of a cruel world on his heart. For this man who had at times drunk deeply from the trough of living, life had degenerated to a valueless bother.

Daisy began calmly shouting as one who has rehearsed the moment. "Alright. The last I see of you, you're sitting on the couch falling asleep in your own clothes. The next thing I know, it's three in the morning, the car's gone and the police are here wanting to know where you are. And they say you burned down an apartment complex."

"What did you tell them?" asked Ray, surprised to feel himself sinking even lower.

"Nothing. What was I supposed to tell them? I didn't know where you were, did I?" Daisy's voice was rising in spite of efforts to remain calm. "I knew Mort was behind this. I call his house and he's not home. Now I want you to tell me where you've been all night, where the car is, where your clothes are, what the Hell you've been doing and why I shouldn't kill you. And God dammit you can leave off the last one." She pushed him in the chest. "Look at me!"

Ray was hanging his head in front of a monstrous gargoyle with teased hair, chubby cheeks, extreme eye shadow and pancake makeup that he once found attractive, even vowed to love and cherish. So this is my life, he vaguely thought as images of past happiness forced themselves fleetingly to his mind: camping in the Rockies, fishing in Mexico, young women. Too overwhelmed for his usual strategy of retaliation and counter accusation, he sighed and remained silent.

"I'll make it easy for you," Daisy screamed. "An apartment complex burned down a block from where our car was parked. Mort brings you home in his shorts at seven o'clock in the morning. I don't see any fish, Ray. You boys been fishing? Where's the fish?"

Ray couldn't make the truth come out. "The car's stolen. I'm going to bed." He squeezed by Daisy before she'd had a chance to inhale.

"Oh, you're not going to bed, Ray. You tell me what happened. Whatever it is, I know Mort talked you into it. I can't help us if I don't know the truth."

Weird extraterrestrial sobbing sounds started coming from Ray as his whole body began to shake. He could cover the car and the late hour but he couldn't think of a logical story for his clothes that wouldn't be worse than the truth. "I burned it down," he said softly. "Is that what you want to hear? I did it. It was all me. Mort had nothing to do with it."

Daisy's locomotive was derailed by the truth. She stepped back and became outwardly calm, refusing to believe what was happening. "Let me get this straight. You went and burned down a perfectly good apartment complex."

"Sure. I burned it. And I'm an axe murderer, too. And I rob a few banks in my spare time."

"What were you doing all night?!?"

"I told you already." Ray felt himself rallying. First buffalo Daisy, then the police. "There's no point talking to you when you're like this. I'm tired and I'm going to bed."

"Where did you get those shorts?"

"I rolled a jogger and stole them after I burned the apartments and before I killed a couple dozen people with a hack saw."

"A bum was sleeping in those apartments." Daisy followed Ray into the living room. "They haven't found him yet."

Ray's spirit dissolved. MURDER! This information was one too many and he slumped onto the box of Cracker Jacks on the Lazy-Boy, curling into the fetal position, trying to become catatonic.

"Why, Ray? Why did you do that? Were you playing around in there and accidentally set it on fire?"

Ray saw a chance but didn't bother. "Nope. Did it on purpose."

"Does this have to do with that stuff you're always spouting off about developers and people moving here and everything? Did you burn down an apartment complex to ease the traffic problem?"

"That's it," came a muffled moan from the back of the chair.

"And you thought of this all by yourself?"

"Yep."

Daisy's voice was becoming more animated again. "Were you at least drunk?"

"Drunker'n Hell."

She moved in closer, arms crossed. "Did we get away with it?"

"I don't know. I think so."

Suddenly Daisy started chuckling. "That's the best thing I ever heard," she screeched. "If that don't beat all," she said with wonder, hands on hips and slumped down on top of the criminal. "This story better hold up, because if I find out you were with some woman, you're going to wish you'd burned up with those apartments."

Daisy looked down at her man, fascinated. "You mean you actually went out and did something for a change instead of just bitching and complaining about it? You mean you've got some guts? Maybe I didn't know just what I was married to. Kiss me, you wild man and tell me what else you've been keeping me in the dark about."

Ray squirmed out of the chair. "Now, let me make sure I've got this right. You're proud of me. Is that right?"

"I'll just say I'm seeing you in a different light."

"Uh huh." Ray let this soak in for a minute. "You should have seen it, Daisy..."

Ray had only stumbled into the eye of the storm, a seductive lull. Like a man who glimpses heaven and is then informed of the error, Ray soon would be buffeted again.

"Sergeant Whatsitabout, we believe Ray Macon burned down those apartments. We have no hard evidence but his car was parked near the site and he wasn't home all night. His wife didn't know where he was. Got brought home by one Mortecai Cohen."

"Anything on Cohen, sir?"

"He's a religious cult leader. And get this. They apparently worship crap."

"So. A bunch of religious fanatics trying to destroy society. They must be stopped, sir."

Police Chief Fosdick stood up behind his desk and gazed out the narrow window. "Exactly right, Whatsitabout. If nothing else turns up, we'll pull him down here and see if Hammer and Nail can crack him."

Another long hour later Ray Macon received a phone call from the Orlando Police Department informing him that his vehicle had been towed and was impounded. Ray responded with appropriate outrage and demanded release of the hostage and compensation. As planned, the police had no recourse but to comply, apologizing for any inconvenience caused by their misjudgment.

18

$\mathcal{A}$ lovely young woman was cross-legged on the bank in wet shorts and t-shirt, dripping temporarily detoured Econlockhatchee River. A ten-year old white Volvo crossed the 419 bridge and pulled onto the limerock track down to the river. Violet Chance stepped out and, surprised by the other woman's presence, sat down beside her.

Without looking at her, Mary Barbarosa said serenely, "It's great out here, isn't it?"

It was an unusual meeting, as though these two already had become friends. As they sat together quietly, not rushing the conversation they knew would come, a small, shiny red pick-up trailing two Sea-Doos pulled off the blacktop and rumbled down the limerock road to the bridge. Three young men were squeezed into the cab. "Alright, Dick. Here we are. You stay with the truck now and you can go when we get back."

"You guys don't take forever. I don't wanta be hanging around here all #!%#ing day."

"Can you believe it?" Violet said, turning to Mary.

"It's just some jet skiers, isn't it?"

Violet patted Mary's knee patiently as she stood up. "I have to do something here."

Corey, George and Dick all worked as respiratory therapists at Orlando Regional Medical Center. They were in their late twenties, overweight and flaccid and they employed their "personal watercraft" as equalizers. In that seat they had speed, agility and power. They might have used motorcycles but the asphalt rushing by was too scary.

As the truck turned around under the bridge to back down to the bank, Violet Chance approached the driver. "Man! Look at this," he said and rolled down his window. A blast of frost burned air hit Violet in the face.

"Hello. What can we do for you?" Corey asked, like a lady's man.

"I'd like it if you don't put those things in here." Violet pointed to the trailer.

"Hey - what's the matter with you people around here? We'll put these things in wherever we damn well please. !☹☺! you."

"No... you won't," Violet said calmly.

"Yeah? Who the Hell you think you are, bitch?" George shouted from the passenger side."

Chance turned away and stepped to the only stretch of bank suitable for launching. She turned her back to the river.

Truck doors slammed. Angered by the incomprehensible, Corey and George stomped over to the obstacle. "Move it or lose it," George shouted so he could brag later about it.

"Look. I don't like to hit a woman," Corey said, glowering at Violet. "Get out of our way. We have as much right to be here as you do."

"That's right. You do, but not your machines. They have no place here. You would roar along on them, seeing nothing and disturbing everything. No, this should be a sanctuary against such things. You may not take them in there." Then Violet suggested brightly, "Why don't you try just walking?"

"Are you crazy? Walk around in there? Now move." Corey started to push Violet.

"You'll have to push two of us," Mary Barbarosa said as she stood beside Miss Chance.

"Whoa! Wet t-shirt contest," hooted George. "I think I'm looking forward to moving these babes out of the way."

"You lay one finger on me," said Mary, "and I'll yell rape so loud and long, the FBI will come after your ancestors."

Violet looked at her ally and a slight, bemused smile came to her full lips.

"Dick! Start backing her down. We'll just drive these bitches into the river."

Dick got out of the cab. "This is your fight, man. Not mine. I wasn't here for whatever happened before, and I don't know what's going on today. I wanted to go to the beach. Let's just get out of this damn jungle and do that."

"Forget it, man. I'll do it myself."

Dick walked over to the two women. "Why don't you just move? That bastard's crazy. He'll run you over."

"You going in too, Dick?" Corey yelled as he jammed the automatic transmission into reverse.

Dick stepped aside and walked to the bridge where he sat on a concrete ledge. He heard a car door open a few feet away and watched Violet reach quickly in. She walked past Dick and smiled.

"You're going in," George taunted as the trailer approached "You bitches are going in."

Corey was concentrating on backing up straight, as all males must do under the critical eye of a woman.

Suddenly the psshhhh of escaping compressed air dominated everyone's senses. "That's the right rear," said Chance, brandishing a large jack-knife. She stepped to the right front. "You can still put your spare on and be out of here before dark."

"Alright, alright," Corey yelled, slamming it back into park and jumping out to examine his wounded soldier. "Son of a bitch!" he shrieked.

"Now can we go to the beach?" Dick whined to Corey, who was sitting on the ground pounding it with his fists and crying.

Violet shocked herself with a war whoop and grabbed Mary and jumped in the river with her. George gazed at them like he assumed they were crazy.

Ah, the fruit of the rare, sweet victories is the bonds they create. Violet and Mary drove three miles to an Eat Gas convenience store for supplies including wine and cheese, then returned to picnic by the bridge and relive their glory. There was no sign the Sea Dooers ever had been there. In the course of the afternoon they learned much about each other. Mary explained that her husband was the developer of a city of forty-thousand people planned for the headwaters of the small river.

"What's he like?" asked Violet, popping a chunk of sharp cheddar.

"Really weird and it's downhill from there." Mary received kudos for her matrimonial choice. "There's just no excuse, I hate to say."

"Does he go out on you?" Violet asked.

"I doubt it. Nobody would be with him, he's so screwy. I did, though. One time. I don't even really know how it happened. Vince is in Tampa on business, I'm bored out of my mind and this cute little guy comes around offering to wash my house. Next thing I know, we're together in his beat-up old truck. He showed me this place. It was just so very nice to be with somebody normal. At least compared to Vincent. It was like I needed it."

"What about this city?" Violet asked.

"Destruction scheduled to start in three weeks."

"We've got to get Mort in on this. He's been fighting this thing all along."

"Who's Mort?"

"A special friend."

"Has he done any good?"

"Not yet," Violet admitted.

Her gaze suddenly distracted into the woods, Violet said, "Did you just hear talking?"

Ray Macon had been sentenced to indefinite house arrest. However, the fall mullet run was in full swing and Warden Daisy granted him an eight hour furlough to Port Canaveral for snook, the only fish she would eat. These delightfully edible fish ambush an endless parade of innocent mullets as they take a wrong turn into the port on their journey south. Well-positioned anglers, in turn, can ambush the surface feeding snook with artificial lures.

It would be tight but Ray calculated he could devote most of the night to a joyous celebration of "no mention in the news of an incinerated bum" and his own continued absence from government jails. Then he would nip over to the Canaveral Locks once he's as drunk as he can drive, and pick up the required fish. At 5:09 p.m. on the road in front of Mortecai's house, Macon popped the trunk and Cohen loaded his medium duty spinning outfit and tackle box on top of Ray's stuff. Ray said, "Reverritt." Mortecai repeated the remark and added a moderate rebel yell. For the first time since the fire, they drove slowly by the razed apartment complex, able to view finally with pleasure Ray's amazing act of revenge.

"Sure as hell gone, isn't it?" Mortecai said, taking a rare, deep look into his friend and firmly shaking his hand.

Ray's soul lit up and he couldn't help beaming.

To ensure success, the two celebrants visited the ABC where Mortecai purchased a pint of Cuervo Gold. Ray didn't do well in the long run on spirits, normally going comatose when the fun ended, so he purchased their finest quart of Old Milwaukee. Highway 50 made a pleasant bar and they wouldn't slow until a worthy dive loomed in sight.

"Hey - look at that," Ray pointed out, astounded by the bumper in front of them. "I SMOKE AND I VOTE".

"Stee-rike 2!" Mortecai declared. "So are we supposed to feel sorry for her?"

"No. She's just a well rounded person. Something you don't know much about. She smokes...and...she votes," Ray said with admiration. "What else is there to life, really? She ought to go on Letterman."

"I can just see it. 'I understand you smoke and you vote. And you're probably a mom, too. How do you fit it all in?'"

"Oh, that's not all, I do, Dave," Ray rendered in falsetto. "I !**!, too."

"Well, we already knew that," said Mort expertly, based on mutual teenage observations establishing cigarets as a beacon for sex.

"Pull alongside, Ray. For the sake of science I must further probe these murky depths."

Ray stowed his beer. "Put your bottle down."

Mortecai hung out the window signaling the driver to roll down hers. It came down halfway. "Hello. I represent a church. Could you please explain to me the point of your bumper sticker?"

A corpulent blonde woman in her early twenties squinted out the top of her window. "Do you smoke?"

"I have been known, on occasion, to smoke a mullet or two." Ray was skillfully matching the Acura's speed.

"You have a big enough mouth, I'm sure. Do you vote?"

"Haven't yet."

"Exactly." The window went up electrically and the car sped away, leaving the interviewer to consider his evidence.

Mortecai turned to Ray. "You know, she wasn't smoking."

"Probably wasn't voting either."

"Not her car, is it?"

Ray twisted his moustache. "Stolen. Let's pull in here and call the cops." A topless place ten years earlier when an exquisite pair of buttocks burned itself permanently into Macon's list of regrets, the White Horse Inn had downgraded to a mere drinking and pool establishment. Still its past glory lingered for the buddies as Ray negotiated the washed-out dirt driveway. Their nostalgic trance was rudely jarred by something inconceivable parked to one side of the door.

"Will you look at that shit," urged Ray.

Mortecai saw it too. "The pestilence is everywhere."

"God damn roach brained, dog ass eating, buzzard anus following..." Ray paused for inspiration.

"...Republican jet skiers have no respect."

"Probably don't even know they're desecrating a shrine."

"I'll kill 'em," vowed Ray.

Ray backed into a space across the dirt parking area. As they passed the offending miniature pick-up, he whipped it out and briefly hosed the driver's door handle. Ray would derive pleasure all night from the knowledge that sometime a Sea Dooer would grab his urine. That easily he boosted the quality of his outing.

"Looks like they had a flat," said Mortecai, noting the wounded tire in the truck bed.

Inside the bar their eyes were instantly assaulted by the orange and blue neon spandex clad trespassers shooting pool.

"God." Ray said loudly. "You know this place has gone downhill if those clowns have been allowed to live."

"Sign of the times, Ray," Mortecai surrendered, scanning the hazy room. "Face it. The world ain't what it ought to be anymore."

Direct provocation, looking people in the eye and frankly expressing displeasure with them, was not Ray's way. He preferred to throw remarks onto the air like flatulence and see where they would go. If someone took offense at an insult, it was his own fault for overhearing it. Ray was blameless, only exercising the right of every American to state his opinion: like when a particularly irritating police officer stands by your car window demanding your license. You turn to your companion and say, "Yes, what an asshole he is." You are innocent of provocation, merely living within the Bill of Rights.

The spandex crowd did not take the bait. In fact they didn't notice it, so embroiled were they in their own anguish. Men may lose their manhood in a variety of settings but they come to a bar to find it back, often with cue and ball. Dick, Corey and George were immersed in the three-way game "cutthroat." Made grave by sinking two in a row,

Corey was deliberately stalking balls around the table with the sincere concentration of a box turtle sneaking up on a grasshopper.

As Cohen and Macon strode to the center, that good old sour aroma of long neglected floor vomit gladdened Ray's nostrils.

"At least it stinks," he observed hopefully.

Macon belched loud and long, his test of a bar crowd's mettle. Congratulations was an acceptable response but apparent oblivion to the blast was the best sign. Three heads lifted slowly from the counter to view the source. Corey's pool persona shattered, the spandex boys suspended their game for ten seconds of disgust, Ray apparently having failed their bar exam.

"There's your answer," said Mortecai. "You see? Three bar flies noticed that. We got a faulty group here."

"Those faggots over there look like I just threw up a baby in front of them," Ray judged.

"Well, we're here. You want to stay for one beer? I'm buying."

"Might the *?!* as well," Ray answered colorfully.

"Let's shoot some poodles."

Ray hunted a relatively unbowed cue while his opponent squatted to insert two quarters, then stood and addressed the trio at the adjacent table. "Looks like you guys got a flat."

"Shit!!" spat Corey, his soft face twisted into frustrated anger as he slammed his stick on the edge of the table straightening it slightly. He ran by Ray who regretted not being able to hose his shoe as he headed for the door.

In a moment Corey was back. "What are you talking about? We don't have a flat."

"Not on the ground," said Mortecai. "The one in your truck. Sorry, man. Didn't mean to give you a heart attack."

Differences between people can coexist peacefully in the outside world that require addressing in the arena that is a redneck bar. The difference can be one of race, dress, nationality, accent or of course, women. For an ornery individual the very temerity to meet his gaze constitutes a challenge.

Mortecai had not challenged the spandex boys, nor displayed any differences with them other than dress and he had that in common with all the other patrons. He had simply enjoyed a little joke at their expense and played dumb. In fact, he had no quarrel with them beyond their actual existence and it is hard to blame a person for that. Mortecai's natural good nature magnified under intoxication. Though only a few miles from the Econlockhatchee, he assumed the jet skiers had been to the coast where their hobby was an annoying but tolerable behavior.

Race, nationality and clothing did nothing for Ray. A New York accent could get under his skin. But when he had drunk a quart of beer in the company of the relatively formidable Cohen, an obvious philosophical difference which could be imagined from any of the other categories was enough to set him off. At the same time beer filled Ray with brotherly love for all of mankind. In the absence of loose women to channel that off on, he and Mortecai fighting a common adversary started to feel like a great way to get over it. Luckily this fantasy never had reached fruition, neither man having had pugilistic experience since junior high school. Even then, Ray had only one, avoiding fighting as an unwarranted risk to the arrangement of his features. Mortecai had been a gentle boy and fought only bullies.

"A goddam bitch slashed the tire," George moaned by way of explanation.

Mortecai lined up on the white ball, took steady aim, shot his arm forward and missed. "Okay. Now for the real one." He lined up again, lowered the cue tip and pushed his right arm forward like a piston, striking the cue ball a glancing blow and skewing it three inches.

"Great break," said Corey. "You must have played this game before. Before teevee."

"Give me the stick," Ray said, hoping to rescue their dignity.

Ray lined up on the cue ball and the jet skiers stopped playing to watch. He missed as the tip led the upward curve of the stick over the ball. "Darn ball's hard to hit, isn't it?" offered Mortecai. Ray missed again and Cohen collapsed on the table laughing. Ray looked up sheepishly. Having at least not touched the ball yet, it was still his break. Focusing intensely on keeping the tip down, this time Ray struck dead center. Mortecai caught the ball just before it hit the terrified triangle. "That was too easy. Do it again."

"What'd you go and do that for?" asked Corey. "He actually hit it."

"Just to show it wasn't an accident. Go ahead, Ray. Do it again."

Ray wanted to quit while he was ahead. "Nah. It's your turn now." He returned the bent stick and slugged down half his beer.

"Hey. You guys want to play for money?" Dick needled as Johnny Cash began igniting a Ring of Fire from the jukebox. "Corey here needs to buy a new tire."

"*$☻* you, man. You should have told me she was coming."

"Hey," said Mortecai, suddenly hearing the conversation. "Some woman slashed your tire?"

"Yeah. A gang of #$%kin' lesbos down at the river. Didn't want us using jet skis in there. Crazier than Hell."

"What river?"

Ray could see where this was going. It was suddenly a bit confrontational for him and he stepped back to watch his outspoken friend in action.

"The f☻*!in' Econ down there. Just a damn stinking ditch. A few months ago, somebody cut all my tires and keyed my Cherokee," George related, sensing a shoulder to cry on.

Mortecai was inclined to take credit now, but he sensed more to be gained with tact. Ray was performing naked cartwheels over heaven.

"What about these women? What did they do?" Mortecai asked, fascinated.

The jet-skiers all came over and started talking at once as Ray edged around behind their table with his fly down and located Corey's half draft. A one jigger urine squirt and he edged on, locating the other two.

Finally Corey shouted, "Let me tell it." His friends became quiet.
Dick returned for his mug and saw Ray feigning attentiveness to the story.

"Here you go." Macon grinned and handed Dick his drink.

"Thanks, man," Dick said, imagining what he'd give to look like this man, even for one month.

Corey began. "It's crazy. These damn lesbo bitches come out of nowhere when I'm backin' down the trailer and one of 'em cuts my damn tire. Then they get behind the trailer and won't let us put in."

George chimed in, "I told 'em 'move your asses or lose 'em, bitches.'"

As George was speaking, Ray enhanced his drink. "What happened then?"

"We don't get rough with women, even their kind, so what could we do? We left."

"How'd you know they were Lesbians?" asked Mortecai, finishing his beer.

"#!5#, man. You can just tell," educated Dick.

Ray was back behind Mortecai again. "Guess you won't be going back there anymore, huh?"

"#?2# that shit. We'll go back there anytime we please. If we see those women again, they better watch out."

Mortecai was feeling an approaching loss of tact. "You wouldn't hurt 'em would you?"

"I'm not saying what we'll do, but I might just show one of 'em what it's like to be with a man," Corey blurted.

"What? You gonna bring pictures?"

Ray was acquainting himself with available weapons and the quickest route to the door.

Dick laughed as Corey sized up the athletic Mortecai and concluded he'd rather continue seeking his manhood with porcelain balls. He was about to suggest a game when Ray approached. As always, when it appeared likely his battle would come true, Ray no longer wanted it. He was carrying fresh beers for himself and Mortecai. "Hey, hold on now," Ray interjected. "I propose a toast." Corey and George groped for their beers. Ray waited until everyone had mug in hand. "To friendship," he said warmly and hoisted his. Ray's happiness was complete as he scanned from face to face, cognizant of the grandeur of the moment, straining to memorize it for all time.

"Man. This got warm," noted George.

"Yeah, but it's still good," said Corey, wishing to preserve the peacemaking gesture.

"That's because it's fresh," Ray said, amazed by his prosperity.

"Let's blow this joint," Mortecai recommended.

Ray said, "Reveritt," and they guzzled their beers.

The Sea Dooers soon recovered from the loss of their new friends and set about with renewed zeal the task at hand. Outside, Ray's empty Honda idled while his partner watched the pool game from the edge of the door.

Ray closed his knife and returned it to the glove compartment as they bounced out the driveway. Cohen looked back with his head out the window and admired how Ray had adjusted the scene in the parking lot to suit better their sensibilities. Mortecai suggested they wait around at a safe distance and observe the Sea-Dooers' reaction to the improvement but Ray was driving and he preferred the run of all possible scenarios his imagination could produce. It could keep him occupied for years.

"The hell with how things used to be," Mortecai said. "It's a lot more fun now."

In everyone's life a few nights stand out, glistening at the zenith and showering pixy dust on the mundane remainder. They rank among those rare times we are absolutely sure were spent to their full potential. When we are in a reflective mood in front of a beer, they fight to the front of our memories and beg to be recounted. This was such a night for Ray, thrust even further beyond ordinary life by his recent hopelessness. Ray and Mortecai could not go fishing then. If they

156

should each become hooked to a leviathan which pulled them skipping across the water, it would be too dull for their spirits. Besides, they were far too happy with life to kill anything. Their world was perfect, made so by their deeds and their intoxicated viewpoint and they would not risk changing it by the life of one snook. The domino effect could be devastating.

They continued south-eastward, reliving events over the thirty mile barless stretch of the dim two lane S.R. 520, reeling together in gut-wrenching laughter whenever they imagined their victims walking into the parking lot. Ray forgot he had peed on the truck door handle, so auspicious were his subsequent acts. A coastal drunk their inevitable fate, Cocoa Beach with its late closing time was just the place for it. If conscious at dawn, Ray would hike up by the ocean side of the Canaveral locks and catch a snook to prove to Daisy that he had indeed gone fishing.

19

"Braaap! Spew!...Braaap! Spew!...Braaap! Spew!..." said the fly.

Conversation between a fly and a mosquito was inhibited by the food in their mouths. In the fly's case, in and out of his mouth. Dissipated by the latest issue of True Developer, featuring the scandalous "Parking Lot" centerfold, Vincent Barbarosa nodded by the indoor swimming pool between sleep and wakefulness with a white bread sandwich in his hand, placed there by Mary Barbarosa.

Faithful to the reputation of such creatures, the fly was chewing and vomiting on the surface of the bread while the mosquito drilled the nearby hand.

Taking a break, the fly said, "@#%$!&½**+(=/%ed."

The mosquito looked over and was about to pull out and reply when two human fingers pinched the skin around her needle. From a nearby table top the fly watched horrified as the trapped mosquito inflated like a balloon.

"Mary! Come and see this!" Vincent cried with enthusiasm.

"Another trophy for your exploded mosquito collection? No thanks."

"Yeah, but this one's still filling up. What capacity!"

The mosquito was struggling to free herself. "So this is how it ends," she thought, trying to slip her nose out. "How ironic."

Suddenly the skin was loose. The mosquito retracted her nose but was able only to roll around on the back of Barbarosa's hand which was engaged in trying to slap away a fly that had buzzed into his ear. The mosquito fell from the hand, wings flapping hopelessly, bounced off his leg and landed on the granite patio with a thud.

"Oh spiders! Oh spiders!" exclaimed the bloodsucker as she lay prostrate holding her belly. "Ooh, it hurts."

"Vincent," Mary said, standing over him, "everything you do is on such a high plane. How do you manage it?"

"Takes practice," he replied gruffly, feigning immunity to the rebuke.

"I guess that story's true, huh? About when your school had a field trip to a petting zoo and you were thrown out for kicking a lamb in the head."

"The son of a bitch tried to bite me. And where'd you hear that, anyway?"

"Your father, of course, but I thought he was just going a bit nutty."

The developer sat up in his chaise lounge. "Is something eating you lately? Suddenly you don't know if you really like what I do for a living. And maybe you're not sure you even like me. But you don't seem to mind the trimmings."

"You don't develop land for a living. You do it for kicks." Mary was looking straight at him. "You've got some kind of a weird grudge against nature, like it was your personal enemy. Why, Vincent? Why?"

"Who the Hell you been talking to?" Vincent Barbarosa was standing inches away from the swollen, agonized mosquito. "Let me tell you something. A few years from now when we're done with this state, it's going to just lay here quivering like some broad who's been gang-banged - every day for the last twenty years. Then maybe it'll sink back into the ocean or something because it'll be no damn good to anybody. But before that happens, you better believe I'm getting my dick in a few times."

"That's good. Because you're not putting it in me anymore."

"And what does that mean?" demanded Vincent, feeling like he'd swallowed a can of blue paint.

"I mean just that. I sure won't miss laying there while you try to get hot by watching the forest fire scene in Bambi. I'm outa here, Vinny. I feel like I just woke up from a bad dream. Life's too short for this shit. Adios Amigo. You get it yet? I'm going to the nearest piece of ocean I can find and dive into a wave. When I walk out, everything on me about you is going to be heading out with the tide. And I'll have self respect again."

Mary patted Vincent's cheek. "I'm leaving."

"And how you think you're leaving?" Vincent menaced, feeling suddenly very desirous.

"I'm driving my car. It is my car," Mary said defensively.

"I gave you that car. I gave you everything you have."

"Oh, no," said Mary, voice trembling. "I paid for it all. Too much. I paid too much."

"You're damn right you did," shouted the developer, advancing on her. "You paid with your soul. I got it right here in my pants and no amount of jumping in the water is going to bring that back."

"All right. Keep your damn car. I'll call a cab."

She turned to walk into the kitchen and took two steps before her husband kicked her posterior, knocking her head into the door frame. Dazed, she turned around and received a punch to the stomach. Vincent Barbarosa grabbed the nearest vcr remote control, popped Bambi into the patio teevee and frantically rewound to the forest fire. The mosquito felt herself bursting between granite and Mary's left breast and then it was all over.

An hour later Mary awoke, rose from the floor of her deserted home, packed a bag, walked out the front door and drove away without looking back. At an ATM she started cleaning out her savings account.

20

"Where's that gorgeous wife of yours, Vince? I haven't seen her in about a month." A man shaped like an upright pig motioned Vincent Barbarosa to sit.

"She had to go take care of her mother in Delaware. Mary used to be a nurse, you know."

"No shit?" he squeaked.

"Yeah. And a good one."

"Well get her back here, wilya? I need to recharge my fantasy life."

Barbarosa was sitting back on the beige leather couch with Barbarosa Development's comptroller, Donny (Fat Penis) Rizzo, sipping a Ron Rico rum and Coke. Rizzo's Fort Myers Beach condominium had the usual stainless steel and beige condo feeling of being not a home, but a furniture showroom with a Gulf view. Donny was treating the boss to his latest underground video purchase, *The Feeling of Death*.

"Say, Vinny, I'm glad your father broke that curse from your great grandfather, about everybody after him had to be named for something on his restaurant menu."

"Are you nuts? Old Ravioli loved that curse. He thought he named me Meatballs but Mama put Vincent Rigatoni on the birth certificate. I heard he'd just be walkin' along and crack up thinkin' about it until he found out."

"Oh, yeah," Rizzo said, looking up with revelation. "I wondered why nobody got Rigatoni. You sure lucked out. Okay. Here we go," he said, pressing the remote control. "Wait'll you see this first one."

Barbarosa leaned forward, immediately seduced by a new voyeuristic journey. "Forking Hell! That's great! They just whack the top of their head off clean as a whistle."

"Now watch 'em spoon out the brains."

"Unbelievable. Where can we get some of that?"

Rizzo sniggered like a nasty doctor. "I can get us some. Wild, too. They're all over Ocala, got left there when they made those old Tarzan flicks."

"Arrange it, Donny." Barbarosa fought back an erection.

"Look at this, Vince. That nigger's about to get dragged in the river by a crocodile. Watch her face." Rizzo quickly dragged a small, hairy hand across his wet mouth and drippy nose to ready himself for adventure.

The African's eyes flew open, wide with terror. In Donny's television she made a desperate, slow motion grab for the grassy bank where her baby sat as the viewers were breathless with laughter.

"God. Where do they get this stuff?" said Vincent after composing himself.

Rizzo rewound, then froze on the woman's face, presenting a backdrop for philosophy.

"Look at her," he said emphatically. "More alive than she's ever been and she's gonna go right from that to dead - nothin'. That's what scares me about dyin', Vinny. It's the first minute I'm not there anymore. You know what I mean?"

"Yeah. Forever don't bother you. It's just making the change."

"Hey - maybe the first minute's just like forever. Maybe there ain't no minutes once you're dead. Just seconds." Rizzo's moist hand was on Barbarosa's knee to communicate the importance of this information. "Maybe when you $%$kin' die... it automatically feels like a zillion years. You're alive, then you're dead as Capone."

"What about Heaven? You don't buy that?"

Donny stared out the window briefly, thinking. "I'll go there long as they keep the niggers out. You believe?"

"Yeah, I think there's somebody stronger than me out there. I think I'll go to Heaven."

"But here's another thing," Donny expanded. "If you're goin' to Heaven, do you go right now, or is there a waiting period? Maybe a few seconds, maybe you gotta be dead fifty jillion years and then you go. It'd be all the same to God."

Barbarosa considered this. "It might depend if you just shoot right up or if God has to see you die."

"Nah. He don't know from time, so you're either knocked out or bored out of your gourd hangin' around. I don't know if it's worth it."

"Yeah. Turn that off for a minute. There's something I want to talk to you about."

Rizzo sent the African to the waiting room with the mash of a button. Barbarosa lit a Camel, took a drag, then leaned back and draped his arms over the back of the sofa. "Somebody broke into the Orlando office. But whoever it was unlocked the door and walked in."

"What'd they get?"

"Don't know. Nothing much anyway. The place was too trashed to really tell. It makes me so god damn mad."

"So who has keys?"

"That's what I want you to find out. I want a list on my desk asap."

"Lock couldn't have been picked?" Donny asked over his shoulder, heading to the fridge.

"Not according to The Weasel."

"Just trashed the office."

"They did leave a message. 'FORK YOU' in five foot letters on one wall."

"Kind of a love note, huh?" Donny popped a bottle of Heineken for his guest and leaned over with it, replacing his mixed drink. The bottle clopped as he placed it on the glass coffee table. "Did it really say "Fork you?""

"Of course not," Vincent returned irritably.

Donny put up his hands. "Alright, alright. None of our people would pull that. Why would they?"

"I don't know. Maybe somebody got their keys stolen. I'm not Columbo."

"Hey - how about the locksmith? That would explain a lot. He goes down there and glues the locks so he can sell new ones. Makes himself a key and sells it to some ##!%ing environmentalists who want to make a statement."

Barbarosa sat forward, relaxed, tan arms on legs, index finger and thumb around the top of his beer. "You may have something there, Donny. Or should I say forking Columbo? We'll have to have a talk with that man. Anyway we're putting a stop to that crap. The Weasel's installing a security camera outside the door. Next time somebody gets cute with our locks, we'll have his picture."

"What the hell's wrong with people, Vince? I understand that Mango bitch is petitioning the DCA about Havalawn."

Barbarosa sneered. "She might as well go tell her mommy on us. We have a friend in the department. They're not going to do anything but make a little stink and fade away. Now what's next on that video?"

"Oh, this next bit's great. Down in Cameroon. Once a month, right out in public, they tie prisoners to poles and they just keep wounding 'em, in the arms and legs. The great part is, they give 'em a drug so they stand there laughing; and that's how they die. They die laughing."

"Wow. One second laughing, next second dead," Barbarosa comprehended.

"That's what I'm talking about. Ain't that something?"

"Leave me will you," Vincent Barbarosa snarled, stalking up the walk past a nude Barbie doll staked with pens and string to a fire ant nest in his xeriscape.

Sighing, he turned the key, opened the front door and stepped through the foyer into his living room.

"At least now the place has some pizzazz," he comforted himself, absently hanging his coat on the eagle-beak clothes tree as he admired the deer, panther and manatee heads scattered about the walls. "Flipper there wasn't cheap, either," appreciating the embryonic dolphin mounted above the entertainment center.

The developer flopped into his Rwandan gorilla-hand chair and set fire to a KOOL. He had arrived at work that morning to find himself glued out and the security camera spray painted. It was eleven o'clock before he could get in and this had made an ordinarily full day a hectic one. On top of that, fifteen people called up wanting to read essays for fifty dollars. He picked up the phone and called his construction manager, Phil Durt.

"Phil, I'm announcing a construction date. I want you to be ready to go a week prior. Yeah. I'm a little worried some of these forkin' nutcases might pull some kind of a protest. You know, chaining themselves to a raccoon or something. We don't need delays like that .... I don't know. Can't stand progress, I guess. This way we get the jump on the assholes. By the time they get out there, it's too late. They're forking screwed." Barbarosa tapped his cigaret over the elephant's foot ash tray to his right. "Get all the materials and equipment ready to go. No. Her mother's gotten much worse. Thanks for asking."

Concluding the conversation, Barbarosa ground his heel into the alligator skin floor mat and walked listlessly into the kitchen, threw a teevee dinner into the microwave and admired September on his Developer Playboy calendar, featuring negligeed women provocatively addressing bulldozer shift levers. Returning to the living room he walked to the mantle and took a pinch of rhino horn from his varnished scrub-jay nest. Then he popped Bambi into the vcr, leaned back in the lazy boy and opened his fly. "It's just not the same," he grieved.

After Vincent had fallen asleep, a figure appeared at the top of the stairs. It descended lightly and, hand on doorknob, stopped briefly to look at him, shuddered, then turned the knob and left.

21

Vincent Barbarosa was marshalling his doomsday forces of mechanized mayhem: graders, backhoes, front end loaders, cranes and last but not least, bulldozers. The phalanx of Tonka Toys loomed grim, cold and unsympathetic at the far end of his den. Across a vast mahogany table a complete layout of Havalawn spread out before him, platted but not built. Deers, bunnies, raccoons and tortoises of various composition, equally unfeeling, sought shelter under plastical oak and palm trees. Through this grim scene wound an alligator infested, red felt, topographically accurate replica of the Econlockhatchee River at low water. Wearing loose cotton shorts and halter, Barbie was sitting beside a tiny picnic basket covered by a red-checkered cloth. Her bare feet were on the red felt and a squirrel was in her lap.

Dean Martin's Greatest Hits surged in casual quadraphonic waves over the developer, clad only in white jockey shorts and black socks pulled up over pale calves. His torso was trim, ceramic white and hairless as milk. With tan hands below a tan neck and face, he mimicked a doll born of scavenged parts. Standing in front of the entertainment center, Barbarosa considered releasing his dolphin embryo from the wall and placing it by a palm tree. "No," he finally decided, "Let Flipper watch from up there." Behind the front-end loaders, a blow-up doll with "Mother Nature" Magic-Marked across its belly leaned petulantly into a corner, arms folded across her chest.

Barbarosa turned and strode across the room. "Mother Nature," he called out. "Why do you stand there like that? You should be laying on your back with your legs spread, unpro-tected, your huge tittypoppers full of squirrel milk and bird milk and owl milk and all that other shit standing straight up like trees." The blow-up doll made no move and Barbie was looking a little miffed. "So. Still not cooperating, eh? You know I can do anything I want with you." His heartbeat accelerated, his breathing deepened. "I've done it before."

Realizing the time was at hand, Barbarosa took his place behind the machines. "You looking Flipper? How about you, Thumper? Enjoy that last carrot? Oh, and what have we here? An innocent blonde maiden with her toes in the water holdin' her pet baby squirrel. How unlucky for her." A malicious grin crept across his heavy jaw, black eyes

shining over his flattish nose. "Hey, Bambi. Guess what! Man is in the forest."

The developer lowered each hand to a bulldozer and was thrown by a high voltage electric shock back against the wormy-chestnut wall.

The blow-up doll looked on dispassionately.

"Oh, that was classic. Left hand ground, right hand positive. Just like your damn car battery, Barbarosa. God, I am sick of you. I only wish your mommy had gone skiing a few years sooner." Mother Nature leaned over and beamed with satisfaction, farting a flock of bluebirds into a field of daisies bursting from the top of her head. "Speaking of God," she worried, "I hope he's still asleep. The big lug wouldn't appreciate me messing with one of his precious 'images'."

"Guess what now, Bambi. Man is on the floor," Mother Nature reported gleefully.

"Big Mama, what are you doing?" a voice like James Earl Jones' the Eskimo echoed around the universe.

"Factories!" spat Mother Nature.

"I said, what are you doing? And where are you, anyway?"

"I'm over here. Just trying to bring one of Your people more in line with Your image. That's all."

"Mother Nature, you will leave that to me," boomed an angry God, the Downe's Syndrome child. "The trouble with you is, you have no patience."

"Hell, God. That's what You said a million years ago. Face it. Evolution isn't working."

"Silence!!" Two white dwarves and a pulsar winked out.

When Barbarosa woke up, his evening of ecstasy had been spoiled. He might have thought he'd had a very life-like dream, but his fingers and arms still tingled and he felt a lump on the back of his head. He leaned over his toys, reassuring himself that they had no electric source, no batteries. He decided that after the initial phases of Havalawn were completed, a long vacation to New York City, where electricity stayed where it belonged, might be in order.

All paperwork hurdles blocking the way of the real yellow monsters had been removed. Environmental Engineering for Florida had seen to that, Barbarosa Development being incompetent to negotiate what mild constraints had been placed by the government on their ambition.

22

Months of scorching tyranny dangled toward autumn like a sweat drop from the Pinocchial nose of the sun god until the heat beast was forced to back off. Finally came the day in Orlando when summer started packing its bags for the long, slow journey to Australia to bake the outback; pushing Aborigines toward coolabah trees and growing melanoma on the skin of the Anglo Saxon invaders. A smidgen of a cold front had dropped cautiously out of Georgia. Not out, only down, the beast emerged again for a few more weeks. City and county work trucks again vied for position under the prime shade oaks as power plants renewed their vows, setting to one final and fearful rumble their vast army of air conditioners.

"Dang, Elliot, can't you find us a decent oak tree to park under? I'm startin' to sweat."

"I'm tryin, Booger, I'm tryin'. Can't join up with them lawn crews like it was a *camp* meetin'. I'll drive over to Blanchard. Bound to be somethin' there."

Booger Pilsbury's bony hand lifted a warm orange soda to his narrow face.

"Hey, Elliot. You ruther be a possum with three laigs or a woman?"

"Does the woman have all her laigs?"

"Sure does."

Elliot Yeats wheeled the city pick-up truck onto a brick road. "Watch your French, Booger."

"I didn't say nothin'."

"You didn't say nothin' right out, but you said somethin'."

171

"Lookit them heat waves in the road. We got to get to some shade."

"Ah'm tryin', dang it!"

"Alright. Well, come on."

"Is the possum a man?"

"Ah'm not sure."

"Whadda you mean you're not sure?"

"Well, you just has to take your chances. Mebbe he is and mebbe she ain't. But you know the woman ain't."

"Dang! Why's the possum have to lose a laig?"

"Stepped on by a elerphant."

"Are you crazy? An elerphant would squash the whole thing."

"Well, if you want to be completely squashed, that's your never-mind. Or you kin jus' be a woman. But if you're a woman, you know what's going to happen to you sooner or later."

"Ooh, yuk, I'd get my ragtime, wouldn' I? Alright. I'll be the possum missin' a laig. I don't think Florena'd be too pleased if I turned into a woman."

"Look, Elliot, there's Blanchard and ain't nobody parked there."

"Thank the Lord."

Elliot positioned the truck perfectly in the thickest shade and turned it off. Both doors opened and the men's skinny legs went up on the dash for better air cooling.

"Now it's my turn. I'm gonna give you a even worse one. Would you ruther be a woman monkey or a woman pig?"

Booger was alarmed. "Hey, you can't have 'em both be a woman. I'll jus' stay me, if it's down to that."

"Shoot. I was givin' you the chance of self improvement, Booger."

For all that, this was a hollow victory and natives knew it was not a replay of summer, only a reminder and a threat, a shaking fist that would return open-handed next June to grab and squeeze the juice out of every living animated object that must wear a suit between offices in the day.

172

Inside the house of Cohen, the rattle of night-rain upon metal roof pervaded a conflab between Mortecai, Doc and Violet.

"Killer. Oh man, that's great. I wish I'd of been there." Doc was pounding his palm with a blend of delight and agony. Violet had just related her jet-ski story and he was running it by himself again as if that could somehow put him in it as the hero, rescuing the woman who haunted his dreams and days.

When Doc informed Violet of his special relationship with Mary Barbarosa, Chance nearly fell off her chair. *"You're* the pressure washer?!?" she rendered incredulously.

"What's so amazing about that?" Doc asked, sorry he'd ever mentioned it.

"Oh, nothing. That husband of hers must really be a freak if he makes you seem normal, that's all. Got good news and bad news for you, Doc. She left her scumbag but she's not seeking male companionship at this time."

After further futile interrogation by Doc about Mary, Mortecai added the White Horse Inn conclusion to the jet-ski story and filled Doc with more regret than one man should be expected to survive.

"Doc, you can't be everywhere," Violet consoled him.

Cohen relieved Stiles of his counter-spy duties and apprised him of the Havalawn update. Lessup had called, cryptically relating that the construction date had been announced, in ten days. Mortecai and Doc decided to check out the scene in two, just to be safe.

Mortecai saw off Doc from the porch and his thoughts returned to the day the Econlockhatchee River changed his world. He was an urban teen joyriding down country roads in his first clunker, bopping to The Ventures on his amazing eight- track tape deck, missing only a gal's shoulders to support his right arm. Spying something odd down the hill,

Mortecai slowed and parked on the roadside. He tied on Keds, left his car behind and descended through grass and sandspurs to the shore of a shallow, red stream. He marvelled at the relic plank bridge standing there on creosote blackened legs like an invitation to a world overlooked. Unfamiliar instincts called him to forge through dense undergrowth hugging the river. He was confident his blue jeans would rescue his legs but he tripped on palmettos, broke spider webs with his face, caught branches in his modest afro and broke through. Young Cohen stopped to gaze, astounded by a meandering wonderland of grassy hills and snow-white sand hidden behind the roadside jungle curtain. At that moment a significant chunk of his future was sealed.

By mid-June his playground was covered by a torrent of tannic water and Cohen feared it gone forever; but the river's charms reappeared like a magic calendar picture between the low sun of winter and the summer floods, as emancipating as when he first looked upon it and the vivid realm shot through those eyes and threw open his brain.

At thirty-five years old he loved that he could dive into the Econlockhatchee's cool embrace and find the teenager still there, swimming under submerged tree trunks, hunting shark's teeth in the bottom sand or chasing a frantic turtle.

"Mort," Violet said, pulling him from his reverie. "There's something else going on out there. Something amazing."

"Well, what is it?"

"I promised not to tell anyone. Including you," Violet anticipated him.

"Then why did you bring it up?"

"I don't know. I guess because I really feel like telling you. And I will, soon."

23

"You missed it," said Mortecai in his ant covered boxer shorts, surprised to see a dozen nattily attired Negroes on his porch.

"Hogwash, Mr. Cohen," said a deep familiar voice. "I've brought more Witnesses to hear what you have to say."

Mortecai agreed to a special Sunday service, but without sacrament, disinclined to share oranges in the season when only the hardiest Valencias remain hanging. He demanded a period of silence during which his cupped ear remained against the mouth of the Immortal Sole.

"That's how he gets his sermons," Jacob Moseby explained.

Taking leave of the miraculous flatfish, Pastor Cohen led his largest ever congregation around the weather side of the house to the backyard. Lacking adequate seating, all stood. The pastor welcomed his new parishioners and then began. "This glorious morning we are praying for the preservation of one of the brightest gems God has sent to earth."

"Yes. He does a few things right," thought Mother Nature, listening in through a pink hibiscus flower next to the house.

"The Econ River Basin is in immediate peril from developers. You folks have more at stake here than I do. I only got thirty, forty years at the most to miss it. You have eternity."

"No, Pastor Cohen. You have just as much at stake," that deep, humorous voice resonated again. "Remember? You've been saved."

"Oh yeah. Hell! Now I'm really mad." Cohen continued gravely. "What portent of things to come in Florida is more prevalent and ominous than the arrival of our state bird, the sand hill crane? In its wake follow marvels of the fifth century a.d., (Columbus' death), devoted chiefly to the subjugation of Mother Nature to the greater glory of men.

" 'Look! See what we can do!' say the men to Good God Almighty as a child calls to his mother, bored by numerous repetitions of the same antic. 'Watch us clear life from the land and pour concrete and hit nails,' they cry in their minds to the Lord above. 'We are fulfilling our destiny. See how we draw away from the other animals.'

"Many people believe what the Bible says and they know they have been made to look just like God, which leads one to wonder if God looks like Sidney Poitier or Don Rickles. Perhaps God made the least of us in his image, a midget or a dwarf. Or a baby. One would suppose the inside mimics him also, so God must have lungs to go with his nose, although it seems unlikely he needs to breathe in Heaven. Maybe he has to make a speech now and then. It is also commonly believed that God can read English and bends down to get his instructions from car bumpers. This is proven by the proliferation of stickers in the last few years exhorting him to bless American soldiers intent on killing his children in other lands. Well, maybe it was a holy war after all."

"I wish God could hear this," Mother Nature was thinking as she smiled at this portrayal of the creator of the solar system.

"Others believe in Darwin, that species are in a constant state of change, adjusting to each others' adjustments and the climate. Most combine these beliefs and suppose that we are steadily evolving toward perfection, the true image of God. They naturally feel that what is new is better than what came before. Since technology and advanced forces of destruction have found us closer to God, they must be good.

"These people simply took a wrong road back at the theory of evolution. They followed the wishful thinking version. Nowhere does it indicate that evolution has a long range goal. We're not getting better; just different. Even if we were headed somewhere as a species, evolving on this planet certainly would not bring us to the qualities of an all merciful god. Humans would simply become more ruthless and cunning. These are the qualities that would be perfected. It is what works

176

here."

The pastor paused to see if anybody was paying attention. "Go on," Mr. Moseby urged him.

"Alright. Here's the big finish: The Theory of Reverse Evolution states that if mankind ever had any cosmic awareness, it had to be early man. Lacking survival value, such a trait would have been culled long ago in the march to perfection.

"Most animals are faster, stronger or more agile than humans. Many are all three. Modern man consoles himself with brain size to weight ratio. This is a favorable category for him, the dolphin the only fly in his ointment. Neanderthal man is another, but time has taken him out of the competition."

"Okay. You can stay, Cohen," Mother Nature decided.

The service finished with a question and answer period during which Cohen urged each Witness to wreck one bulldozer a week and instructed them how. The congregation all shook Mortecai's hand. Jacob Moseby lingered.

"That fish told you all that?"

"Not exactly. He just kind of gives me an overview."

"Well, it was a fine sermon. It was short." He took Mortecai's hand again, then caught up with the rest of the crowd fanning out for some impromptu Sunday morning persuasion.

An hour later Mortecai met Doc Stiles at the Econlockhatchee River's Snow Hill Road Bridge and they drove Cohen's van from there for a reconnoiter at the headwaters.

"What do you think we should do, Cohen, if the stuff is there? Burn everything and make a statement? Or give those machines the slow death?"

"I sure like the idea of burning 'em but it wouldn't do much real damage. I vote for the slow, grinding, complete death."

"So be it. I have rock-polishing abrasives," Doc revealed proudly, shoving a leg out the window and resting his foot on the rear-view mirror.

"Alright! Sand and actual abrasives in the oil," Cohen rejoiced.

"To top it off, how about some super high octane gas in the diesel? If we don't grind those suckers, we'll melt 'em down."

"Sounds good to me, Doc. Sounds mighty good to me. I'm beginning to look forward to this now."

"Now we just have to decide who drops who off."

"I vote for who."

On reaching the area, they checked both road accesses to the proposed destruction and found nothing changed.

"Maybe it's not gonna happen," Doc suggested hopefully.

"Yeah. Wouldn't that be nice."

"Take me back, man. As long as we're not doing anything, I have to go to Crystal River and wash a shopping center."

"What a value you are to society, Doc."

They returned to the bridge and Mortecai parked on the shoulder of the road in front of Doc's truck. "Sure you don't want to come out, Doc. You're here, man."

"I hope you get snakebit, Cohen."

"Well, if I die, you could probably beat me in tennis."

"Later. On the court."

As the thunder of Doc's truck diminished in the direction of Chuluota, Mortecai grabbed his light spinning rod from the back of the van. He transferred a few select lures from tackle box to pocket, walked through the sandspurs that always and only grow by the road, then kicked off his sneakers and carried them as he ran down the bridge embankment. He tossed the shoes under a palmetto frond and headed upstream. Cohen knew just where he wanted to be - a soft sugar sand bluff in the dappled shade of a few scrub oaks. It was a warm, clear early-September day with an intermittent breeze. When Mortecai reached his spot, he looked all around him, tried to absorb it into his soul and gave thanks that he was alive and where he was. Cohen rested his rod against a tree and lay on his back, hands behind his head. This was one of the rare places where a person can scrunch into the planet until it conforms perfectly to his body. Mortecai liked to picture himself part of the earth's surface as it spun through space. After he rode this image into sleep, he dreamed that the local fauna had tired of waiting for the good people to defeat the bad, gnawing apart hydraulic hoses and chewing up tires, coordinating the effort in English.

Meanwhile flatbed trucks began arriving at the headwaters with bulldozers, front end loaders, graders, a ditchwitch and two scrapers with 2-wheeled tractor.

24

At eight pm Mortecai sat on his bed trying to pick a spot on the map to go sell his bags. The phone rang. It was another cryptic call from Lessup. "Hello, Mortecai. Just calling to see how you're doing."

"I'm doing fine, Jake. And yourself?" Mortecai rejoined, leaning his back against the wall. "And how's your pet giraffe?"

"All doing fine. Well, things are happening now. Gotta go."

The moment was upon him that he had hoped never would come and Mortecai felt his stomach twist. Quickly he called Doc but got no reply. Still in Crystal River. He realized he was on his own. Instead of being dropped off, he'd have to drive himself out, park inconspicuously a few miles away and hike to the site.

Cohen went to Albertson's for rubber gloves but he didn't go. The engine of his van growled when he turned the key but would not join his cause. Mortecai crossed the battery posts with a screw driver and got plenty of spark, checked the cable connections, crossed the terminals of the starter from under the van. The starter worked, the engine didn't. He checked the plug wires and dried the inside of the distributor cap. He called Violet. No answer. He called Ray Macon.

"Me and Ray," he thought as the phone rang. "That's how it ought to be, anyway."

When Ray answered the phone, Daisy pulled to within earshot in the kitchen.

"No. We really can't afford to give to the Police Benevolent Association. Especially since they upped the speeding fines."

"Come on Ray. It's Barbarosa!"

"Forget it. What did the police ever do for me anyway? You call 911 and they take fifteen minutes to arrive."

"You don't have to do anything. Just drop me off on 50. I'll walk the rest of the way."

"Sure it's risky. But nobody forced them to join the police," Ray went on. "They could have been plain clothes criminals."

"If we get caught, I'll swear you had no idea what I was doing. I just asked you to drop me off and pick me up later. Let me call back and you tell Daisy I'm broken down out by the St. John's. While you're out there you might as well do some fishing." Ray hung up the phone.

"Ray, I can't believe you were so smart-mouth with the police," Daisy said suspiciously.

"That's not the police. They just hire companies to call for them. The phone services get most of the money."

The phone rang again and Ray answered it. "You just called this number. I'm still not giving."

Ray cradled the phone with a nagging sense of loss.

Ten minutes later the neighborhood quietude was broken. "You work all week, all day. We never see you. Then when you do get off early, you have to go to Mort's. Well, you're not going anywhere," Daisy stated in reasonable tones for a woman threatening mayhem.

"If it wasn't for Mort, I'd be in jail now."

"If it wasn't for Mort, you wouldn't have done what you did in the first place. Just trying to show off for him."

Ray dug deep for courage and was somewhat surprised that he found some. "Daisy, I'm a grown man. I have the right to do what I want. Now I'm being honest with you. I've told you where I'm going."

Daisy grabbed Ray by the arm and slammed him against a dining room wall, his dramatically sculptured face offering a stark contrast to the smooth, round Hewlett Packard thermostat. "Alright. Maybe you are a man after all," she said with a slight tremble in her voice. "You go do what you've got to do but by God, you'd better make it back!"

He stood out from the wall and looked at Daisy as a partner. "I'm going to Mort's. I have to."

Ray Macon walked out the house dead sober, Daisy standing in the door.

Ray stepped out of a sulphuric cloud he had thought was his world. Blue sky and sunshine filled his soul, freedom from sneaking and politicking his new road. "Honesty," he thought. "Just simple honesty is the best policy. That damn Cohen was right."

As the emancipated man started to step into his car, a maroon sedan pulled up behind the Civic. Two men in suits walked up to Ray and asked his name and requested identification. One detective read him his Miranda rights as the other cuffed him behind his back, too tight.

Mortecai felt the desperation of helplessness in the face of calamity. Trying to see through sweat and tears by a dimming flashlight, he worked furiously over and under his van, banging his head, cutting his hands, receiving dislodged crud in his eyes. As mosquitoes relentlessly buzzed his ears and mined his face, he wiggled every wire to nudge the electrons all the way to the distributor, then he'd try to start it, over and over again. "All the talking, all the bullshit, everything for nothing," he lashed himself. "I think I'm so great. Then the time comes to actually do something and here I am trying to fix my goddamn van." He found a spare coil in his box of parts and swapped it in. With little justification for hope, still he hoped as he slid into the driver seat and turned the key to the same maddening result. At 1:30 the last glow of flashlight disappeared and at 2 am the van battery turned the engine over one last time and quit trying. Cohen jumped off the seat, slammed the door like he hoped to knock the van over with it and kicked and punched it in the side, growling, "???! you, you goddamn piece of shit!" when it still stood. Then he stomped up on the porch and collapsed fully clothed and greased, into the hammock, hoping for a day's grace.

While Mortecai Cohen toiled miserably on his van, Mary and Violet had gone for an evening drive in the country and found themselves staring at big yellow machines.

"Shit," said Violet. "I wonder if Mort knows about this."

"We don't need your Mort," Mary said. "I've been preparing for this moment." Mary popped her car trunk revealing cans of gasoline additive, alcohol, rubber gloves, funnels, crescent wrenches, red-cellophaned flashlights, WD-40, bags of white rice and Dave Foreman's creative maintenance manual. "I've been walking through Caterpillar yards and construction sites with diagrams, memorizing these things, mainly the gas and oil inputs."

Violet looked with reverence at Mary.

"What!?!" she said, loading her backpack.

"Somebody better get your car out of here," Violet said. "How much time do you need?"

"The rest of my life," Mary said. "But give me an hour."

Violet shook her hand, then drove to the junkyard town of Bithlo to drink coffee in a truck stop.

The yellow monsters had been left unprotected, so confident was Vincent Barbarosa that he was one step ahead of his enemies. Mary approached her first bulldozer. She popped open a side panel and unscrewed the oil cap, then bent down and scooped some sand. "Here you go, you stupid son of a bitch," she said, picturing the yellow funnel as her husband's mouth while she poured in the sand. "What?!? Not your flavor?" She aimed the WD-40. "Well, just imagine this is Bambi pissing down your throat." With a small crescent wrench she unscrewed the oil filter. "Here. Have some of this," she insisted, and crammed sand up her husband's ass, then replaced the filter canister. "What's the matter? Too gritty?" She walked to the front and poured rice into the radiator. "Eat this." Searching for the fuel cap, she spotted the hydraulic lines. "Say," she said. "Looks like you have some varicose veins." Nope, she thought, don't mess with those. We want these babies looking good.

She twisted open the fuel cap, squeezed Vincent's neck into it and watched him gag as she sanded the diesel, washing it down with alcohol and octane booster.

Though she had heard nothing, seen no headlights, Mary's sixth sense was trying to tell her that a car had stopped nearby; but Mary was having too good a time to pay any attention to stick-in-the-mud inklings. She kept working. I can do this, she was thinking. I *am* doing it. Her sixth sense started pounding on the door, trying to tell her she was being watched; but the door was bolted and she was not answering. Mary still had patients in need of medicine. She moved on down the line. After dosing another dozer she froze, then slowly turned around until she saw at the edge of the pine-woods a dim human figure. She couldn't tell if it was man or woman or how old it might be. The only feature she was certain of was the police uniform. It was in fact a local sheriff deputy, born and raised in that rural area, fishing and hunting whenever he could. He knew the terrain. The figure did not move.

She gazed at it for a long moment. "What are you looking at?" she demanded. "This is between him and me." Mary had no thought to flee, felt not obliged to cease and desist. She returned to her task. Halfway through a front-end loader she stopped again. Her sixth sense was not needed to detect the branches crunching under a grown man walking or the loudly shutting squad-car door or the wild Rebel yell from a quarter mile down the road.

An hour after she had started to work, Mary foraged a dry cabbage-palm frond and retraced her steps, dragging it behind. Every machine had been cured. Still they slumbered. Who knew if these dormant disasters were angry at the time bombs they had been force fed? They could not express themselves. Maybe they would resist starting but probably not. The coming day, all their pandemonium might be directed inward and they would commit suicide, more or less together.

When Violet returned, Mary was waiting in the roadside shadows.

"Mort'll be so ph?!king pleased!" Chance said as she hugged her taller friend and lifted her. "God damn, we're good."

Mary had the proof she needed that she was no longer Mrs. Barbarosa. They hugged again and Mary returned to her apartment feeling a long forgotten serenity as Violet headed for Mortecai's.

Her plan of cuddling up to him and whispering sweet sabotage in his ear was detoured by his industrial coating.

"Mort," she said, shaking him awake. "I think I understand about that 'getaway' feeling now."

On learning what Violet and Mary had been up to, Cohen was further devastated that the relatively risk-free first blow had been squandered recklessly by a woman seeking to annoy her husband.

"Shit. Now I wish I'd told you I was planning on dealing with it. You have to really nail them the first time, when you have the element of surprise," he chastised, sitting up. "And anyway, since when do you approve of this kind of thing?"

"I didn't see anybody else doing it, did I?" she said. "God damn, you're an asshole. We save your river for you and that's not good enough. Doesn't count if you didn't do it, does it?" Chance headed for her Volvo. "I should have let you slowly die out there."

"Yeah, I guess so," he said to himself and dropped back down.

As planned by God, Sun crept up to the eastern horizon that morning, dividing and conquering Darkness with shafts of blue and gold. Having given fair warning of its approach, the source of all warmth in the solar system and in our hearts, all our happiness and woe, our own thermonuclear orb burst upon the scene from behind an ocean thunderhead, bringing to life the early birds, the breeze, airborne amoebas, honey bees and the very ground itself, switching plants from carbon dioxide production to the good old oxygen everyone would need for the day. As planned by Vincent Barbarosa and Barbarosa Development, a number of heavy equipment operators, construction foremen and surveyors would sit crumpled on the edge of their beds rubbing their crotches as if trying to flip an uncooperative starter switch, light a cigaret and carry it with them to the crapper, twenty minutes later emerging to embrace the joy and fecundity of life on earth.

They came together at their new job, the future site of Havalawn. The operators intended to ride their black-smoke belching metal maniacs through a community of life with an eye to a lunar landscape.

25

The pine trees nearest the road would not cower and would not run from bulldozers fueled by their ancestors bearing down on them. Bulldozers cannot go around, will not share, are incapable of compromise. Their office is intolerance. A pine tree is the unlikely result of a pine cone. It was chosen by all the unimaginable interconnected forces that prevail upon this planet and for years it has done its damnedest to fulfill its role in the grand design. It had withstood wind, drought, lightning, wild boars and the dreams of termites. Its destiny was altered by an element of chaos. The many fingered roots of the great plant, grabbing and pulling tight to the sand, could not hold up against the inventions of modern man.

On the other hand, the bulldozers weren't feeling so good that morning. Something like heartburn. A front-end loader started, engaged gears and jerked into motion, crawling along its halftrack into a young, supple pine with a bmmf. The skin was torn but the tree held fast. As the machine reversed ten feet to deal another blow, its engine was running a fever, as if its fuel's octane were too high. Two feet from its victim with the bucket lowered for leverage, meltdown occurred and the behemoth rolled harmlessly up to the damaged bark and shuddered to a stop, steam and stink billowing from every orifice. Redundantly, its human marveled at the temperature gauge. At this moment, Superintendent Phil Durt tripped on a root, wrenching his knee. Meanwhile loaders and graders were starting up and roaring off on giant doughnut tires to their own targets. A grader screeched to a halt, great geysers of steam leaving it like its soul if it had one. Durt looked up from his knee as if he were awakening from a stupor and frantically limped around yelling for all

187

engines to shut down. Already moving away, a grader jockey and two bulldozer drivers couldn't hear him. One, seeing the second dying machine, left his engine running as he dropped down to investigate. As he did so, the engine on his dozer dozed. For good.

Quicker than sand and more devastating, the gasoline additive had taken charge of the project, burning much hotter than the easy going diesel and melting the pistons. When the tally was in, it was three fewer bulldozers, two fewer graders and three fewer front-end loaders operating in Florida. The state finally had been improved.

Mr. and Mrs. Rabbit poked their brown faces out from the palmetto thicket where they had hidden. The children tried to hop out and were cuffed back. "You stay put," said Mrs. Rabbit, her nose twitching rapidly.

After a while Mr. Rabbit turned to his misses. "It is true, is it not? They cannot come in here."

26

own at the police station, around a small round table, detectives Hammer and Nail were questioning the most low down Ray Macon in history.

"Give it up, pretty man," snarled Hammer. "What other stuff did you do? And who's this guy Mortecai Cohen? Friend of yours? Maybe he's the leader, eh? Brainwashed you. Tell us about Cohen and we'll go easy on you."

As Hammer circled around behind him, Ray was silent, his only thought concerning whom to contact with his one call. He decided on Mortecai. It was a superfluous decision because Daisy's sister had arrived to watch the kids and the love of Ray Macon's life was en route to her man.

"Lemme at the son-of-a-bitch," blurted Nail as Hammer restrained him. "You %!!kin' drug dealers make me sick!"

Hammer winced and took Nail aside. "He's not a drug dealer, you moron," Hammer whispered. "He's in for torching a construction site."

"God."

Ray was sorrier than a beached jellyfish. If he would have a life after arrest it would be scarier than his past, knowing he had so much farther to fall. For some an uplifting of the spirit can create this effect. For Ray it was the usual deepening of the abyss.

Two pedestrians jumped as car brakes screeched in the street outside the police station. The driver's door slammed and a tornado like thing with lightning bolts crackling over it, evil spirits hovering around it and the spine-tingling yelping of an Apache war party

189

accompanying it, came blasting across to the peril of the traffic. Gnats hunkered down as it swirled through the steel doors. At the information window the special effects eased up and a woman of medium build with teased blonde hair appeared from the chaos. "Could I see Ray Macon?" she asked pleasantly.

"Is he employed here?" the lady cadet asked.

This question exceeded the breaking point of Daisy's calm facade and a hideous demon took its place. She grabbed the bars and screamed, "They handcuffed him and brought him down here in the back seat of a squad car. Is that how you usually get your cops to come to work?"

"Uh, let me get the sergeant," the shaken information officer replied.

"You do that!"

Responding to the urgent call from the lobby, Sergeant Whatsitabout appeared from the elevator and addressed Daisy in a paternal tone. "Now, what's it about?"

"What's it about?" Daisy shrieked. "You want to know what's it about? I've been married for twelve years to a lying, sneaking, uncaring, gutless wonder. And to top that off, you know what? He's a goddam fisherman!! 'Daisy, my dear wife,' he says, 'I've been working from dawn to dusk and haven't seen you all week, but now I got to go fishing with my $%#*ing friend Mort. You have fun here with the kids like you do all the live long day and if you feel like having a conversation with an adult, call 911 or something. Bye'. So what am I supposed to do? Do I ever get free time? When can I go to the mall? I have three kids to watch."

The sergeant was fighting an instinctive impulse to put his hands over his ears. "Uh, I mean, why are you here?"

"Why am I here? Well, excuse the hell out of me. I must have left the kids home alone drowning in our luxurious Olympic size swimming pool. Shit. I forgot it's the maid's day off." Daisy paused to size the man up, read his mind. "You think raising monsters isn't a full time job? Are you insane?? I got 'em all day and I got 'em all night. I don't go fishing. I'm just a goddam slave. Maybe you think I ought to be glad I'm allowed to live."

As Daisy inhaled, Sergeant Whatsitabout saw a chance to gain ground. "Just a moment ma'am." He turned gratefully to the information officer. "Is this woman's husband by chance here?"

"Yes, he is. One Ray Macon. He's on the spit at the moment. Hammer and Nail."

"Shoot. I'll tell you right now he's too tough for them to crack. Bail?"

"Three thousand dollars."

"What are you two talking about over there? I want my husband out of here. If he's taking time off from work, I'll be damned if he's gonna spend it here when there's stuff to be done around the house. Well, answer me!"

"Do you have three thousand dollars ma'am?" The brave lawman flinched.

Daisy's "face" assumed a puppy-like, quizzical look as it dawned on her that she was dealing with mere children here. "Oh yeah, sure, Mr. Policeman. I think I've got that on me somewhere." With some difficulty she pulled out a front pocket of her tight bright jeans. "Nope," she said with surprise, "not in here. Just some lint. Let me try the other ones. I know I've got it somewhere." She disemboweled the other front pocket, then shook her head at the sad sight. "Nope. Not here either." She looked up at her victim, standing with powerful arms crossed and foot tapping. "Wait a minute. I know. I must have bought a new car or something on my way here."

He leaned back in to the information window. "Connect me to the chief."

After a cogent explanation by Sergeant Whatsitabout of the situation, Chief Fosdick understood they were wasting their time grilling a veteran of such training. Perhaps they would do better to concentrate on the cult leader, Cohen. He further understood that Macon's wife could be a foe more formidable than they would care to deal with. All this led Fireball to release Ray on his own recognizance pending a possible court date.

"He'll be down shortly, ma'am." The Sergeant touched his bill respectfully as he bowed slightly to Daisy and then hurried off to more pressing duties.

Fifteen minutes later, a dissolved Ray Macon ambled into the lobby a free man, saw his deliverer and considered voluntary incarceration. Daisy walked quickly to him and took his hand. "Come on, honey," she said softly, "let's go home."

27

When Ray Macon came over the next night and showed Mortecai Cohen the front page story detailing "ecotage" as the Orlando Goofy Gazette called it, Mortecai recognized a better job than he might have done himself. The damage was estimated at $120,000 and 105 man-hours lost. He struggled out of the hammock and bounded over the railing onto the front lawn, kissed his van and informed the neighborhood with a blood curdling whoop. Next door, Pete shot up in bed. "Man," he said, "Mort's woman sure knows how to make him feel good."

"You know, Ray," Cohen said after he'd calmed down, "I never buy flowers. But something tells me if I pick some, I'll just be in more trouble."

"You better walk around in the rain some, too," Ray advised.

Barbarosa Development held an emergency board meeting, their financial outlook having been altered. No company would risk their earth-moving machines anywhere near the Econlockhatchee headwaters without an escrow account to absorb the cost of euthanized equipment, so Barbarosa needed to project further costs attending Havalawn. They would have either more unauthorized maintenance or the security costs to prevent it. Or both. As a project spreads out, it is inconvenient and time and fuel consuming at the end of the work day to drive back all the earthmovers to a central, fenced, lighted compound. And with all that, it is not foolproof. Security guards cost three thousand dollars a month each with dubious effect. Over the strained plea of President Vincent Barbarosa, Havalawn was relegated to a low priority while the costs were refigured. "It's not just this. Look what happened to the Twin Rivers Golf Course. Considering what we're planning on doing to these yokels, it's safe to assume that this is an organized effort," said Vincent's Uncle Ziti. "This project has been a headache from day one."

"Let's just let things cool off. We're not losing anything," Vincent was consoled by his Uncle Spumoni. "The land will only increase in value. Who knows? Maybe some day the Nature Conservancy will have enough money to buy it off us." There was raspy laughter all around.

"Let me get this straight," a near hysterical developer demanded, standing up to glare at his elders. "We spend the last seven years greasing all the right palms, getting people in office, jumping through hoops, hiring a big-shot architect and when we're finally ready to clear the land, some god damn, low life, motherforking piece of white trash shit puts a stop to it by vandalizing some machinery. Is that correct?"

Around the table knowing glances were exchanged. "Not stopped, Vince. Just delayed," Uncle Tomatopaste tried to placate him. "It's what your father would have done. Bottom line, he was a smart businessman."

"Somebody also got cute with our computers and added a zero to everybody's paycheck," added Uncle Cannoli. "Unfortunately we'd just made a rather large deposit. Thirty-two employees cashed their checks and quit. You know what that cost us? You know what they think about that in Reno?"

"I don't care what they think about that in Reno. Two weeks," Vincent blurted, nearly hyperventilating. "I'll give you two weeks, and you tell those accountants to make those numbers work, because we will build Havalawn. And fork anybody who tries to stop me."

Spumoni Barbarosa looked compassionately upon his nephew. "Vincent, you don't have to say fork. We're all adults here," he said.

194

"I know that. For some damn reason I can't say what I'm trying to say. Every time I try to say 'fork' I say fork."

Uncle Ziti asked, "can you say duck?"

"Yes, I can say duck. When I want to say duck, it doesn't come out dork, I say duck."

"And can you say luck?" Uncle Macaroni asked so politely.

"Yes, I can say luck," said Vincent. "It doesn't come out lork. I can say luck. Listen to me luck, luck, luck, duck, duck, duck, not lork and dork; but when I try to use 'f' it always makes fork."

"He always says fork," the uncles agreed as one.

"Oh, I wish I wasn't stuck," said Vincent. "I'd so like not to say fork when I mean fork."

"Clearly you can't say it, Vinny," said Uncle Ziti. "What's the meaning of this muck? You can say luck and duck but you cannot say #&@%."

The room was aghast at this alien sound.

"It looks like you can't say it either," stated Vincent triumphant.

"Two weeks," Vincent repeated and stomped out of the long room.

Then the uncles stood, all nine of them, and with one mighty chorus, bellowed Ode to Joy loud enough to level a forest.

The uncles reseated, quite pleased with themselves.

28

vast mist arrived, stretching ground to sky and all points of the compass; a reluctant, barely wet rise in humidity from 99 ½ percent to 100 ½. It seemed to spread all over the calendar with no end imaginable and no distinct memory of its beginning, Sun having regained the mythological status of Brave Helios who drove his flaming chariot down the road and out of town. Mushrooms hijacked the earth as Drizzle became the medium of existence, distilling a once sensational world down to simply damp. Floridians saw only soak, heard only splatter, smelled only mold and dreamed only of sun drenched tropical isles. The rain barrel by the back of Mortecai Cohen's house had been overflowing for days. A tropical storm was hurling threats from the Atlantic.

A 1972 Chevy pick-up rattled, moaned and splashed up the road like the tires themselves must be gripping the wet asphalt and pulling it along. It slowed down slightly and gratefully ceased in front of the house, pooping out a backfire as if each journey accomplished now deserved an exclamation point. The driver door popped loudly and swung open. Doc Stiles sprang out like an adventurous frog, looked up and down the street, then slogged up the driveway. He leaped into the shelter of the roof overhang and hopped up the three steps to Mortecai Cohen's porch. "Somebody want to wring me out?" he said. "I feel like a sponge."

The vaporous swirl of counterclockwise fury from Africa was skimming the ocean aimed for 150 miles south of Miami's Cuban sandwich district. Coinciding with his recent upgrade from a tropical storm, Hurricane Howie had upped his forward speed a couple knots to seventeen, as though   eager to strut his stuff close up for the weathermen. Six hundred miles of still- warm energizing autumn ocean lay between Howie and his first likely landfall.

Doc let a shiver run through him, shook it out his leg, then dropped into the wicker chair next to Violet Chance. Several hurricane attractors were lined up on the cypress railing of the front porch. Doc emptied the one he'd arrived with and leaned forward to place it for best effect.

"You know, Doc, it's not where you set one individual can, it's the combined power of them all that's going to bring Howie here," Violet instructed.

"There's where you're wrong. That can, all by itself will do it. Don't you see how it stands out?" No one answered. "All right. Just to show how confident I am, I'll knock all these other superfluous cans off."

"No, Doc." Violet rose from her wicker chair. "To show how sure I am..." She turned his Budweiser around and moved it along two inches.

"Hey. Hey." Doc was alarmed. "I hope you know what you've done."

"Alright. Stop fighting amongst ourselves," Pastor Cohen admonished from the colorful string hammock at the camphor tree end of the porch. "You superstitious natives with your primitive ideas kill me. I'm from New York. I believe it's the power of prayer that'll bring our man in. Let us pray."

"Shove it, Cohen and pass me a beer. I think I hear some wind coming."

"You must be physic," Mortecai noted, farting as he leaned precariously out of the hammock to fish one out of the cooler for Doc. He made an underhand toss. "Could be a monster by the time it gets here." He lifted his Molson. "Here's to high tide."

"You got that right."

Violet added a Busch can to the array and bent out to view the sky beyond the eve.

Far out over the desolate Atlantic Ocean, Hurricane Howie was stalking the waves for want of any real victims, a nebulous nest of demons hungering for children, a mass murderer alone in the world, stronger by the minute, pulling himself together, compacting, honing winds so thick and hard they approached solidity. A hovering, slowly rotating two hundred mile octopus at play, he threw out black funnel clouds like so many wooden tops, to career about sucking up hundred-year old green sea turtles, giving them the ride of their lives.

Flying flying in the sky
turtle know no reason why
he be up not down there plump
soon be skidding on his rump

Howie's route, his itinerary, his life span and his ultimate powers all had been set the moment his first molecule of moisture rose from the urine of a wart hog dying on the Ivory Coast. But something unforeseen was tugging Howie now. He slowed his forward speed to consider.

"See, Vi? You messed us up. Nothing out there, is there? You got to learn to leave these things to an expert. Now for one thing, get this Busch can out of here." Doc removed it with a flourish and tossed it to Cohen who quickly placed the detriment on the plank floor. "You're not going to attract anything with a Busch can." He reset his Budweiser, aiming the opening to the southeast. "Now, for the final touch, Cohen! Toss me that Molson bottle."

"Not playing fair, are you Doc?"

"Tough times call for tough measures, dad. There." Doc laid the green bottle on top of the Bud can, pointing also southeast. "Can almost feel it sucking old Howie in, can't you?"

A howling, catastrophic maelstrom no longer lonely, no longer a simple pawn of fate, made contact. Mother Nature saw to it. He resumed forward speed. Weather satellites soon would note not a turn, but an almost imperceptible tendency to the north.

Though surprised and puzzled by Howie's new track, weather forecasters, being scientists, were not at a loss to explain it. "This slight movement to the north is not a trend, but a rare result of the Coreolus Effect", said Channel nine meteorologist Lester Stump. "As the cold front drops out of Georgia, Howie will likely revert to his original more southerly heading. There shouldn't be any cause for concern in the Sunshine State, beyond maybe the Keys."

The local Christian teevee station featured not a weatherman but God Himself, channeled through a nattily attired human vessel with slicked back black hair, standing in front of and dwarfing a satellite photo of earth. The difference was, this oracle didn't predict the weather, He inflicted it upon his viewers. His planned disasters lacked the geographic specificity to cause alarm and when they did not materialize anywhere, were interpreted as warnings followed by a merciful pulling back. When He actually did follow through on one, this was seen as clear proof the viewers were glued to the right channel and the targeted area was infested with Democrats. Having been well trained for such mental latitude by years of watching professional wrestling, the faithful followed easily. A landfall for a devastating hurricane was announced for the North American coast.

Within a few days the mortal weather forecasts started to include the possibility of a Florida hit. Potent, vast and enthusiastic, with a scary barometric pressure lower than the 1935 Hurricane that leveled the Keys, Howie had used his travel time well. He was heralded well in advance and he was aimed right at Melbourne's Condominium Row.

Condo he so hard and grand,
gonna make a mighty stand.
Howie comin tough and fast,
see if condo built to last.

No one would be caught unawares. For days people had been evacuating the barrier islands, a great boon for the off-season Orlando motels, now bursting at the seams, and the westside business women. For best effect Hurricane Howie needed to come in with high tide because wind without water would be like a state legislator without obfuscation. It just wouldn't get the job done. Howie seemed to have allowed even for this.

29

It was two days after Howie's turn. Ziti Barbarosa had called and given his nephew the incontrovertible word. Havalawn was indefinitely on hold. Furthermore, Vincent was directed to approach the state to buy the land for a park. If a decent profit could be turned, this would be an easy way out for Barbarosa Development; and probably it could be used to mitigate untold acres of wetland filling elsewhere. He mashed the phone into the floor with his shoe and screamed in pain.

As was their custom with great storms, Mortecai Cohen and Ray Macon were setting out to greet Howie. Aware that no one else would be there, they wanted to be sure he felt welcome. They were taking Ray's Honda, being the more likely of their two vehicles to keep running, and carrying far less sail than the van. Wind was steady at forty, gusting to sixty and the barometric pressure diving, but who knows from barometric pressure? They've named it wrong. If it were the "sense of foreboding indicator" or the "something don't feel quite right in your nerve endings scale" people could relate a little better. Mortecai and Ray were simply drawn to the source of that drop. They wanted to see what happens when hurricane and beach meet, they craved to root for the waves encroaching on the concrete wasteland and they needed to feel the wind. They left friends and family safe, buffered by at least forty miles of gale tempering land. They did not bring beer, beer being pointless on such an excursion.

Riding Highway 50 east, they were astounded by the constant stream of headlights aimed for Orlando. Ten miles east of town they crossed the Econlockhatchee River, and Mortecai had the fleeting impression that he saw someone run from a car down the bank. Maybe just a wind blown shadow, he thought. Beyond the river headlights rarely appeared north of the center line and the daring Honda had no company at all going east. The small car was buffeted on all sides, slapped all over the lane. When they met rain, it was so thick Ray could orient himself only by the occasional headlights emerging from the distorted gloom ahead. The Honda's forward progress dipped below wind speed.

"This is really something, isn't it?" Cohen said, flinching as a club of rain thumped his window.

"It's a bitch to drive in," Ray stated, hoping for appreciation.

"Hey - there's no traffic. I thought you'd be happy."

Ray had his nose pressed against the windshield. "We should have left sooner."

"Yeah. As it was, I think I heard Daisy all the way to my house."

"That was just because Muffin clawed her in the nipple."

"Figured that was a good time to leave?"

"She wasn't really that bad about it. Daisy understands there are some things a man has to do."

"Fart, belch and go to work was all she used to recognize. Probably figures 'go see hurricane' ain't gonna happen enough to matter."

"Jesus! This rain's something else."

"To tell you the truth, I don't think we're going to make it."

At that moment a gust like a mighty piston hit the Honda in the face and sprang the windshield wipers. Ray praised the event eloquently and then with great care eased over and found the shoulder of the road, much farther than he thought.

"Might as well park in the middle, man."

"Isn't that some shit? Well, that's it and here we sit." Ray sat back and twirled his moustache. "What do you want to do now?"

"Send out for champagne?"

On slick, hard soled shoes, Vincent Barbarosa skied and stumbled from the road down to the bank of the rising Econlockhatchee River. A brand new, lovingly fueled McCulloch chainsaw with shiny black sixteen-inch bar was in his right hand, and Barbie was tucked up to her tits in his pleated pants behind the zipper. Cypress tops were flailing in all directions while the sheltered current carried on unmolested, sometimes a wind sheen painted on its surface. Only turtles were about, occasionally pushing a head through the wet-dry line for a breath of hurricane. Everyone else was shut up tighter than a Republican's ass at a suppository party. Raccoons and squirrels were hoping they had chosen substantial treehouses. Cardinals and ospreys hoped they had skillfully prepared their nests as they struggled to stay low and face into the swirling wind. Male rabbits complimented their mates on the impervious burrows they had dug. Alligators slept on the bottom, bored sullen by the infernal monotony of their lives.

Striving for the confidence of the schooling fish and the soldier, each an anonymous piece of a greater thing, the developer had arrived in the uniform of his calling: the slacks, white cuff-linked shirt, ornate watch, tie and coat that says, "My wearer is a twentieth century businessman. See by his costume how he conforms to the standards of that vast alliance. Know by this tie that serves only as a vestigial bib, that he will embrace the debauchery of government and will lubricate himself through it as smoothly as his coat goes through the cleaners. Smell these feet that he binds and tortures in leather to prove he is civilized, admire the timepiece with which he embraces the thief that one day will flee with his life." He had clothed himself like some ultra-conservative circus clown to distinguish himself from those laborers, toilers and dreamers who follow the dollar and play the game only because they feel they must, not because they love it. Vincent Barbarosa needed to feel the strength of the whole because that night he was going to war. He wore his flag and he wore it proudly.

"You're here tonight," he shouted with words blasted and shattered at his lips into something only thought about. He pulled the doll slowly from his pants and leaned her, scowling, against a cypress knee. "You're here in spades," he lip synched. "You're here to fork yourself, but I'm still in ahead of you." Vincent felt strong, vital, energized by the tumult surrounding him. The champion of downtrodden developers everywhere, he held Manifest Destiny in his soft grasp. He tried to laugh derisively but a wind fist shoved him backward and he tripped, dropping his weapon and splashing into shallow water that seared like hot grease. He lurched back onto the shore ripping the still burning clothes from his body.

"*Now* what the forking Hell goddamn?" he thought. "First the jacket to get at the shirt. The cuff links! Aighh! The damn cuff links, damn fingers!"

One off, then the other, he was human popcorn, hopping, jumping, running amok as his still tender fingers wrestled clumsily with his Windsor knot. Tripping, falling and rolling, he tore open the agony, buttons flying, pulled his arms through and dropped the shirt on the dead tie, followed by sleeveless undershirt and watch. His rapidly drying torso came cool and right but still the fire burned below his waist. Not until the businessman stood naked did the flames subside. The charms of the Econlockhatchee are unavailable to space travelers and developers.

Every man is naked at some time in his life. Vincent Barbarosa had suddenly joined a new club: "all the naked men in the world." At the same time he was more cloaked than before because a bare man is mysterious. While revealing what every man has in common, his appearance tells us nothing of his differences. Barbarosa at this moment was everyman, faced once again with a choice of apparel.

Fifty feet up, Howie tore loose a dead palm frond and dropped it with a crash and rustle on top of Disgruntled Barbie. Barbarosa saw only a gauntlet. "Alright," he cried to nobody. "So that's the way you want it? That's the way you'll get it." He looked upward at the green, indistinct sky and saw a Titanic woman with rain forest pubic hairs and pastoral foothill breasts. His instrument rose and he spotted the lump of his chainsaw under the discarded jacket. Touching the article of clothing, he found it no longer hot. He moved it away and took chainsaw in hand. "Look, you forking tree huggers," he yelled silently, thrusting his weapon overhead, pain in his dark eyes and rain flowing down his square cheeks. He started to shiver.

Vincent never had operated a chainsaw but at Home Depot the salesman demonstrated how to start it and advised reading the instructions thoroughly, especially the safety guidelines. Being a careful man, Barbarosa did just that and nowhere did it say "Never use with an erection." He pulled out the choke with great ceremony. Then, holding the tool aloft in his left hand, he gripped the black starter cord handle and jerked it until he succeeded on the fifth pull. The small engine buzzed like a shoebox of angry bees and a microphone, then settled down and percolated arrogantly, eager for something living to chew, somehow well audible over the roar of wind and rasping of trees. He pushed the choke back in with solemnity and defiance, scanning the sky for Mother Nature. Barbarosa's index finger revved the throttle, spinning the barracuda mouth around the bar. A sudden gust slung cabbage palm tops around like pom-poms, and a wall of rain walked across the river and strode over him. The developer's right bicep lapsed and the gas powered mayhem rode lower and closer to his body. As easily and quickly as slicing through a puff of smoke, the tiny blades released the end of his penis which he saw hovering momentarily before it disappeared in an updraft like a fairy's pink parasol.

Barbarosa hadn't recognized what he was looking at. It was several seconds before the diminished man realized he had joined another club. When he did, he threw down the treacherous machine and howled with horror, unheard in the throat of Howie. An alligator floated to the surface, breathed for awhile, spied something large behaving erratically on the bank, logged it for future reference and sank back to its place of eternal contemplation.

Not yet reconciled to his new fate, Vincent Barbarosa embarked upon the irresistible quest of all men separated from the business end of their penis. This adventure includes none of the joyful anticipation attending a childhood Easter egg hunt nor the adolescent hunt for true love. Indeed it cannot even be compared to the search for a pen to record the gas company's phone number. Blame these shortcomings on the mood of the participant, whose emotional range is limited. Desperate and sick at heart, he is frantically scouring the vicinity, with no chance to feel pride in his performance. With luck it happened in a small tiled room. At the other end of the scale, the valued terminus departed while he stood knee deep in a huge vat of cooked mushrooms. Somewhere in between, Vincent searched at night in a hurricane among weeds, cypress knees, roots and mud.

But he could not be kept from it, even if we were there to try, any more than a Springer spaniel can be told not to chase the ball, or a toddler deterred from seeking his navel. Indeed he probably would entreat our aid and being good citizens, we might give it. There we all would be in the howling winds of fate hunting insincerely for this pervert's penis. Or maybe somebody would just hand him a flashlight. Such are the whims of the universe.

Resting on his tie, the watch ticked like a gong, violently invading his brain. Refereeing this contest, it ticked off blood loss. The man had to achieve his goal and get it to a seamstress before bleeding to death. In response to this, he had wretchedly fashioned a tourniquet from his red satin tie, perhaps the real, hidden use for this adornment. The watch was monitoring the tip also, its wind-up key of life and freshness, of stimulation and ecstasy winding down.

With no idea where to look, the developer's immense despair was compounded by futility and self loathing. He staggered about aimlessly, tripped on the idling saw, bashed his right temple on one of the ubiquitous knees, furiously inspected the ground and rose to stagger and fall again. Meanwhile Barbarosa's corona had ridden up over the tree canopy and floated there with a rare perspective on its former owner. It leveled off next to a mosquito who couldn't believe her luck and took a mad stab at the delicacy before kissing her ass good-bye. The fleshy tidbit then drifted into some sinking air and fluttered back down, landing on Vincent's disrupted hair. Had he found it then, who knows what the outcome might have been? Instead he scuttled along like a giant armadillo, scattering leaves and sticks with his hands until the missing part slid down to his neck. Slapping it instinctively, his hand closed. On opening it before his eyes, he felt true gratitude for the first time since birth. The developer stood and turned quickly, poking out his left eye on a dead branch.

Barbarosa moved to save himself, his own clock ticking very loudly. He focused on his wife, angel of mercy, nurse. The name Mary filled his brain. "Mary. Must get to Mary," his only thought. Sliding uphill while bleeding to death with an eye poked out turned out to be far more taxing than the I.R.S. His tie loosened and fell into the wet weeds, and the fountain spouted with renewed gusto. Clutching his prize, the stricken businessman couldn't retie the knot so he squeezed off the flow with a familiar hand. He stood and was blown down. Crawling back up the embankment with one fist and the last of his strength, he reached the road. His body had accumulated sandspurs like a plush carpet would but he did not notice them. Vincent rolled over the guardrail and dragged himself on his side across pebbly asphalt, through roadwater to his Cadillac. Still trying to win, he reached up to the handle and found the door locked. The hand splashed into an oily pool as the suggestion of headlights appeared in the distant west.

Gradually the lights became indisputable. A faded blue 1973 Ford Thunderbird, duct tape banners flying from the perforated vinyl roof, was thundering through the opaque deluge on a mission.

"You really think we need to come out here in this?" the passenger asked.

"The man said he's goin' to sell it to the first one there. I reckon that'll be you."

"If'n we live."

"I'm willin' to take that chance, Booger. Does that tell you how tah'rd I am of havin' to drive you ev'rywhere?"

"You feel that bump, Elliot?"

"Think it was a dawg. Already dead."

"No, it felt bigger than a dawg and there was a car there."

"You think it was a person?"

"Well, I don't know. Feel awful bad if'n we see somebody lyin' there on the way back. And then it's hit and run."

"Okay, we'll make a quick turn around and see. Lookin' at this rain, I'd say we got time."

"Hey Elliot - what would you rather be? A blin' man with his dick cut off or a dawg with ev'rythin'?"

"Whooee! That's a tough one, Booger." Elliot rubbed his chin thoughtfully. "But I reckon I'd hafta be the dawg."

"You're a onselfish man, Elliot Yeats. Always thinkin' of the wife."

"Hafto."

Vincent Barbarosa had been flipped onto his back by the Thunderbird's rear tire. Elliot drove to within a few feet of him, then he and Booger rushed out.

"Elliot, look what you done," Booger said with awe, oblivious to the wind and rain. "You knocked his clothes clean off."

"Oh, Gawd," Elliot moaned, noticing the altered groin. "That ain't all I knocked off."

As Booger and Elliot bent over the nude developer in a hurricane, painting him with their dinner, a Highway Patrol car pulled in behind them.

30

With both heads stung and battered out the window trying to see the road lines, Ray had managed another mile to the Bee Line Highway overpass, which afforded some slight buffer against the tornadic atmosphere. There he and Cohen waited to view the damage in the morning and then boogie-board the hurricane swell. They wished they had brought intoxicants. Their perspective was that of worn blue jeans in an agitation washer, tired old images rising to the surface.

Cohen began. "Did I tell you about when me and Vi were camping up at Halfmoon Lake? And I'm standing in the water fishing naked up to about my waist?"

"If you're trying to get me excited, forget it. I'd rather have Stiles."

"Yeah, he wants you, too. Anyway, I'm standing there casting an artificial worm and I get a strike but it's not on the worm."

"Bluegill?"

"Yep."

"Was he smiling?"

"I wasn't. It was amazing how much that hurt. Anyway I took it as a warning. What if it had been a mudfish or a gar?"

Ray smiled slightly and twirled his moustache. "That would be a rough way to become a woman, alright. Did you jump?"

"Hell, yes. I'll tell you one thing. I don't wade naked anymore."

At that point in the conversation, the small car lifted like a helicopter, spun around and set back down in the same spot facing west. "Jesus! Let's get out of here," said Ray, white as Donnie Osmond.

"I'm way ahead of you," Mortecai said halfway out the door.

If you run up the concrete embankment under an overpass, you will find just below the bottom of the road an uncommon sanctuary against all the usual plagues except severe flooding. It is the only earthly refuge from ants. In cold weather it captures warmth. Normally a narrow ledge has been included for sitting or sleeping on, offering a unique vantage point on a hurricane. Completely sheltered, the storm tries to get at you in fascinating ways. You can sit and watch tiny tornadoes spin off below and climb, always squashed by the roadbed before reaching you. Also water scales the concrete, oddly seeking its level in defiance of gravity. The wind cannot support it all the way and you remain dry. The various voices of the gale achieve a character unheard anywhere else; and you may thrill to their chorus with the added excitement of being technically outdoors. This is how Ray and Mortecai greeted Howie. If he was insulted by the lack of pomp, he didn't let on. The Honda danced a few more jigs in the night and hovered again, never straying far from the spot Ray left it. When the air pressure dropped below the air pressure in the tires, they blew, one by one as Ray watched, stricken.

"God damn!" Mortecai remarked. "I hope they weren't new."

The muffled explosion inside the trunk had a surrealistic quality.

31

*A*t 6:30 a.m. on April twentieth, 1971, a person could travel Highway A1A from Melbourne Beach fifty miles to Vero Beach and ride alongside a coastline that mostly resembled the view one-eyed pirates gleaned through their spy glasses with the Jolly Roger a flyin', iron hard, tattooed, untamed crewmates throwing their dirty underwear at each other, cleaning their weapons or drunkenly cursing the heavens. A1A was invisible from the beach as was the beach from A1A, blocked by an impenetrable thicket of palmettos, prickly pear and thorn bushes. At 6:35, about midway along this stretch, a gopher tortoise lumbered out of his burrow and extended his neck. A great white glob of pelican shit slammed his chin to the sand. Discouraged by such a start to the day, he cleaned the mess with his front legs and sand and slid back into his burrow to try again a little later. Prospects would not improve. At 7 a.m. a small amount of sand made way for a stake and a disease was injected there that spread north and south killing everything and leaving in its dreadful wake colossal concrete scars. For ten years the beach was racked by this sickness which moved through the ground with astounding speed. Some people who loved the beach searched their government for a cure but found none. It slowed of its own accord after most of the beach had been killed, popping up occasionally like the rare cases of bubonic plague, more deadly in the United States than most places because it is typically misdiagnosed here. As late as 1990, the state attempted to buy a small piece of what was left because it was an important sea turtle spawning area. Before the money could be raised, "development" came.

Hurricane Howie had begun removal of the scar tissue. Aquarius Beach and Racquet Club was first in line as wind and tide rose together. A little ahead of peak high tide, Howie slowed as he approached the coast and when the time was right, they came in as one. Beach erosion had been terrific throughout the day and little buffer remained between ocean and condominium. A Sledgehammer sea broke beyond the sea wall and purged the swimming pool of chlorinated water. Again and again the pool was refilled as the ocean could come no further. Howie's henchmen waited, needing a battering ram to enter the building. It was coming. Howie had brought with him a double wave, one which had caught up with another and piled on. In an Atlantic of gargantuan swells, a titan had risen among them. It rushed on undiminished, pure energy flowing through its medium. As all waves must break, this wave broke every pane of glass in the Aquarius Beach and Racquet Club, oceanfront and roadfront, smashed every mirror with the memory of every face that looked to itself instead of the world around it; every human who checked scrupulously for an infinitesimal new line or blackhead but could not see the annihilation of an entire ecosystem. The door was open and Howie came in. A tentacle writhed down to earth and sent a small tornado spinning through the first floor, collapsing walls, detonating plumbing, ejecting furniture. Another tentacle dropped and spun one into the fourth floor. A washer and dryer wound up five blocks north in the rubble of The Miramar. As the twenty mile Cyclops eye of the monster approached, three black arms lashed a concrete telephone pole yanking it from the cooperative earth and plunging it through two load bearing third floor walls. The roof sagged under great pools of rainwater.

As suddenly as an air conditioner going off, all was calm. As Howie's eye floated over the Aquarius surveying the damage, round two, the finishing touches, the other side of the eye, was around the corner.

And so it went - condominium to condominium, Hurricane Howie showing the same respect for the creations of man as the builders had shown for the creations of God. The Dolphin, The Sea Turtle,

Northerner's Haven, Oceanville, every high rise from Orchid Island to Melbourne Beach, neutralized. Weakened by his exercises over land, Howie pulled even with Orlando and spawned on his western edge a line of thunderstorms. On all the news shows that night were interviews with DisneyWorld customers who claimed they saw a huge image of Walt appear in defense of Cinderella's Castle. As a bolt of lightning flashed from the black sky, they said he caught it in his right hand, looked at it, looked at the castle, seemed to consider, then said, "Duck it!" in his cheery voice and flung the thing into what had been the top of the entrance to the Magic Kingdom. There was rabid applause from the few onlookers, who thought it a marvelous effect until the emergency equipment started arriving.

Hurricane Howie never really came inland. By the time he reached Melbourne Beach, his fringe winds had blown asunder Doc Stiles' directional device so he simply turned north and did sporadic damage up the coast to Flagler Beach before heading back out to sea. The ever cooler waters of the northern Atlantic were killing Howie. Perhaps he could turn back to the tropics, strengthen and do it again, live forever by wintering in the Caribbean. But the great tempest could no more head back south than a spent butterfly can become a caterpillar. Hurricane Howie howling in protest, trying to marshal his draining forces, was dragged kicking and screaming to his anticlimax. For the residents of Scotland he was only a few days of torrential rain instead of the usual drizzle. Held up there by the highlands and a stationary front to the north, Howie's last drop landed on the head of a spider trapezing between two gorse bushes. Rolling down around the mouth, it was taken inside.

"And what are you smiling at, Mother Nature?"

"Oh, just admiring one of those cute little tricks you play on your people things now and then."

"Yes, they have to be reminded. What was it?"

"A hurricane."

"Ah, the one where I let them show how they can build things and then I come along and blow them down. Yes, that's a good one."

"Some of those edifices didn't go down, you know."

"The devil you say!"

"Yes. They build them out of a mixture of sand and water and you can't blow them down."

"I know what you're trying to do, Big Mama and it won't work. Do you think I'm stupid enough to fall for that childish trick? I'm God, dammit. Still, it might bear looking into."

32

The Gallup poll on "How many Americans rode out Hurricane Howie under highway overpasses" never came out. Likely a few hitchhikers. Dawn featured no sunrise at all, that effect apparently blown away in the night. Wind held at sixty knots with overcast and light rain.

Ray and Mortecai ran down the concrete slope to the savaged transportation, extricated wave riding equipment from the trunk and filled with wonder at the shredded spare. Then they waited for a lift. "I don't think anybody'll steal it," Mortecai consoled his friend.

Considering them a possible news item, a Channel Nine "I'mwitless News" truck picked up the pair. On the way to the coast, Cohen explained that the flat-tired Honda had been abandoned by two naked Cuban men who popped the tires and then ran up onto the highway. He and Ray were simply homeless and living in the overpass, sleeping on their boogie boards and feasting on the abundant road kill, "More than any two guys could want. Now I'm not saying you ought to collect it along the way. The key is being there when the animal is hit."

"Then you know it's fresh," added Ray.

"Just don't come moving into our spot. We've been there awhile. Don't think you can call your friends up and move them in while we're at the beach. It doesn't work that way."

"Don't worry, man. Nobody I know wants to go live under some bridge."

"Yeah, right," said Ray.

The reporter returned his gaze to the road.

"Look, I'm not trying to be unfriendly or anything 'cause we appreciate the ride. You just need to know where you stand, that's all." Mortecai leaned back and stretched.

The newsman turned back around. "Listen. I drive a brand new twenty thousand dollar car. I live in a nice apartment with a stereo, teevee, a bed, a door, all kinds of stuff. And I date. I actually have a place to bring women back to. Now why in hell would I want to go out there and live under that road?"

"Hey," said Mortecai. "We're glad you feel that way. We're not into converting anybody, that's for sure. Are we, Rufus?"

"Nope. But you'd be surprised how many women come wandering down that road looking for a warm place to stay the night. Good looking, too."

"Oh yeah. I'll bet they're real foxes."

"Got them too," said Ray.

"Of course, if you look at it this way," said Mortecai, "who's going to work today and who's going boogie boarding?"

The reporter turned his attention to the driver. "So Dave. How's your Vette running?"

Florida Power was already out clearing roads of downed wires. The vagabonds were transported as far as the Holiday Inn Cocoa Beach, newly undermined and leaning eastward, the swimming pool cracked and half filled with dirty salt water. If you walked near the motel, you crunched shattered glass. The destruction was complete; all the vacations and memories of future vacations, photos, life conceived on the beds, television watched and kids yelled at sucked up into the sky to waft down now and then elsewhere, an eternal rain of history changed, lives altered, canceled, reinstated.

Though not particularly gladdened by the demise of a Holiday Inn, which, after all, had a bar, the men took it as a hopeful sign of the fate of the despised condominia. Then on to something requiring immediate attention - the surf of a lifetime. Used to the small waves of Florida, the ten foot hurricane swell that menaced Ray and Mortecai was too much of a good thing. They waited for a lull and then, excited and terrified, the two pals ran into the surf and flopped onto their boards paddling desperately. Too slow, they soon found themselves cowering under a breaking wave twice their own height. They dove under but nearly lost their arms when the tremendous force caught their attached vehicles.

Beaten and pummeled into the sand for awhile, they eventually washed up and out of the tumult. "I think I'm satisfied," said Mortecai, but he saw on Ray's face something he had learned to fear. It was the grin, scarier still because Macon was totally sober.

"I have to ride one."

Shamed into trying again, Mortecai joined his insane buddy in the next attempt. Driven by fear they made it beyond the breaker line. Their swell came, they looked at each other one last time and then paddled and kicked for their lives, making it to the crest which seemed much higher than it did from below. They felt in control like a mouse on the wildly salivating tongue of a tiger, then over the top they went. When next the surfers saw each other, they no longer owned boogie boards. Luckily, the Velcro gave way before their arms did. Ray had a dislocated shoulder and a thumb he could extend back to his arm. Mortecai had a sore neck and abrased face from its repeated drubbing into the sand.

"Uh, awesome, dood," Mortecai mentioned as they lay crumpled on the sand like the ocean had vomited them out. "Wanta go again? This time without boards."

And where was Violet Chance when Howie came ashore? She had invited Mary to join her at a hurricane party at Ann Hinga's Fishhouse and Tavern. For a night they were part of a small, hardy band of revelers toasting one of the world's most spectacular phenomena. When the electricity disappeared, Tom the bartender lit oil lamps and Violet told a joke about a frayed knot. Doc Stiles weathered the storm at home because his truck wouldn't start. He watched it from his bed, was startled by each random explosion of an Orlando Utilities transformer and marveled at the hand to hand combat between hurricane winds and oak trees, their roots betrayed by their canopies and the sodden ground.

The muscled air gained a death grip on the green hair of a laurel oak behind his apartment and threw it onto the middle of the one story block house next door.

"Killer. Unbelievable. I can't believe I saw that," he said to himself.

33

Violet waited on a plastic chair among the mockingbirds and cardinals of the back yard. Wearing a cervical collar, the pastor soon emerged with navel orange sections, obtained with Ray in the nighttime raid of an excellent Narcoosee grove. He was surprised to see Jacob Moseby and Doc Stiles also there, and went back for more sections.

From a perfect, brand new Uranus box, the pastor raised a section to Violet. "Thanks be to Florida."

"Now prepare yourselves, because I have profound news this morning:" Pastor Cohen paused. "The Immortal Sole has gone silent. This can mean one of only two things. Either he is..."

"She!" Violet interjected.

Cohen smiled with forbearance. "Either she is dead, or her mission here is done. I suspect it is the latter. Good God Almighty answered our supplications and sent us Howie. We have regained a large section of our coast (cheers from Violet and Doc) and the rubble remaining will serve long into the future to remind people that buildings are what define beach erosion. Good God also has taken from us one Vincent Barbarosa, through a pair of county groundskeepers from Tennessee who did him in mountain style, though modestly they are refusing to take credit for it. It is a grave loss to environme'talists everywhere and with him goes the immediate threat to the Econ. We wish his soul well on its trip to New York."

"That's not where his soul's going," interrupted Doc Stiles. "It's going to British Columbia or someplace where it can suffer for eternity."

"It is only fitting that my last service should finish with a theological correction from the learned Stiles. Accordingly, the Church of Florida, that ambitious endeavor to raise the awareness of a community of zombies and avoid income tax, is folding its tent."

Agonized exclamations of horror, sobbing and wailing filled the air around a perplexed Moseby.

"Sure, I know it hurts, but you must get on with your lives. When you walk away from today's service, I want you all, you multitudes to stride into and embrace the world without looking back."

"Man, Cohen," moaned Doc Stiles, "That's going to ruin my whole routine."

"All I can say, Doc, is I'm sorry. You'll just have to get a new routine. It hurts to stand in one place too long, so I just want to say, thanks to a very special friend of Violet's who is not here today and whom, in fact, I have never met, though Doc says he has. I thank her very much."

As the former Pastor Cohen stepped ceremoniously away from the pulpit, Jacob Moseby extended his hand. "I'm sorry you're quitting, Mr. Cohen. What will you do now?"

"Sleep longer."

"What happened to your neck?"

"Oh, just a little swimming accident."

"You know, we sort of had a vote at our church about whether we ought to get involved in trying to preserve things for later."

"Oh yeah? How'd it go?"

"It turned out to be a complicated matter. I said, 'If we aren't concerned about what happens to this place while we're alive, maybe we're not doing our job. Maybe that's why we're here now. To safeguard our eternity. Maybe,' I said, 'if we're not interested in protecting this place, then we don't really believe we're coming back here. It could be a test of faith.'"

"Excellent point," said Mortecai.

"Then one woman stood up and said, 'So are we supposed to become environmentalists to convince ourselves that we believe? Besides, I say let 'em build as much as they can. We'll have that many more houses to stay in after they're gone.'"

Mortecai cringed.

"And a lot of them felt like God was going to make it just right for them anyway so why worry about it."

"Well, at least you thought about it. Can't make people think the way you want them to. That's one thing I've learned."

"What it amounts to after you cut through all the rhetoric, Mr. Cohen, is most folks just don't want to get up and deal with anything. I hope you never get that way."

"Heck. I already am."

"Amen."

After everyone had gone, Violet and the former pastor took a stroll over to Lake Gasoila. "Mort, remember I told you there was something going on out at the river that I promised I wouldn't tell anybody about?"

"Vaguely. It seems like a lot's happened since then."

When they got to a thoroughly lawned street corner, Violet stopped Mortecai and looked him dead in the eye. "They understand English."

"Puerto Ricans?"

"No. The animals out at the Econ. Mary and I discovered it one day."

"Let me guess. They learned it from a pet raccoon somebody set free."

"How did you know?" Violet squealed.

"I had a dream like that myself," Mortecai said wistfully.

"It almost seems like a dream now. But at the time I was so sure."

"Yeah. Aren't we all."

Walking hand in hand, they reached the top of the hill overlooking Lake Gasoila.

"Look at that, Mort. No evil fish feeder."

Mortecai squeezed Violet's hand.

"Remember," she said, "I'm just over here to bring you back."

Cohen and Chance sat on the bank. "Doc's going to be a father," Violet said factually.

"Well, I suppose most of us are," Mortecai said. "What about it?"

"I mean Mary O'hara is pregnant. She doesn't want him to know until after the baby's born. Then she'll see where they stand. Right now she's back in Delaware renewing her nursing certificate."

"From what Doc told me, under intense interrogation, I might add, he never really got the chance to make that happen."

"I know. But I guess it only takes one. And she's sure it was his."

"Wow! This isn't supposed to occur between species. Human evolution could be set back permanently."

"Well, if it's a girl, maybe it will be like Tinker Bell."

"He'll be so excited," Cohen said, picking up a stone and sidearming it in.

"You think so?"

"For sure. Especially if she'd marry him. But why'd you tell me? Now I have to not tell him."

"Mary just wanted to know what you'd think he'd think about it."

"What if in the meantime he kills himself out of despair? What a tragedy."

"Yeah. Then one second later his phone rings."

"I'm hopin' it's just a bill collector. I couldn't stand that."

"I never knew you were such a softy," Violet said, squeezing Mortecai with one arm. "But we're still not telling him."

Back on the porch, the two criminals reclined together in the hammock.

"You know, Viol, I think we've beaten Fish and Game in hand to hand combat."

"Actually," Juice said, "the whole thing was my idea."

Mortecai and Violet just stared at him.

From a mercenary's diary

I've seen lots of alligators - in a variety of positions. Though I'd never seen one seated on a barstool, there was no doubt this was authentic, although a fake one would have fit in nicely with Ann Hinga's decor. The only empty stool was next to it and I claimed it. Still beats standing, I thought.

Having failed to introduce ourselves initially, we embarked on a period of lonely silence. I was pretty interested in gaining a foothold with the bartender anyway. After securing a brew, I felt relaxed enough to gaze to my right. It was staring straight ahead, little hands on the empty counter. From its lower jaw hung a silver ring, and a safety pin highlighted its left eyelid.

It caught my stare but said nothing.

I nodded at the drinkless space and the alligator grimaced sheepishly. "Gatorade", I ordered, "with, umm, maybe five straws." Using skill and tenacity I constructed the drinking pipe. Gratitude is an incongruous aspect to an amphibian's face, but there it was. I looked away.

We concentrated on our drinks and I scanned the crowd for familiar faces, finding none. I started working on familiar body parts in general and found plenty.

By the second round, we'd both loosened up. The gator spoke first. "Come here often?"

I might have hoped for something less mundane, but we were, after all, in a bar. "Uh, sometimes, Yeah. Say, if you don't mind my asking, why the body piercing?"

Though crocodilians have a naturally sly presence anyway, this one looked at me suspiciously. "Why not?" came the inscrutable reply, as its chin rested in the hand not drumming the countertop with scaly fingers.

"No reason. I just always wanted to ask somebody about it."

"So you chose me."

"No offense intended," I offered, as the swing band struck up Minnie the Moocher. "It seemed like a good opportunity."

"My belly button's pierced, too. You want to see?," it said softly, swinging around.

"Well, no, not... oh yes. Very nice. Look," I said, "I know you're not a person."

Its chin nudged away the mug as the full length of the great green head came to rest glumly on the bar. "It was the gar tattoo, wasn't it?" it mumbled straight ahead to the draft handles.

"I never saw the tattoo. Believe me, ..."

"You want to see it?" it said, perking up. "It's right..."

"No, I really don't," I stated strongly. "It's just obvious. No one would have used that line."

"Drought! And I thought it sounded so human."

I saw it glancing out the window. "So what are you doing here?"

"Promise you won't laugh?"

I nodded gravely.

"I'd been living in Lake Putridia for years. Grew up there, really. I did alright, plenty of ducks and turtles. Then the worst day of my life, I'm sunning on the dock and some guy from the land of ice and snow moves in, sees me and has a heart attack.

224

Next thing I know, there's a "Persecutor" stepping out of his truck. I settle to the bottom so he can't shoot me and next day it's goodbye to home, and crawl into the south storm drain pipe, hoping I might find my way to a river."

"That must have been miserable, living underground," I responded, establishing a rapport.

It seemed to relax and become more candid. "It had its good points and bad, like anything. You know what I mean. Eating was no problem. Rats all over the place, one day I even got a cat. Didn't really care for all that fur, though. It's the sun that I missed. I finally came out on Michigan Street. How's that for irony? I saw the name of this bar and I thought, if one of those dumb snakebirds can impersonate a human and open up a bar, I should be able to at least hang out. Got this disguise and I've been biding my time here ever since."

"But why would anybody want to shoot you? You have a right to live."

It shot me the mother of all withering glances. "Sure. We were here first. We're part of the ecosystem. I'm more harmless than a typical twelve year old human. Try telling that to some clown who just landed here from Michigan and thinks I'm going to bash down his door and snarf him up while he's watching Rosie O'Donnell."

"How do you know about Michigan and television?"

"I'm an alligator- not an ignoramus."

I took a long slug of beer, then set down my mug and looked him in an eye. "Been on the road long?"

"You trying to be funny? Because I'm really not in the mood."

"No. I'm interested," I said a little too defensively.

"You're not going to make any cracks about back alleygators or anything?"

I flooded his eye with sincerity.

"All right. About four days. I've been in this place for three. At last call I lean into a corner and remove my disguise until everybody clears out."

I started wondering which of the other decorations were faking it. "Not getting very far, are you?"

"To be honest, I'm scared to go back out."

I sat quietly thinking, then finished off my Corona.

"Come on," I said, putting my arm around its shoulders, "I think I can help you."

"Those are the words I've been waiting to hear," my bumpy buddy said in a trembling voice, an alligator tear streaking its leather jaw.

We walked together out the front door and I can say in all good conscience that he never knew what hit him. Bam! Bam! and it was over.

"It ain't easy makin' Florida just a warm version of Minnesota, but we're doin' it," my jubilant partner grunted as we dragged the fugitive to the pick-up.

"Yep," I said, heaving it in, "we must never forget the prime directive: swans - not gators. Swans - not gators. Come on. There's another one at Popeye's. Wearin' a sailor suit."

"Say - this explains that naked sailor the other night."

I nodded knowingly. "It's going to be an ugly millennium."

OUTTAKES

Ray, looking for all the world like he was going to belch powerfully, farted silently instead.

After administering horse tranquilizers, Vincent Barbarosa has scx in Fidel Castro's beard.

A happy dream of squirrel-size dolphins cracked into unwelcome shards of reality as Mortecai Cohen fell out of the colorful Yucatan hammock.

After requesting a colonic from Doc Stiles' pressure washer, Mary Barbarosa became Mortecai Cohen's best customer.

...baby dangling from her right zeppelin

Both 35, Mortecai and Ray, searching for their true identities, met in a gay bar.

Vincent Barbarosa made love to his chainsaw, then broke up with it.

Ray looked like a coconut with a face painted on it.

"Look at her teats, Ray."
"Forget the teats, Mort. Look at her butt."

"Oh man, dimples. I love that."

The chainsaw rode lower and closer to Barbarosa's body and sliced off his dick. "Forking Hell?" he said. "What next?"

The alligator looked over and bit the guy's head off.

Lastly...

Several people helped me bring this book from a lump of words to this lump of words. I implicate them now.

Thanks to Lynne Jenne for always doing what she can, Bob Mervine, Jim Crescitelli and Kiley the Kiwi librarian for looking at an early manuscript, and Bob Morris for his encouraging words. Jeff Weakley for scorning the very heart of my original effort, Eyal Goldshmid for murdering it and Dave Richey for giving all the constructive criticism he could stummick. Michele shooed away some loitering characters, cartoons and dreams and shored up the plot. Meanwhile Cathy Hettinger attacked the dangling participles. Thanks, Steve, for the ducks.

A special thank-you to Jerry McBride for going where no man had gone before and copy-editing it.

Check out defiantworm.com